PURSUIT OF FEAR

Also by William Beechcroft:

POSITION OF ULTIMATE TRUST
IMAGE OF EVIL
CHAIN OF VENGEANCE
THE REBUILT MAN
SECRET KILLS

PURSUIT OF FEAR

William Beechcroft

Carroll & Graf Publishers, Inc.
New York

First Carroll & Graf edition 1990

Carroll & Graf Publishers, Inc
260 Fifth Avenue
New York, NY 10001

Library of Congress Cataloging-in-Publication Data

Beechcroft, William.
Pursuit of fear / William Beechcroft. — 1st ed.
p. cm.
ISBN: 0-88184-510-8 : $17.95
I. Title.
PS3552.E32P8 1990
813′.54—dc20 89-27673
CIP

Manufactured in the United States of America

1.

Thirty-one miles out of Maui's Kahului Airport, with fewer than twenty miles to go, Jim Gammon realized he was being tailed.

The drive on Hawaii 36, the Hana Highway, had begun easily on a spear of smooth, two-lane macadam along the gentle green foothills of Haleakala, the island's massive, dormant volcano that jutted ten thousand feet through a crown of fluffy cumulus clouds high upslope to his right.

A few miles past the little settlement of Haiku, the road had begun to undulate. Then the alignment swung steeply right, switched back hard left, then veered right again to begin its infamous serpentine convulutions and soaring valley crossings the length of Haleakala's northeastern slope: the 617 curves and fifty-seven bridges that had earned the "Highway to Heaven" an international reputation as one hell of a tough road.

Since he deplaned less than an hour ago at Kahului and rented the Nissan, Gammon had wondered why Van Hayden had insisted on meeting him here. On Maui in general, which itself could be considered isolated; in Hana in particular, which every twisting mile told Gammon wasn't only isolated. It was remote.

When Van Hayden had called him from Honolulu, Gammon had been surprised by that much removal from Washington. But the old man's urgency had set aside Gammon's uncertainty about the marathon flight out of Dulles. Not that Van Hayden had told him much. Only a blurted, "I've got to see you immediately. *Got* to, Jim. Colony Surf, north of Waikiki. Ask at the desk."

Was that worth dropping everything for? Everything he was beginning to uncover?

"For God's sake, Jim," Van Hayden had barked, "it's part of it. Get here!" The call had come on Saturday.

Gammon had sweated through Sunday, then had done it on Monday with no notice at all. Rushed aboard a United 727 to Chicago. Grabbed a 747 out of there. He was in Honolulu by nightfall, exhausted, then inordinately pissed off to find at the Colony Surf not Van Hayden, but a sealed note from him—and that not until Gammon had produced ID for the desk clerk. The note gave him the Hana address and directions to reach it. It was unmistakably written in Van Hayden's old man's scrawl. Gammon was used to that, but its unevenness told him it had been written by a frightened man.

Gammon stayed the night at the Colony Surf, which Van Hayden had anticipated: the old man had even reserved and prepaid a room for him. In the morning, Gammon had checked out, taken the limo to Honolulu International's Inter Island Terminal, and never once noticed the car that followed him from the Colony Surf's entrance on Kalakaua Avenue.

At Kahului Airport, he had rented the Nissan, asked the muumuu-clad clerk for a Maui Drive guide, then headed out on Route 36, the Hana Highway.

Shortly past the first set of switchbacks, the narrowing blacktop had begun to arch high around lava promontories upholstered in brilliant green, then dove precipitously into lush rain forest valleys. Abruptly, the pavement dwindled to little more than a back country lane, its macadam suddenly potholed, then little more than loose gravel. A brief stretch of this, then it was macadam again. Tropical rains cascading down Haleakala's slope did this periodically, Gammon deduced, followed by hasty repairs to keep the road open.

Just past the turnoff for Wailua, a tiny village barely visible far downslope at the Pacific's breaker-creamed rim, he noticed the white Chevy. It came up fast. Moments ago, across the highway's hairpin swing around a fold between towering lava escarpments, he had seen only a mile of empty road behind him. Four minutes later, there was the white Chevy. It closed rapidly, then it decelerated to pace him a hundred yards back.

Gammon felt a prickle of apprehension. Then he forced himself to think, damn it. *Think.*

How could FRETSAW's people have known he was rushing hell-bent for Hana in this underpowered little Nissan that he had rented in such a hurry at Kahului Airport? Could they possibly know why? The note that had awaited him at the Colony Surf had obviously been intended as a break in Van Hayden's trail, should FRETSAW be dogging him. And Gammon hadn't been all that obvious about his own actions: hadn't told his secretary where he was going, hadn't even told Marcie; had bought his own ticket at Dulles . . . with a credit card. Damn! With a credit card. But that had been unavoidable on such short notice. And even if they thought to initiate one, wouldn't a computer scan take time? How could they possibly be on him this quickly?

They couldn't, Jim Gammon decided. The Chevy was no more threatening than a pair of tourists earning the right to an I SURVIVED THE ROAD TO HANA bumper sticker.

He scruffed the Nissan around yet another hairpin switchback, this one skirting a niche with a tiny waterfall set deep in its drapery of huge *ape-ape* leaves and trailing lianas. A small white stone cross edged the pavement. Apparently some poor sucker hadn't made the turn here. Probably slammed head-on into the lava behind the lush foliage. At night, maybe, after one mai tai too many. There were a lot of such crosses along the crazy road, Gammon realized. Jesus, what a drive! His chest muscles had begun to ache from wrenching the wheel through endless switchbacks and around sudden potholes and runoff ruts.

His eyes darted to the rear-view mirror again, made out two people in the Chevy before its image was blanked by another high-flying turn to skirt an outcrop. Hell, yes, a couple of tourists. He put his full attention on the road.

The impossible alignment skittered the Nissan's rear wheels toward the outside of a tight rightward bend. He pumped the brakes judiciously, avoided a skid on the loose gravel, jinked the car straight again, and broke out of forest gloom into wide-open space. Now he drummed along a rare straight stretch, five hundred feet above the churning froth line where Pacific rollers thundered into Haleakala's lava skirt. The sea had washed the mountain's oceanside edge to shiny black. A tangle of vegetation began above the contrasting strips of white foam and black lava to blanket the mountainside in green carpeting, slit through horizontally by the Hana Highway. Incredible place for a road.

Suddenly, the Chevy loomed huge in his mirrors, its grille big as a truck's.

Close enough for Gammon to recognize its driver. *Kolker!* God!

How? I've been so damned careful, Gammon told himself desperately. Obviously not careful enough. He felt a curious emotional crossfire. Fear, for sure. The spiced scent of the rain forest was abruptly overridden by the smell of his own sweat. Yet, shafting through the fear was a sense of vindication. Goddamn it, he was right! FRETSAW was a lot more than he'd been led to believe. Kolker, contract chief of security, was *here.* On top of him. That proved plenty.

And, Gammon realized, I'm leading him and whoever that other guy is with him, straight to Van Hayden.

Better to bluff it out. Pull over and talk. He could come up with some plausible reason for being here on the eastern tip of Maui when he was supposedly back in D.C. attending to FRETSAW funding.

The Chevy tailgated in earnest, riding his bumper only inches from contact. Jesus . . .

A woman. Would Kolker go for that? I'm here for a stolen weekend of sun, surf, and skin. Cheating on Marcie just a little. A guilty grin, a nudge. You know how it is, Kolker. Weren't you a married man once, yourself? A little variety helps keep it up, right? Met her at a conference at the L'Enfant Plaza, set this up then. Marcie thinks I'm on Foundation business. Don't blow it for me, buddy.

Okay, Kolker let's lay that on you. Gammon slowed the Nissan. Too abruptly. His head flew back against the headrest. Christsake, Kolker!

He jerked his foot off the accelerator, but the Nissan failed to slow further. He tapped the brake. Then he rammed it hard. The little car skidded into the outside lane.

God, he was being *shoved* across the road by the big Chevy! The sons of bitches had to be crazy!

Not until the Nissan's canted front wheels banged off the pitted blacktop and through the roadside weeds did Jim Gammon realize that Kolker intended to kill him.

The Nissan's left front tire thudded into a hidden rock. The front end was catapulted upward. The neck-twisting bounces stopped. He was riding on air. Literally. The Nissan flew away from the edge of the Hana Highway in a long, graceful parabola, its engine idling softly.

Gammon rode the brakes all the way down, the steering wheel still cramped full right.

He plunged four hundred vertical feet to his point of impact forty yards above the shoreline. He had time to think about the damndest things. How clear the air was. How it's not the long fall that kills you—one of Steve's quips.

Halfway down, wind began to whistle past the plunging car with increasing shrillness. He was glad he wore the seatbelt. All right so far. Insanity, this was insanity!

The little white automobile nosed straight down. The trees began to grow large. Like falling into a thick, green rug. But what was under it? *Jesus God!*

Marcie, I'm sorry. Thought it was a legit job should have known better Steve goddammit *do something about this! You'll know, because on your birthday . . .*

The trees soared like broaching green whales. The Nissan crashed through a huge African tulip in an explosion of brittle branches. It was deflected a few degrees by a thick limb that sheared off the car's roof.

The decapitated Nissan and its decapitated driver smashed into the forest floor, flint-hard beneath its mat of rotted vegetation.

The sound of the impact was not dramatic, muffled as it was by the heavy rain forest canopy. But the energy built up by the four-hundred-foot free-fall had compacted the Nissan to two-thirds of its original length.

A liana, thick as a man's forearm, was displaced by the air blast. It swung slowly back into place over the wreckage. The forest had already begun to absorb the abrupt intrusion.

Sweating in his out-of-place charcoal business suit, white shirt, and red-striped blue tie, Milo Kolker said, "You can get back in the car now, Georgie."

"I thought we were only supposed to stop him." It wasn't an accusation. George Prescott's cleanly chiseled face wore something approaching a grin.

"Consider him stopped." Kolker wished he could have assigned somebody else to this operation with him. But Prescott was the only other wet-work specialist the agency had. The cobra-jawed kid's impulsiveness sure was a contrast, he thought, with his own deliberate planning. Prescott's ample blow-dried, black hair and his clean-cut yuppie look were contrasts, too. Kolker had often thought of himself as a potential Marlboro Man, if he hadn't been born just a shade squatty—and in Rhode Island. At five feet seven, he was as crag-faced as that epitome of the cigarette-worshipping American male, but Kolker expected to live longer because he didn't smoke. Never had. Didn't drink, either. He despised the weakness of those who did.

Georgie Prescott did a lot of both. He was firing up one of those damned little brown things of his right now. With slightly shaking fingers.

"I thought the car would burn." Georgie's voice around the stupid girlie cigar was only a half decibel above a whisper. Kolker glanced at him. The son of a bitch was enjoying this.

Kolker took a last speculative look over the edge of the highway's overgrown berm. "That's on TV. They always burn on TV because special effects puts in gas containers with detonators. That down there is real life."

Prescott squinted downward again. "You can barely see where he went in. If you didn't know where to look, you wouldn't see it at all."

"Doesn't make much difference. An accident is an accident." Why was he standing here explaining basics to this little preppie? In his own establishment-image dark suit, Prescott looked like what he was—a recent grad of Hotchkiss or Lawrenceville, one of those fancy Eastern boarding schools. Kids. They're giving me kids to work with.

Kolker ran a clubby hand across his balding, short-cropped ash-gray scalp. He was surprised that it came away sweaty.

"Too damned hot to stand here," he growled, though the morning was only pleasantly warm. "Too damned risky, too." He checked the shoulder where the Nissan had gone over. Some churned-up shrubbery, but the gravelly macadam showed only two short skid marks. He scruffed them away with his polished black shoe. Then he bent down to peer at the Chevy's front bumper. "Only scuffs. Could be from anything."

Still staring downhill, Prescott hadn't moved from the edge of the drop-off. Kolker grabbed his arm. "Come on, Georgie. That down there is only half the assignment. Put out the damned cheroot, and let's move."

Ninety minutes later, the Chevy, now with Prescott at the wheel, rolled out of the incredible snake of the mountain road, drummed through abruptly open country, then entered the sleepy village of Hana.

The highway split at the north end of town, near the medical center. Kolker squinted at the map he'd bought at the airport's news kiosk. "Take the high road, to the right."

At forty-miles-per-hour, they cut through upper Hana in no time, a real anticlimax, Kolker decided, after the attention-focusing drive to get here. He'd ordered Prescott behind the wheel when they'd gotten back in after taking care of the Gammon problem. Kolker had wanted to handle that part of the assignment personally. The rest of the trip here had been routine, if anyone could call the second half of the Hana Highway routine.

The paralleling lower road, visible now and then far downslope near the small harbor, looked as if it cut through the resort area he'd expected Hana to be. Up here could have been almost any sparse rural settlement. When they reached the south side of town, the pavement deteriorated into ruts and bumps, still drivable, but a fast getaway would shake their teeth out.

He wasn't sure how they would handle Van Hayden, but the orders were specific. Use own resources for terminal disaster control: accidental mode. Kolker knew exactly what that meant. The initiative was his, and FRETSAW didn't want Van Hayden to make it out of Hana.

The entranceway that had been described to him soared uphill, to the right of the main road. The turn was sharp, more than ninety degrees, and Prescott overshot. He braked hard. The tires scuffed gravel. He threw the gear selector into reverse, let the Chevy jerk back a couple of yards to clear the hedgerow of brilliant red bougainvillea on the left. He swore, spun twin fans of loose stones and dust behind the rear wheels. He was a rough driver. They fishtailed up the hill, then Prescott got the car straightened out.

"Christ," Kolker muttered.

For a quarter mile, they climbed between twin hedgerows of hibiscus and frangipani. Then the drive bent leftward into a level parking area. The house lay below, an expensive ramble of dark-stained wood and tinted glass. Through breaks in the dense landscaping, the glass looked as opaque as steel. One car, a rented Toyota, was parked up here. Van Hayden's, Kolker assumed. They'd told him the man was alone. The owner of the place, a college classmate of retired attorney Walker Van Hayden, lived stateside six months, here six months. Stateside now, he'd given Van Hayden the key.

The substantial grounds appeared to be encompassed by chain link, seven feet high with three strands of barbed wire strung along outwardly canted braces at its top. So this was how the retired CEO of Garvin Industries spent his winters on the Valley Isle: luxuriously fortified like a paranoid godfather. No wonder Van Hayden had sought refuge up here.

An electronically operated gate gave access to flagstone steps down to a walkway from the parking plateau. Kolker pushed the button beneath the built-in speaker.

Nothing. Then a shaky, "Gammon? Jim Gammon?" The voice was as dry as shuffled papers. So Van Hayden couldn't see the gate from inside the house, and there was out here no visible TV remote camera. Some security.

"Yes," Kolker said.

The gate lock clicked. How easy could this get? Prescott followed Kolker in, his customary little grin back on his face. In tandem, they walked down the long, imported flagstone path to the house, through a meticulously tended group of coconut palms, past a stand of pampas grass that bent gently in the soft breeze, through a trellised arch of some vine that bloomed lavender. Kolker didn't know what some of this stuff was, but it all smelled good, and somebody had a full-time job taking care of it. Just one car back there, though. He was reasonably sure Van Hayden was alone in Garvin's isolated paradise.

The sound of running water pulled the security specialist's eyes away from the house. Swimming pool over there, to the left. The soft air carried a faint tang of chlorine behind the dominant scent of tropical flowers. He motioned Prescott to stay in place. Kolker edged his head around a planting of tall ferns.

The splashing sound came from a chromed pipe that recirculated filtered water. No one was out there.

"Okay," he told Prescott. They walked in tandem up to the Mexican-styled carved door. It had a crosshatched pattern in a mellow, reddish wood. A little security lens was set in it at eye level.

"Stand off to one side," he ordered Prescott, "away from that lens."

This was some back door, or was it the main entrance? Kolker thumbed the mother-of-pearl button set in the door's wide jamb. The chime was faint. A tightly built house. Maybe even concrete or cinder block walls behind wood veneer. With bullet-resistant glass in those picture windows? He'd read somewhere that Garvin was worth $300 million.

After some twenty seconds, Kolker heard the metallic sound of a well-oiled dead bolt being retracted. The ornate wrought iron latch vibrated under the light finger pressure. The door cracked open an inch.

"Thank God, Gammon." The voice was high and thin with strain. "I'd begun to think you'd never—"

Kolker rammed his shoulder against the door and shoved it wide.

"My God!" Van Hayden shrilled. He recoiled halfway across the terrazzoed entrance hall, a stunned old man in powder-blue slacks, an open-throated white Hawaiian shirt with a green palm frond pattern, and thong sandals on his uncoordinated sockless feet. "You're not Gammon!"

Kolker, with Prescott now in the hall behind him, said, "No, we're not Gammon, Mr. Van Hayden. Mr. Gammon will not be coming. Georgie, close the door, please."

The big door thunked shut like a massive main gate of a prison, Kolker thought. It was Van Hayden's prison now. His death cell.

The old man made an admirable effort to get hold of

himself, forced his slender body erect, attempted to straighten his disheveled white mane with a trembling hand. "Who . . ." he began, then swallowed. "Who in the hell do you think you are, bursting in here? This is a private residence."

The voice was stronger now, but Kolker could see fear in Van Hayden's watery gray eyes.

"Take a look around, Georgie," Kolker ordered. "A good look. You find anyone else, bring them back here. And use a handkerchief, you understand? No prints." He turned to the old man. "You want to sit down, Mr. Van Hayden?"

The retired lawyer shook his head. They stood there, Kolker near the door, Van Hayden across the hall, both silent. Kolker heard George Prescott open doors progressively further down a long corridor to the left of the entrance hall.

Abruptly, Van Hayden said, "I've seen you before."

Kolker felt his chest lurch. Then he calmed down. What did it matter? Van Hayden wasn't going anywhere. "Now just where have you seen me before?"

"Nuremberg."

"Where's that? Sounds like New York State."

"Germany. I assisted at the trials."

Kolker was puzzled, then comprehension hit him. Son of a bitch. "I'm an all-American, Mr. Van Hayden. Following orders. Nothing personal at all about this. I'm following orders."

"That defense didn't work there."

"That was then. This is now. I don't question what I'm told to do. It's for the good of the country."

"It always is."

"That'll be enough talk, Mr. Van Hayden." Did the old man suspect why they had come? Kolker wished Prescott would snap it up a bit.

"How do they find you?" Van Hayden asked. "How do they inevitably find you?"

"I said that was enough talk." The old man's newfound calmness was getting to him. The clever bastard was trying for control. Kolker could see through that.

Prescott finally strode back into the entrance area, shaking his head. "Nobody here but the three of us."

"We'll go to your room now, Mr. Van Hayden." Kolker kept his voice matter-of-fact, like he imagined a doctor might. The less hysteria, the easier this would be.

"I assume you are armed?" Van Hayden seemed to want an excuse for compliance.

"Does it make any difference?"

"Good point. In addition to our obvious age differences, I am afraid I am sans-a-belt in karate."

Kolker wished Van Hayden hadn't said that. He felt a sudden and unwelcome touch of liking for the old man. That wouldn't make any difference, either. It just made this assignment a degree less easy.

The guest bedroom Van Hayden was using was at the end of the central corridor, near the swimming pool. The room was large, had twin double beds with expensive rainbow-hued spreads, sturdy white bamboo-motif furniture, and huge tinted picture windows on the two corner walls. The windows were shaded with vertical overlapping cream cloth slats, a kind of window covering Kolker hadn't seen before.

"How do you work these?" he asked Van Hayden.

"Why should I contribute to your criminal intrusion?" The old man's voice was cold as winter air now. Kolker almost smiled. Didn't matter. The midday light outside was so bright, nobody could have seen through the tinted glass anyway. And this end of the house was secluded by heavy plantings. Kolker couldn't see any of the fence from here.

"You brought swimming trunks, Mr. Van Hayden?"

The old man wasn't cooperating now.

"Georgie?"

Prescott reached for the drawer pulls on the bamboo-trimmed dresser.

"Your handkerchief, Georgie." God, how did he endure working with such kids?

Prescott finally found the trunks draped over the shower

curtain rod in the adjoining bathroom. The obvious place, Kolker reflected, since Van Hayden had been here a reported day and a half. A tiny slip, not having Georgie look in there first, but enough of a slip to warn Kolker that they might be losing a little of their edge. Better get on with this and get out of here.

"Put on those trunks, Mr. Van Hayden."

"And if I refuse?"

"We'll put them on for you." Kolker believed the old man would opt for dignity. He hoped so. He didn't want to have to take the chance of marking him. He waited a second or two, then he said, "Georgie—"

Van Hayden reached out, took the burgundy trunks from Prescott, turned toward the bathroom.

"No, you'll do it out here." Damned if he was going to give the old man an opportunity to mark himself or take some unusual substance, or do anything else that might derail the accidental death verdict Kolker intended to arrange for Maui County Police records.

Van Hayden seemed to have gone through three stages: anger, disbelief, defiance. Now he was near stage four. Acceptance. Maybe it was easier when you were almost ninety, Kolker thought. Maybe the anxiety reflex deteriorates. Was that why old people so often waited calmly, looked death straight in the eye, then quietly went?

The old man unbuttoned his shirt and dropped it on the pale green rug. No undershirt.

"Neatly, on the chair," Kolker ordered. "You're going for a casual swim."

Van Hayden's mouth tightened. He bent down, retrieved the shirt, lay it across the chair arm. He had a thin chest with a wiry white thatch, but surprisingly muscular shoulders.

The slacks bunched on the floor. Van Hayden picked them up, folded them neatly across the chair back. He wore white boxer shorts with thin red striping. He stripped off the shorts, flipped them upward with a foot, dropped them on the chair seat.

He stood naked save for the thong sandals, glaring at Kolker. A spare old man, leg muscles stringy and without a pot in his flat abdomen. Pubic hair white as the hair on his chest and head. Penis and scrotum loose. Van Hayden was eighty-seven, but he stood military-straight, a gutsy old man.

Then the scrotum began to tighten, draw up, nearly disappear. So the old man wasn't immune to fear, after all. Prescott saw it and grinned.

Van Hayden said, his voice scratchy, "Are you interested in hearing the truth about whom you are working for?"

"The swimming trunks, Van Hayden."

"I thought not. Truth means nothing to the robot mind."

Kolker ignored that. "You, too, Georgie," he said.

"Me too, what?"

"Strip."

Prescott's face turned dead-white. "Strip for what?"

"You want to get back in the car with your clothes sopping wet?"

"Oh. But I don't have a suit."

"God gave you skin."

"Interesting," Van Hayden said, "that you should mention God." His voice was faltering, but Kolker had to give him credit for trying.

"Put the trunks on, Mr. Van Hayden."

Prescott stacked his clothes on the bed. He had a surprisingly good build, the kind you get in a gym, Kolker decided. Without calluses. Then he saw that Prescott was beginning to get an erection. That explained some things about the boy's qualifications, didn't it? Not gay, or he wouldn't have gotten through the screening. But he sure was turning on by what he was about to do.

"Gentleman, we are going to the pool. Georgie, you will need a towel."

A door at the end of the corridor opened on another flagstone path, which swung around the corner of the residence, then led to the broad Mexican-tiled patio that framed the pool. Van Hayden, in his floppy burgundy trunks, was in the lead, followed closely by Prescott, fully erect now under the towel around his waist and walking in a sort of embarrassed half crouch in an ineffective effort to conceal it. Kolker followed a few paces behind.

The only sounds he picked up were the burble of water from the recirculating outlet at the far end of the pool, the deep end, and an occasional bird cry in the shrubbery that concealed the fencing and the driveway beyond. The smell of chlorine was strong, overriding the scent of some nearby flowering shrubs. Gardenias, Kolker thought. Chlorine and gardenias.

He selected a white wrought iron garden chair near poolside, sat down and threw a leg over one of its arms. Might as well be comfortable.

"Into the pool, Mr. Van Hayden."

The old man stood at the top of the steps and glared at him. "If you have any interest in history at all," he said with startling evenness now, "none of those at Nuremberg succeeded with the 'orders are orders' defense. They were hanged."

"Not Goering."

"He poisoned himself."

"Not Hess."

"Life imprisonment, and probable insanity. Is that the best you're hoping for?"

"I hope I'm helping my country."

"You poor bastard." Van Hayden turned away and walked slowly down the steps at the shallow end. Acceptance.

Prescott looked back at Kolker. From his chair, Kolker nodded. Prescott tossed his towel aside and followed Van Hayden into the pool.

Then he arced his naked butt in a surface dive. Van Hayden jumped aside. Kolker wondered what the old man hoped to accomplish by that. Reflex response, he guessed; the way a man would make a desperate attempt to escape a shark in his pool.

Prescott turned out to be adept in the water. He seized Van Hayden's thin ankles, yanked him off his feet, and pulled him beneath the surface. The struggle in the crystal-clear, five-foot-deep water was brief. Prescott rolled the old man on his back on the pool bottom, then stood on his chest to pin him there.

When Prescott's head broke water, Kolker stood at pool edge. "Don't mark him, Georgie," he called. "Don't break any ribs."

Prescott rode the struggling old man like an underwater log roll, grinning, lurching to keep his balance. Under the distorting surface roil, Kolker saw Van Hayden's arms waver upward, claw at Prescott's calves, fall away, then drift. A final gout of expelled air broke the surface. Now Van Hayden's lungs were satisfactorily taking in water.

Prescott had to have felt the final spasm through his feet. His face changed. Slackened, then took on a silly smile. Kolker figured the weird son of a bitch had actually gotten off on this. Took all kinds, this work. Took all kinds.

"Get up out of there, Georgie. Dry yourself, get dressed, and let's haul ass."

It had been a near thing, he realized, as Prescott drove them back down to the Hana high road. It could have blown FRETSAW sky high, according to Buttonwood, and all of them with it. But he and idiot boy here had corked the potential leak.

Why did it have to be so damned difficult and dangerous to do for your country what everyone else lacked the guts to do?

2.

Steve Gammon checked his den clock again. Damned near midnight. Jim had never stretched it out this long. Not since they had started the tradition.

It had come about when their parents had died in the crash of a Grand Canyon sightseeing charter. Steve had rushed from Fort Myers to Chicago to—face it—to do what he could for his kid brother. Jim had been twenty-two then, still living at home; Steve was seven years older, not quite eighteen months out of air force intelligence and already deep in his developing civilian career. The agreement had been born out of Jim's stunned reaction to the tragedy. He'd never had it fully together, anyway, and the shock out of Arizona had thrown him into near helpless confusion.

Steve had found the wills and gotten them to probate, had expedited paperwork, loaned—hell, given—Jim a couple thousand of his own to get the kid going. "My God, Jimbo, you can't stay a boy all your life. You've got a degree in English. That's good in any business."

With the money, he had also given his disorganized brother his favorite lecture on the virtue of persistence. "If you've got that, you don't need an overload of talent, Jim. That's why we get low-cal persistent politicians in the White House instead of intellectual heavyweights who can't stick out the campaign lumps."

"So to the second-raters with staying power go the spoils?"

"That's not quite what I meant, but get the idea, will you?"

Steve had been torn between a moral obligation to stay to help Jim limp into real life, and the need to get back to Fort Myers and keep his own momentum going. Westmore Development had just signed on, and Westmore was a lot more impressive a client than the local developers who had used Steve's services to date.

Westmore won out. Steve left Jim with the logistics of clearing out the old West Chicago homestead, putting it on the market and finding himself an apartment, a job. A life of his own. Steve also left Jim with the promise that he would keep in touch. A lot, at first. Then only monthly. Then, after Jimbo had suddenly caught fire as a pretty damned effective fund-raiser, only sporadically. Finally, it evolved into an absolutely ironclad, mutually agreed tradition. Each faithfully called the other on his birthday.

Today, Steve had waited. The point was to be available, at either home or work, or to arrange for call-forwarding. No call had come to his office. No call had come this evening. The gold hands of the little desk clock inched toward midnight. Then past.

First time in fifteen years. *Fifteen* years.

No call.

What the hell? So Jim couldn't get to a phone. Simple as that. Had to be. He wouldn't have forgotten. They'd been proud of the fact that through all the years, neither of them had ever forgotten a birthday call. Now, with more than a thousand miles separating them, it was the only family ritual left.

Steve lay aside the report draft on which he'd been unable to concentrate, shoved up from the deep leather chair, and his wide mouth tightened. Come on, Jim.

This was stupid, he thought. A forty-four-year-old man sweating out a routine phone call from his thirty-seven-year-old brother. He stood at the den window and gazed across San Carlos Bay. The house stood on a point of low-lying land at the mouth of the Caloosahatchee River. The view of the low gray-green islands that dotted the bay was arresting by day, spectacular at sunset, hypnotic now—a few moonlit minutes after midnight.

Steve lingered at the picture window, hands clasped behind his back. Tomorrow, he would try to track Jim down, find out what had prompted his memory lapse. Tomorrow he—

The phone's shrill made him start. Why was he so edgy over this? Then a little ripple of relief swept through him. Better late than not at all, kid.

"Steve?" Her voice was high with obvious strain, but he recognized it.

"Marcie, what is it?"

"Did Jim call? The birthday call?"

"Isn't he there with you?"

"No. No, he isn't. He packed suddenly and left two days ago. Business, he told me."

"Where?" Steve kept his voice calm, matter-of-fact. She sounded as if she could easily escalate into hysteria.

"He wouldn't say where. I asked him, and he refused to tell me. He just said, 'If you don't know, then nobody can make you tell.' "

The hairs on the back of Steve's neck suddenly felt bristly. "He said that? Has he ever left like this before—not told you where he was going?"

"Never. I was hoping that wherever he is, he would remember your birthday, and you could tell me where . . ." Her voice trailed off.

"He hasn't called, Marcie."

"Oh, God."

"Maybe we're both making too much of this. It's only a birthday call."

"It's more than a casual call, Steve, and you know that. Jim told me it's been going on fifteen years. I know you're trying to minimize this for my sake. I appreciate that, but something's *wrong*. I know it is. But I don't know what to do about it."

"You said he's been away three days. Have you called the Foundation?"

"They don't know anything. Or they said they didn't."

"You don't think they're telling the truth?"

"I don't know what to think, Steve. Some things Jim had said . . . I just don't know."

"What things?" What was she talking about?

The line hissed faintly, then he heard Marcie clear her throat. "Things like, 'I'm not sure what I've gotten myself into' and, 'This isn't what I expected.' He'd begun to say things like that."

"Jornigan & Hall has had him assigned to the Foundation for nearly a year. When did he start that kind of talk?"

"In the past couple of weeks. As if he'd come across something that disturbed him, Steve." She sounded calmer now, but an undercurrent of apprehension persisted.

"That's all he told you? That he felt he might be into something different from what he'd expected?"

"That's all. But you could see more than that in his face. In the way he acted. Our . . . life together."

"Your life together?"

"He's been increasingly irritable—no, that's not quite the word. Preoccupied. Worried. We've always done a lot together, but he's become more and more, well, distant. Even our love life." She paused, and he said nothing, giving her a chance to pull back or rephrase.

"It hasn't been much lately." Her voice had become increasingly tight, now on the edge of tears.

"Hey, Marcie, steady now." He juggled appointments in his head. Adair's people could be put off a few days. Erica could handle the Travis account by herself. He'd hired her as a secretary, and she'd shown him she could handle that much before midmorning coffee. Now she was officially a Gammon Consultants associate, the only one. Lenny Travis might bridle a bit at being temporarily turned over to Erica Brindell, but he would quickly discover she had an IQ beyond Mensa's average reach. It would work out.

Beyond Adair and Travis, nothing pended that couldn't be postponed. "You sit tight, Marcie. I'll be up there tomorrow."

"That isn't why I called, Steve. I didn't intend that you—"

"What's a brother-in-law for? Delta will put me into Washington around midday, if I remember my schedules. I'll rent a car."

"Steve . . ." it was a pro forma protest. He could already hear relief in her voice.

He hadn't slept well. Had he slept at all? The earliest flight out of Southwest Florida Regional Airport was at 7:40 A.M. He'd called Erica from the terminal, filled her in on the Travis arrangement. She'd had to hear it only once, asked two highly technical questions concerning the prime marketing area demographics, and said she would expect Steve's return when she saw him.

As the DC-9 angled up from the reclaimed wetlands west of Fort Myers, Steve reconciled himself to the thought that maybe Erica's confident iron-gray eyes and cool good looks would be politically expedient to take on Lenny Travis, at this stage anyway. Travis was a short man with a barely suppressed uneasiness in taller company. Steve had become aware that his own powerful build, rugged, fairly decent looks, and penetrating hazel eyes could be disconcerting to potential clients who had expected a real estate development feasibility consultant to be more of a spectacled accountant type.

And he had Cary Grant's chin. That apparently had sold Lizabeth Palmer on maneuvering him into a marriage that had foundered just two years out of the starting gate. A sheen of champagne hair, a sleek body with an impact somewhere between that of a panther and a Ferrari, a few high voltage weekends in Nassau, Scottsdale, and Sugar Notch, and a bedtime competency that should have made him wonder much earlier on just who was whose toy. Because after he made it legal, their relationship turned out to be not much more than one of their weekends extended into twenty-three months. They parted with short-lived anguish, mitigated by long-term relief.

Far more compelling had been the growing demand for Steve's consultant services. Could Westmore's projected Mirabel Estates outside Savannah be economically cleared and backfilled to yield two hundred residential sites? What would be the minimum investment, were Hibbing Developers to take over the stalled new town west of Mobile?

Then had come the Adair contract, primarily because of Steve's growing reputation for persistence in a field where a superficial report could doom an investor. He had the tenacity to push for detail until he had the picture in depth. The Adair contract was one hell of a big assignment, fourteen thousand acres available in Central Illinois. Steve flew out there, checked the potential from every conceivable vantage and disadvantage point, came back to Fort Myers with a go recommendation—providing Adair set up five straw companies to purchase the acreage.

Adair had been impressed, and now Steve was at work on a full report and detailed recommendation for Maxon City, Phase II, due by mid-July.

He gazed through the DC-9's oval window. Savannah drifted below.

Where the hell *was* Jim? On the trail of some potential major donor? He'd flailed around after they'd closed out and sold the house in West Chicago. Tried real estate, car sales, repping for a garage tool manufacturer, and he had flopped miserably. Then, in desperation, Jim had taken a minor office job with the local cancer society chapter. To his own amazement, he had blossomed. He was damned good at the specialized art of fund-raising.

From the cancer group, he switched to WTTW, the Chicago public TV station, and he boosted its membership support by 38 percent in his second year there. In his third year, he became a national legend in that tiny industry, and in his fourth, he succumbed to a startlingly high offer from the professional fund-raising firm of Jornigan & Hall on Wacker Drive. Which organization had, eleven months ago, assigned him full-time to the Freedom Through Specialized Awareness Foundation in Washington, one of the myriad of nonprofits headquartered in the District to produce and expend funds for a variety of causes.

Married two years, with a degree of connubial success that made Steve feel benign but undeniable envy, Jim and Marcie had moved from Chicago to D.C., expenses paid by the Foundation, and set up housekeeping in an apartment on upper Connecticut Avenue. The salary was that good.

A cloud layer had glided beneath the jet. Steve turned away from its unremitting opaqueness and reached absently for the in-flight magazine in the pocket behind the seat in front of him.

Maybe Jim's salary was too good. Maybe Brother Jim was really off and running, and there wasn't any need for the birthday call anymore. God knew they hadn't kept in touch lately much more than that.

Hell, Steve, that's an unworthy thought if you've ever had one! Marcie had been one apprehensive woman.

He tried to doze, but his brain began to reel off scenarios unbidden. A mugging in the wilds of downtown Washington? An automobile accident on a lonely Maryland road?

Another woman? The magazine slid off his lap.

He snapped awake. He didn't need this kind of imagining. When the DC-9 had worked its way through the inevitable stack of aircraft over Atlanta, he welcomed the enforced diversion of the plane change.

Fifty minutes after he had hurried up the debarkation ramp into Baltimore-Washington International's unaccountably black-painted pier, Steve pulled his rented Buick Skyhawk into the parking garage beneath the Crossmoor Arms Apartments. The acne-scarred attendant refused to open the entrance gate until Marcie Gammon's voice on his kiosk speaker acknowledged Steve's visit, and Steve had shown him acceptable ID. Then Steve was directed to an unoccupied parking space stenciled VISITOR. He took the nearby elevator to the fourth floor.

"Oh, God, Steve, I'm so damned glad to see you!" Marcie fell into his arms. She smelled of ginger. Her navy slacks had floury smears, and the sleeves of her white man's shirt, worn tails-out, were rolled up. The spicy tang of baking welled through the apartment door.

He realized how long it had been since he'd held a woman. She felt soft, vulnerable. Then she felt like someone else's wife.

"I'm making cookies," she said abruptly. She shut the apartment door and led him through a short hallway to the kitchen. "Isn't that insane? I couldn't sit still. Couldn't do any writing. Some women clean. I bake."

"How's the writing coming?" He had found it impressive that she had managed to sell three stories to *Redbook,* two to *McCall's,* and a scattering of pieces to lesser markets in the three years she and Jim had been married. Just the beginning, apparently; she was only twenty-nine, eight years Jim's junior.

"I'm in the middle of revising a near-miss for *Family Circle.* An article. About moving."

"A how-to piece."

"More of a how-not-to." There her superficial banter ended. She leaned on the kitchen table with both arms, and her amber eyes clouded. "Steve, something is terribly, terribly wrong."

"Come on, now. Ease up. We'll find him."

She looked so damned pretty standing there, teary-eyed, her uptilted nose only slightly red, smooth lips compressed with tension, auburn hair needing a comb just a little. Steve had seen her only twice since the wedding, during trips that had brought him briefly to Chicago, then to Washington. He'd been impressed by her brainy beauty; captivated by her mouth, of all things. Lips a trifle thin, but smooth as pink satin. She used a minimum of makeup. How had Jim, the family bumbler, managed to find such a charismatic, sensitive woman, Steve wondered, while his own marriage had been an impulsive disaster?

"Damn. The cookies!" She grabbed a hot pad, yanked open the oven door, and slid out a sheet of golden ginger cookies. The abrupt switch from concern for a missing husband to her baking demands struck Steve as incongruous. Then the hot cookie sheet rattled as she set it on the stainless steel countertop next to the stove. She might be barely hanging on.

"You said you last saw Jim Monday?"

"Monday morning. Something had been bothering him all weekend. I couldn't get through to him, Steve. He wasn't like himself. He paced. He stared out the window. He barely talked to me. On Sunday morning, he wouldn't . . . we usually . . ." She reddened. "He wasn't interested. It was as if I wasn't even there. It just wasn't like him, Steve. And he's never been like that before."

"You have any idea what was eating him? Was he sick?"

"It had to be his job. I told you on the phone what he said."

"That he wasn't sure what he'd gotten himself into, and it wasn't what he'd expected?"

"He said that a week or so before, and after that he seemed . . . preoccupied. But after the phone call, he was worse." She leaned against the sink, her hands unable to stay still. Then she snatched up a spatula and began to flip the warm cookies off the steel sheet onto a length of waxed paper to cool. She worked in nervous darts, impatient with the fragrant discs that wouldn't come loose readily.

"A phone call?" he prompted.

"Saturday morning. Early. He thought I was still asleep."

"Who was it? Did he say?"

"I don't know who it was. He didn't tell me anything about it. He was out here in the kitchen, making coffee. On weekends, we get our own breakfasts whenever we feel like it. He couldn't sleep, I guess, so he was out here when the phone rang. All I heard him say was, "Will Monday be okay?" And Monday, he packed a suitcase and left without breakfast. Around eight. Usually he didn't leave until eight-thirty."

She turned to the little window above the sink. Beyond it, he saw only the brickwork of the building next door. Not much of a view.

"He wouldn't tell you where he was going?"

"That was when he said, 'If you don't know, then nobody can make you tell.' I thought he was joking, but now I find it frightening."

Her voice broke. Steve said nothing, but he felt a little icicle skid along his spine. "You said you called the Foundation."

"Tuesday morning. Jim's secretary told me he hadn't shown up Monday at all. She thought he was here, sick."

"How about the police?"

She shook her head. "I just couldn't get myself to do that, Steve."

"Marcie, after forty-eight hours he was technically a missing person."

"I know, but I couldn't admit to myself that something might . . . I called you, Steve."

He shoved back his chair."I need a phone. No, not that one. Is there one in another room?"

She looked at him blankly, then seemed to understand that he was trying to spare her the cold checking procedure he was about to get into. "In the spare bedroom. Jim uses it for a home office. At the end of the hall."

The bedroom office was twelve-by-twelve with a daybed that doubled as a sofa, a small bleached oak flat-top desk, an oak captain's chair, and a blond-wood chest of drawers. He pulled out the chair and reached for the desk phone.

The District of Columbia Police Public Information Branch, after a lengthy wait, had nothing at all on a Gammon, James J. No DWI rap, no accident report, no John Doe incident that fit the description. Using the Yellow Pages he found in the desk's center drawer, Steve began a laborious check of area hospitals and emergency clinics. That took half an hour and led nowhere. To his relief. But the blanket negative didn't do a thing for his growing sense of frustration.

He glanced at the room's closed door, then he systematically went through all five drawers of the small desk. Suburban Bank of Chevy Chase checkbook, a small rubber-banded sheaf of current bills, assorted stationery items, Rolodex address file, which he flipped through but failed to find anything that seemed significant, thick District and Maryland suburban phone books, a couple of dogeared fund-raising manuals. The bottom drawer on the right-hand pedestal was empty. If he'd expected anything significant to jump out at him, he was disappointed.

He slapped the packet of unpaid bills against his palm. Jimbo, what the hell are you into that's so all-fired secret?

Steve returned to the kitchen, frustrated and depressed and trying not to show it.

"Good news, in a way. No police report, and he's not in any area hospital."

She had taken a second batch out of the oven. He wondered if she would keep on manufacturing ginger cookies until Jim turned up. Then she turned from the stove and spread her arms in a gesture of helplessness. "Oh, *damn,* Steve! Where *is* he?"

"It's past four. I'll go find a hotel. Then tomorrow I'm going to pay a visit to the Foundation."

"Not a hotel, Steve. Stay here. Please."

He met her eyes, hesitated. Then he said quietly, "All right, Marcie. I'll get my bag from the car."

For a while, he wished he hadn't agreed to stay. She was everything Lizabeth had failed to be. He wondered how he would react if she were to offer encouragement. She was warm, sweet, and smelled of ginger. And she was Jim's wife.

In the sparsely furnished bedroom-office, he lay sleepless on the daybed for a long time.

3.

The building was a converted townhouse on a quiet side street off Dupont Circle in northwest Washington. The narrow, three-story red stone structure appeared at first glance to have weathered the city's bitter winters and notoriously muggy summers far better than the time-scarred white frame buildings that flanked it in mid-block. But as Steve mounted the four gritty stone entrance steps, he noticed that the cream paint of its window frames and sills was chalky and flaking.

The brass plate bolted to the stone facade near the wrought iron and glass entrance door had been carefully polished, though, and its engraved lettering stood out boldly: FREEDOM THROUGH SPECIALIZED AWARENESS FOUNDATION, INC.

The heavy door swung into an outdated black- and white-tiled vestibule. The oak door inside opened on a parquet-floored hallway that ran the length of the building. It was partially blocked at its near end by a beautifully preserved Queen Anne desk just beyond the entrance. Behind the desk perched a middle-aged receptionist, her gray hair mercilessly moussed into a helmet-like swirl that looked as if it would crack were she to move her head too rapidly.

"Yes, sir?" Her voice had a razory edge, no doubt honed daily by reaction to the corps of supplicants who surely made tireless rounds of Washington foundations. MISS SIMMONS, read the bronze-on-walnut nameplate on her desk. MISS, not MS.

"I would like to see Mr. Pope, please." Richardson Pope, Marcie had told him, was the Foundation's president.

"I'm sorry, Mr. . . . ?" She cocked her head upward expectantly.

"Gammon. Steven Gammon. Fort Myers, Florida."

"Gammon? A relation of the Gammon we have on staff, James Gammon?"

She was quick, despite her fuddy demeanor.

"My brother. Missing, I understand, since Monday."

"I'm sure there is a logical explanation," Miss Simmons said evenly. "Mr. Pope, I'm afraid, is not in. Perhaps you would care to speak with Mr. Buttonwood?"

"Who's he?" Steve wondered where, in all of Washington, she had managed to find her burgundy dress that zipped to the throat and sported a startlingly white Peter Pan collar.

"Mr. Buttonwood is our executive director, in charge of day-to-day operations. Perhaps he can give you a few minutes." She reached for her multibuttoned Call Director phone.

Shortly, a blonde with slender legs that burgeoned into a wicked-looking pair of hips beneath her tight beige knit sheath clicked down the dark wood staircase midway along the hall.

"I'm Alix Cortland." She gave him a practiced smile. "Mr. Buttonwood's executive assistant. Come with me, please."

He followed the drum-tight skirt up the stairs. The converted townhouse was larger than it had appeared from the street. It smelled of lemon-scented furniture polish, mimeo ink, and sandalwood, the last drifting in Alix Cortland's wake.

At the second floor landing, she led him along a carpeted hallway toward the front of the building, past several rooms he deduced had once been bedrooms. Now they served as office space, crammed with what looked like too many employees in each, young men and women seated along both sides of wide tables that had been partitioned into phone carrels. Bucket shops, three of them. On the floor above, he heard the muted clatter of office machines. The Foundation was busy up there, too.

She led Steve through an outer office at the end of the hall. Her nameplate was engraved walnut. MISS again. Mossbacked tradition or rock-nosed management policy?

Miss Cortland rapped discreetly just below the eye-level brass nameplate on the heavy oak door in the rear of her watchdog office.

"Come." The voice within was deep, rich and confident.

Miss Cortland swung open the door, stood aside, and Steve passed through her sandalwood aura.

"Horace Buttonwood, sir. Welcome to the Foundation." The man who strode from behind his gleaming Victorian mahogany desk with his hand already outstretched had the build of a linebacker, the blue pinstripes of a neatly bearded banker, and a Jerry Falwellian vocal resonance. Extreme unction, Steve thought ungraciously. Buttonwood's handshake was warm, dry, and firm. A fund-raiser's grip.

"Sit down, sir. Sit down. No, not here across the desk. Let's use the sofa there by the window. I prefer informality." He chuckled. His eyes were such a sparkling green that Steve wondered if he were wearing tinted contacts. "Coming from Florida, you no doubt have quite a different concept of informality." He chuckled disarmingly again.

"Now, Mr. Gammon," he said from the depths of the yielding cushions of his big midnight-blue sofa, "I assume you are wondering what has happened to your brother."

"I'd call that a reasonable assumption." Steve couldn't decide whether Buttonwood's near-cloying affability was a genuine personality trait or a defensive veneer. The paintings that decorated Buttonwood's walls—four chaotic splats of acrylic over acrylic—were as enigmatic as the man.

"All I can tell you is that we are wondering the same thing ourselves. He simply did not show up here Monday at all. And there has been no communication from him since." Buttonwood leaned back and spread his hands, palms upward. "I don't know what else to tell you."

"What is he working on? What's his current project?"

"His overall assignment, obviously, is to raise money for FRETSAW."

"FRETSAW?"

Buttonwood seemed surprised. "Freedom Through Specialized Awareness. FRE-T-S-AW. FRETSAW, we call ourselves informally. The acronym is much easier on the tongue than the Foundation's full name. Your brother's work specifically? He is one of our first floor people."

"Which means?"

"One-on-one solicitations of major donors for planned giving. He is one of our three in-person financial counselors." Buttonwood stroked his short-cropped chestnut beard. "You aren't familiar with the funding business? Planned giving involves the Foundation in a major benefactor's overall financial structure. At the very least, we strive to be remembered in the will. At the optimum, we assume overall management of a donor's investments, with the proceeds going to him or her during his or her lifetime."

"And at death, the investments become the Foundation's property?"

"That is the way it is done, yes. But at considerable tax savings during the benefactor's lifetime."

Steve sat forward, arms resting on his knees. The sofa's yielding cushions were far too comfortable. By design, he decided. "And that's what Jim does? Planned giving, you called it."

"Exactly. A first floor man. That's where we put our best people. The second floor is used for our telephone solicitation specialists—and for these administration offices. On the third floor is our direct mail operation. You no doubt heard the processing machinery in full swing as Miss Cortland brought you up the hall."

"You seem very well organized, Mr. Buttonwood." Steve glanced at the three-shelf bookcase on the opposite wall with its neat rows of fund-raising and management texts, and a complete set of all current Marquis *Who's Who* volumes.

"We like to think so, sir." Buttonwood ran a thumb and forefinger down the V of his bearded jawline. The beard, Steve noticed, did not grow quite high enough to conceal completely a strawberry birthmark the size of a thumbprint on Buttonwood's left cheek.

"For what?"

"I beg your pardon, Mr. Gammon?"

"What is all the money being raised for?"

Buttonwood's black eyebrows arched toward his low hairline. "I thought your brother would have told you that."

"He hasn't been exactly garrulous concerning his employment."

"We, ah, serve as a voice of the public conscience, you might say. We are an information service." Buttonwood cleared his throat. "Would you care for coffee, Mr. Gammon? I can have Miss Cortland—"

"Left-wing or right-wing, Mr. Buttonwood?" Which way had Brother Jim leaped?

"We don't think of ourselves as politically aligned. We simply strive to bring the truth to public attention."

"What truth is that, Mr. Buttonwood?"

"Quite succinctly, the awareness of the threat the Soviet Bloc poses to the world today."

Right-wing. "And how is that accomplished?"

"Through publications, Mr. Gammon. Advertisements in such respected newspapers as *The New York Times, The Los Angeles Times, The Wall Street Journal.* Such periodicals as *Forbes, Business Week, Money* magazine. And through our own newsletter to a large subscriber list with a leadership demographic profile, including members of Congress, subscribers in the executive branch, the Fortune 500. We are highly respected, sir."

"Highly respected, well organized, smoothly run, yet you

don't know where one of your key employees is after he's been missing almost five days."

"I don't consider that fair," Buttonwood bristled. His face reddened above the beard's wiry curls, the strawberry mark now livid. "The man failed to appear, failed to call in, failed to communicate with us in any way. We are fund-raisers, Mr. Gammon, not clairvoyants." He glanced at his wristwatch, a gold Omega. "I'm sorry I can't be of more help, and I do have another visitor scheduled."

Buttonwood had been professional, courteous, apparently open, and no help at all. Steve sensed that nothing was to be gained here. Was the man as earnestly ignorant of Jim's whereabouts as he seemed, or was this a sample of Washington's infamous stonewalling?

Steve pushed up from the sofa's encompassing depths. Buttonwood was perhaps a little too glib. Steve wondered what Buttonwood might not have told him.

"I'll have Miss Cortland show you out." The fund-raiser touched a button on his complex desk phone.

On the stairs, Steve told her, "Mr. Buttonwood said it would be okay for me to take a look at Jim's office." A small lie of convenience, that. He purposely hadn't asked Buttonwood because he had begun to get a sense of unreality about this place. A direct mail operation, telephone banks, a planned giving department—big bucks. All this to underwrite an ad campaign? A newsletter? He hadn't wanted to give Buttonwood the opportunity to deny him access, yet he couldn't put his finger on why he felt this way.

Was he losing his objectivity in his concern over Jim's unexplained disappearance? Hell, he probably ought to turn the thing over to the cops, help Marcie glue herself back together as best he could, then get on the next plane to Florida.

"Mr. Gammon's office is to the left, Mr. Gammon." Miss Cortland's voice was blonde, too. Low and husky. He smelled the sandalwood again. "His administrative assistant is Mrs. Rossmyer."

A clone of the front hall's watchdog? That assumption was promptly dismissed when the tight-skirted Miss Cortland ushered him into the office midway along the ground floor hall. Mrs. Rossmyer was tiny, with a pony tail of straight blue-black hair, owl-class pink-tinted glasses that rode the tip of her nose, and a pursed little mouth she had accented with lipstick the shade and intensity of a brake light. A small, gold Star of David rode the black-sweatered contour of her not-so-tiny bosom.

"Becky, this is Mr. Gammon's brother, Mr. Steven Gammon. Mr. Buttonwood said it would be all right for him to visit Mr. Gammon's office."

He found it interesting that Becky Rossmyer waited until Buttonwood's assistant was on her way back upstairs before she said, in a voice so low he had to strain to catch the words, "For God's sake, Mr. Gammon, where *is* he?"

He caught her furtive glance past him into the hall, and he motioned his head toward Jim's office door at the rear of her cubicle. She preceded him into Jim's office, and he shut the door behind them.

"Something about her worries you?"

"Something about this place, Mr. Gammon."

Becky Rossmyer's little space had been half the size of Miss Cortland's, and Jim's office was smaller than Buttonwood's. But its Oriental rug helped, and the desk was yet another certifiable antique in rich cherry. The twin filing cabinets were cherry as well. The two guest chairs were nicely upholstered in subdued gray and blue stripes, and Jim's desk chair was an impressively high-backed swivel in rough navy weave. Altogether, this was a cosy enough office for a contract junior exec.

He leaned against the desk and folded his arms. Bad body language, but he was feeling defensive as hell. This place, for all its formal courtesy and impressive antique decor, had an unsettling aura. "So, what do you think might have happened to him, Mrs. Rossmyer?"

"Becky, please." Her voice sounded as if she were about to run out of breath. Was that its natural quality, or was it the result of emotional strain? She stood flat against the closed door as if she could keep out something threatening by standing there. "I don't have any idea what's happened to him."

"I'm hoping you might know something that could help, Becky. Come on, let's sit down." He took one of the guest chairs. She sank uneasily into the other and smoothed her white skirt over her knees. He hitched around to face her.

"He didn't show up here Monday at all? Didn't call?"

She fingered the star on its delicate gold chain. "No, sir."

"Steve, please."

"The last time I saw him was Friday afternoon. He said he was going to call on a client Monday morning, so he wouldn't be in until around eleven. But he didn't come in at all. And he didn't call. That was odd, I thought, because he's always been meticulous about that."

"He's good to work for?"

"Oh, yes. I've been here almost seven months, and Mr. Gammon has been very nice."

"Your duties consist of what, Becky?"

She smiled briefly, and he caught an almost subliminal little twist of cynicism. "They call it administrative assistant, but that's just another way of saying secretary. I type correspondence, handle the phone, type his proposals, do the filing. You know, that kind of thing."

She dropped her hand to her lap and made a show of studying her crimson fingernails.

"What are you afraid of, Becky?" He said that conversationally, but she seemed to jump a little, then she met his eyes. Her irises were so dark they looked like hugely dilated pupils.

"I . . . It's the atmosphere. Everything is so prim and proper. And . . . subdued. Like a funeral home. I worked for a printing company before I came here. Maybe it's the contrast."

"If it's getting to you so much, why do you stay?"

"Mr. Gammon. I love working for him." Her mouth twitched into her quirky little smile. "And the money. I'm making almost forty percent more here."

"Nothing specific, then?"

"About what?"

"There's no particular person or incident that's put you off? Only the atmosphere, you said."

"Mr. Pope is kind of . . . creepy, but I've never really had any, uh, direct contact with him."

"Mr. Pope, the Foundation's president?"

She nodded, again studying her hands.

"I tried to get to see him, but he's not in."

"Sure he is. I saw him in the hall this morning. He avoids people. Everybody gets sent to Mr. Buttonwood."

"Why?"

"Maybe Mr. Pope is too busy or something." She glanced at him and just as quickly dropped her eyes again.

"What prompts you to say that, Becky?"

"Things I've heard. Do you know he doesn't have an executive assistant? No secretary. He's the only executive here who does everything himself. Doesn't that strike you as strange?"

Was it? "I don't know how this place operates. He may get along fine without clerical help, so he's saving the Foundation a secretarial salary." Steve stood and stepped to Jim's desk. "You mind if I take a look?"

She rose abruptly and turned toward the door.

"I'd appreciate it if you'd stay," he said. "I might need some help with this." He didn't want her back in her cubicle telling Foundation passers-by that Jim Gammon's brother was in there rifling his desk. She had been outspoken with him. That could mean she was as outspoken with everybody.

Jim was a corporate neatnik. That was unexpected. He'd been the family slob. The desktop held only a brass reading lamp, six-button phone, gold-plated Cross pen and pencil set in a walnut base, a half dozen fund-raising texts between brass elephant bookends, and a spotless green blotter on a blotter pad with tooled green leather edges. Steve had thought desk blotters went out when ballpoint pens came in, but the blotter looked at home in this decor of dated elegance.

As in Jim's home office desk, one of the drawers was barren. Lower right. The drawer above it brimmed with fund solicitation proposals, each neatly typed and bound in a clear acetate cover held in place by a green plastic backbone.

The center drawer was the equipment repository with a flat wooden tray sectioned for paper clips, colored pencils, a stapling machine and staples, the central supply for the green plastic channels used to bind Jim's proposals. Steve found his feeling of depression grow stronger with each drawer opening. This was too much like going through an inventory after a death. And it revealed no more than a fastidiousness he'd never known his brother had.

The lower left-hand drawer held stacks of yellow pads, interoffice memo blanks, scratch pads.

Sterile, all of it. Then Steve opened the last drawer, upper left. A mess. Here was the apparent detritus of the desktop. "So this is how he keeps such a neat office."

"At the end of the day," Becky said, "he sweeps the desktop into that drawer. When it's full, he dumps it in the wastebasket. He won't let me touch it because it has all his notes and phone calls."

Steve picked out the top layer of papers. Last in, first out. These were assorted scrawled notes, presumably to himself. Steve glanced through them. All appeared to be unhelpfully work-related. There were several memo pad sheets of doodlings: circles and stars, and dollar signs. Lots of dollar signs. He must have been fiddling away the time during dull conversations or meetings. Four pink phone message slips, dated May 1. Last Friday.

He pushed the collection across the desk. "Any of this mean anything to you?"

She spread out the papers. "Just the phone slips. He was out of the office for a couple of hours after lunch to call on a potential donor at the Wardman Towers. These calls came in while he was out."

"Routine?"

She leafed through the four slips again. "Mr. Emmart is a donor in Cleveland. I think he wants to make sure his name is listed in the next *New York Times* ad the Foundation places."

"You can buy your way into an ad?"

"For $5,000 or more." She held up another slip. "This call from the Catlett Company was about some plaques we ordered. For $2,500, you get a laser-engraved plaque for your desk."

"How about the other two calls, both from a Van-somebody?"

"Mr. Van Hayden? I don't know why he was trying to reach Mr. Gammon."

"Let me see those again." Steve reached across the desk, then studied the two message slips. "He called at three-ten then again at three-forty. Says on the last one that he would call Jim at home. Sounds fairly urgent. Who is he?"

"One of the Foundation's Advisory Council members. There's a seven-person Board of Trustees that meets quarterly. And there's an Advisory Council that doesn't meet at all." She gave him that cynical little smile. "You get on it by contributing at least five-figures' worth." Then Becky Rossmyer's face tightened. "Please don't tell anyone that I told you about that. I don't think I'm supposed to know."

He offered what he hoped was a reassuring grin. "You think Van Hayden was angling to get his money back? Hell, I don't see anything helpful here." He swept the scraps of paper back in the cluttered drawer. "What about Jim's travel arrangements?"

"I always make his reservations for Foundation trips. We have an account with a D.C. travel agency. I handle his vacation travel, too, but he has me use his own American Express account for that."

Steve thought a moment. "I don't like asking this, but have you ever been aware of his 'going on vacation' with anyone other than his wife?"

"With another woman? No, he did not. And there was nothing going on in this office, either. I'm a definitely married woman who is . . . trying hard to become a mother. If you knew what I'm going through—well, you wouldn't ask such a question."

"I didn't ask it."

"You would have. Anyway, I can't conceive of his doing anything like that." She flicked him a tiny smile. "Pardon the pun."

"Okay, so he's a clean guy, sticks strictly to business, and he's been missing since Monday. Now it's Friday. No area police or accident report."

"You're sure of that?"

"I checked. His wife told me he packed a bag when he left home Monday. Might he have made his own arrangements with the Foundation's travel agency?"

"I already thought of that. He didn't."

"How about on his own with his Amex card, Becky? Do you have his account number?" A long shot, but he didn't have many shots left.

"In my desk." She was out and back in seconds, carefully closed the door again, and handed him a file card with a typed fifteen-digit number.

Steve pulled out his own American Express plastic, studied it, then picked up Jim's desk phone.

"Last button for an outside line," she said.

He clicked in the 800 number printed on his card, waited, got a customer service rep with a voice like Lauren Bacall's, and gave her Jim's account number and name.

Lauren, in 800 number limbo, was eager to please. "Recent postings, Mr. Gammon? There's a $64.60 charge April fourteenth from Thom McAn Shoes in Bethesda. A $506 charge from United Airlines."

Steve's chest thudded. "What date?"

"May fourth. Another charge was posted May fifth from Hawaiian Air."

"Hawaiian Air? You have the destination?"

"Maui, Mr. Gammon."

Maui? "Any hotel charges? Anything after that?"

"That's the last posting we have, sir. It was telexed in."

Steve cradled the desk phone and looked up at Becky Rossmyer. "Maui," he said. "What in hell was Jim doing on Maui?"

In his second floor office, Horace Buttonwood picked up his phone and punched in 444, his direct line to Richardson Pope in the rear of the building a floor below. Damn Gammon's brother, so brazenly assuring Alix Cortland that he'd been given clearance to Gammon's office. Damn Cortland for so readily believing him. And damn himself for not having cleared out Gammon's desk. But then, he couldn't, could he? The presumption had to be that the Foundation expected Jim Gammon to reappear and explain himself.

Buttonwood had no idea what Steve Gammon could find in that office, but he knew instinctively that it was potentially dangerous to let him prowl through his brother's effects. At first, Buttonwood had assumed Steven Gammon to be no more than an understandably concerned elder brother going through the expected motions. He had revised that impression when the man had bluntly asked him what FRETSAW's money was earmarked for. The question hadn't done it; what had set off Horace Buttonwood's alarm bell was the abrupt way it was thrown at him. Then Gammon had conned Cortland into taking him to his brother's office.

He could have asked me, Buttonwood realized, and I would have been forced to grant permission. But had Gammon realized he would have made a quick and significant phone call to Rebecca Rossmyer? Muffling Rossmyer, though she may have known nothing at all, would have been SOP.

"Yes?" Richardson Pope's metallic voice was flat and irritated.

"Pope," Buttonwood said with a twinge of instant anguish, "I'm afraid we may have a problem."

4.

The flight to Honolulu International was god-awful long in coach class. All Steve could get on short notice. Dulles to LA, wedged between two industrial salesman types, both of whom used their briefcases as desks. One of them had a printout calculator that clicked and buzzed all the way to the Rockies while Steve tried unsuccessfully to doze away the hours.

Too many questions. Why had Jim gone so suddenly to Maui, of all places? Why had he been afraid to tell Marcie? *If you don't know, they can't make you tell.* What had prompted that chilling statement? Was Becky Rossmyer understandably uptight because of her frustrating efforts to become pregnant, or was her edginess justified by the atmosphere at FRETSAW? He hadn't found that so damned reassuring himself.

The layover at Los Angeles International didn't help. He downed a single brandy at the airport bar, impatiently prowled the terminal's shops, bought a *Los Angeles Times* and returned to the departure dock to find he couldn't concentrate on more than the headlines. Then he was aboard an Oahu-bound 747 crammed with the excited buyers of two bargain tours: a white-haired AARP group out of Worcester, Massachusetts, and a swarm of balding business types with their tightly corseted wives, all of them wearing white plastic discs imprinted BUCKSAVERS INTERNATIONAL. Most of the Bucksavers had Deep South accents.

Steve drew an aisle seat next to an ancient, bespectacled AARPer who muttered that he wanted to see Hawaii before he died, then added with a horse-toothed grin that he hoped they had a tailwind because he'd been feeling "a mite peaked" since breakfast. That was his last stab at conversation for the next several hours. Steve did manage to sleep most of the way after that. He'd been awake half the night in Marcie's spare room, had napped fitfully during the Dulles-LAX leg. But the 747, syrup-smooth at forty-thousand feet, was soporific.

Yet his sleep wasn't exactly serene. More questions raced through his brain. Maybe Richardson Pope didn't like visitors, but, by God, if one of my men was missing, Steve realized, I'd see anybody who was remotely connected with him. And why had Horace Buttonwood been so distant about Jim's failure to show up or check in for five straight days?

He wasn't sure what he "had gotten into," Jim had told Marcie. Then he'd apparently come to some kind of decision after he'd gotten that phone call early last Saturday. A call at home.

Steve snapped fully awake. "Will call at home," the second Van Hayden phone slip had said. Was it reasonable to assume Van Hayden had called Jim Saturday morning, and that call had triggered Jim's disappearance?

Steve leaned forward to look past the dozing New Englander and his frail wife. The cloud layer that stretched to the horizon was tinted gold. The sun they were chasing had dipped into late afternoon—and probably right into the captain's eyes. Steve checked his watch. Still on eastern daylight time. He made a time zone calculation. No daylight saving in Hawaii. They should be on the ground just after sunset. He would stay in Oahu, near the airport, then catch a Hawaiian Air or Aloha flight to Maui early the next day.

The flight attendants, now wearing flowered muumuus, began to move down the aisles to check seat backs and tray tables. The old man beside Steve yawned.

"Looks like you'll see Hawaii, all right," Steve told him.

"Not there yet," the oldster grumped. Then he allowed himself a wry smile. "But I am feeling a touch better."

In the rear of the cavernous 747, a youngish man in the smoking section stubbed out his thin, brown cigarette. His gray suit and red tie were out of place in this crowd of sports-shirted vacationers. He would have to pick up an aloha shirt at an airport shop, if he could take the few minutes to do that. Maybe while Gammon was picking up his baggage.

This was the second time he had been in Hawaii in five days. When Kolker had put him on James Gammon's brother yesterday, he'd figured it for an easy tail and stakeout. He had spent a lot of time in his own Camaro outside the Connecticut Avenue apartment building he knew had been James Gammon's address. Brother Steve was staying there with Brother Jim's wife. Interesting. To be expected, he supposed, but potentially interesting.

In the morning—this morning—Brother Steve had led him out to the Capital Beltway, then way the hell into Virginia on the four-laner that ended at Dulles. Dulles? There, Brother Steve had bought a ticket and gotten on a goddamned airplane.

So he'd bought a ticket and followed, as ordered. Not hard to do when you carried this assignment's "Edward Johnson" plastic. In Los Angeles, he bought another ticket after Brother Steve settled in to read his paper in the Hawaiian flight departure dock. Hawaii again, and he'd drawn one of the last available seats, right in the ass end of the airplane. At least he could smoke—and wonder what Kolker's reaction would have been if he hadn't made it aboard.

When Gammon shuffled out the 747's side door into the exit ramp at Honolulu International, Georgie Prescott stayed nearly a hundred people behind, wondering whether he would have time to buy a Hawaiian shirt and shed his Eastern Establishment look.

Not quite twelve hours later, a few minutes after 8:00 A.M., a Hawaiian Air DC-9 left Honolulu's Inter Island Terminal and delivered Steve to Maui's Kahului Airport in twenty-six minutes. This was an up-then-down flight, with the two copper-skinned cabin attendants pushing their beverage cart uphill from aft to forward, then back uphill from forward to aft when the jet nosed into its approach past the green-clad humps of the West Maui Mountains.

Only seventeen passengers debarked at Kahului, descending the unloading stairway in single file and keeping that same loose line into the small terminal, open along its east side to the island's benign breeze. Eight of the debarking passengers were members of a Nebraska schoolteachers' tour group, staying at the Hilton Hawaiian Village on Waikiki, a taffy-haired science teacher had told seatmate Steve, but today they were taking a side trip to Maui to ride to the top of Haleakala.

The other passengers were three young couples—honeymooners, Steve guessed, plus a dour, cranelike businessman with a battered sample case, and a clean-cut younger man wearing an aloha shirt that had a blue, white, and yellow hibiscus pattern.

The Indian file of newly arrived Hawaiian Air passengers snaked into the terminal and milled into the crowd already in there, the touring teachers re-forming on the exit side to look for their chartered van.

Now that he was here, Steve realized he'd come to the end of the skimpy documentation he had been able to gather concerning Jim's actions from the last moment Marcie had seen him Monday morning. Now what? Most logically, Jim would have rented a car.

The auto rental counters were ranked along the north side of the terminal, side-by-side open booths. He began with Hertz.

The clerk, a tall Oriental woman, was perfectly willing to backtrack five days' worth through her computer. She drew a blank.

Same at Avis. And Budget. Damn.

Would Jim have used another name? Steve doubted that. Jim had left an easily obtained American Express trail to this point, probably assuming that he would be out of here before he could be tracked—or that no one would track him at all.

Maybe he'd been met here, or had taken a taxi or limo van to one of Maui's resorts. In that case, Steve realized with a twist in his gut, the trail could very well end right here.

At National, the fortyish, freckled, coffee-and-cream black clerk looked up at him sharply. Her lips were a startling and shiny raspberry.

"What was that name again, honey?"

"Gammon. James Gammon. He would have rented a car on May fifth. Last Tuesday."

This was the fifth time he'd said that, and he was close to deciding this was all quite useless.

"Gammon? Just a minute, honey." She pulled a slip of yellow paper from beneath the counter. "Is that G-A-double M-O-N, James J.?"

He hadn't given her Jim's middle initial. He felt his pulse rate jump.

"White Nissan, on the fifth like you said. Says here he was going to bring it back here the same day." She shrugged. "But he didn't."

"Could he have turned it in somewhere else on the island?"

"We checked. Uh-uh. Changed his plans, I guess. But we like to know about that. There's only so many cars available, and we have scheduling problems."

He barely heard her. "Do you remember anything else he might have said? Anything at all?"

"Honey, I was on duty at the time it says he took the car, but I don't even remember him."

"Tall man, dark hair, good-looking. Thirty-seven. Wore steel-rimmed glasses."

"Oh. The doctor."

"No, he's not a doctor." Hell.

"I mean, I remember I thought he looked like a doctor with glasses like that. I play a game, guessing what people are. You said steel rims. That's a doctor. Black rims, that's an accountant. No rims, that's somebody wants you not to notice he's wearing glasses at all."

"Okay, you remember he was here. What he looked like. Where was he staying? Don't you record that on your rental form?" This reminded him of a case he'd handled in the air force, skip-tracing a missing colonel.

"He wasn't staying anyplace. Just wanted the car for the day. I told you that. He asked for a map. And . . ." Her chubby, freckled face grimaced in concentration. "I got it now. He asked how to get on the road to Hana."

"Hana? Where's that?"

"You never been to Maui before?"

"I've been to Oahu once before on business, but not to this island."

"Hana's on the east end of Maui. You go out the airport road till you get to Route 36. That's it, the Hana Highway. Turn left and make sure you buckle your seatbelt. Nice and flat for a while, then you going to hit curves like you never hit before. That's the road to Hana."

"And that's where he went?"

She shrugged ample shoulders again. "That's where he asked about. I can't guarantee where he went."

"You got a car for me?"

"That's what we're here for, honey." She turned to check her scheduling board.

He hit the first of the double switchbacks before 10:00, when the sun was still low enough to throw deep shadows across the now twisting, climbing, and diving macadam.

More than two hours later, wrung out and uncomfortably damp despite the Toyota's air-conditioning, Steve emerged among the gentle slopes north of Hana. There had been a hundred places where a car could ski off the road's precipitous fill, crash down the mountainside, disappear in the dense foliage below. Places where cars *had* done just that, evidenced by the ominous little roadside crosses. But he had seen nothing that would point to a recent accident.

He drove slowly into Hana. Where the highway forked, he took the road to the left, Uake Road, the route that took him downslope near the harbor. If there were hotels in this modest little burg, they would be near the waterfront, he reasoned.

He was right. The Hotel Hana Maui, a ramble of low buildings among impressive gardens and a meandering golf course, was in the center of the waterfront resort section.

The little dark-haired desk clerk was obliging, but not James Gammon had registered there last Tuesday or anytime since. Steve visited several lesser tourist accommodations, but the result was the same. Had Jim registered under an alias—and why would he? Or had he not reached here at all?

Fact: Jim had set out for Hana. That much, Steve could reasonably assume. Either he had gotten here, or he hadn't.

Steve toured the town slowly, swung up Hauoli Road at the end of Uake, backtracked along the upper highway to Keawa Place, turned down Keawa, then headed north again on Uake to cut left up twisting Keanni Drive. He toured Hana's streets slowly, looking everywhere for a white Nissan.

He found one on his climb up Mill Place. His heart banged his chest wall. But the license failed to match the plate number the National rental clerk had given him.

He found another white Nissan parked at the end of the narrow road that swept along the harbor's south rim toward Kauiki Lookout. A National rental sticker was on its rear bumper, but again the license plate number didn't match.

Back on the upper highway, he saw a third white car a

quarter mile behind him and slowed to let it pass. A Plymouth, rented from Avis.

Hana was a tiny town. He had covered it all by 1:30, and he stopped for a quick lunch at a ramshackle frame restaurant at the end of a long drive upslope from the upper highway. Halfway through his grilled cheese with pineapple, he realized something he should have done hours ago, asked for a phone book, and used the restaurant's pay phone to call Maui County Police in Lahaina.

No, a Sergeant Holo assured him, they had no reports at all on that particular rental car. Except . . . just a minute sir; except a notification from National at Kahului Airport that it was overdue for return.

Steve went back to his table at a window overlooking the town and Hana Harbor far downslope. He was playing long odds, now. Seven days ago, Jim had gotten a call at home, logically from Van Hayden. It appeared to have been disturbing enough to impel him to leave suddenly for Hawaii without notice to anyone; to refuse to tell even Marcie where he was going so that she couldn't be *forced* to reveal that information. And he had forgotten—or had been unable—to make the traditional birthday call.

Now Steve knew, or could reasonably assume, that Jim had set out on the Hana Highway. Then he evaporated. Odds were . . . Face it, Steve told himself. Unless he's holed up somewhere beyond Hana, odds are that your kid brother went over the side.

He studied the drive guide he'd been given by the car rental clerk. Beyond Hana, there wasn't much more than additional miles of tough road. Yet in the fifty miles of god-awful highway he'd just driven, nothing had confirmed the possibility that Jim had come to grief back there. Steve had scoured every mile of roadside for telltale tracks. Surely the police had done the same thing, or at least had been conscious of the potential during their routine patrols.

Or was all this empty supposition on his part, based on the

flimsiest of tangible evidence; two American Express charges and a car rental? Damn it, that wasn't so flimsy. He'd have a tough time living with himself if he didn't go as far as he could with this.

On his way out of the restaurant's sloped parking area, he spotted the white Plymouth again. This time, he caught a flash of the young driver's aloha shirt. Blue, white, and yellow.

As Steve slowed for his leftward swing into the upper highway, he was almost sideswiped by an oncoming unmarked car with a flashing red light on its dash. He jumped the Toyota to the shoulder as the tan Mercury whistled past, its siren howling, rocketing south. A hundred feet behind the Merc, a blocky ambulance added its siren to the passing din. It screeched by, closing the distance between the two vehicles, and they disappeared down the narrow road. Hana wasn't so sleepy, after all.

Steve completed the turn northward into the Hana Highway and began the grueling drive back to Kahului. If he found nothing on the way back, there still might be a way to take a final, desperate shot at this.

The helicopter, a red and white, four-place Bell Jetranger, lifted off the helipad at the edge of the Kapalua golf course in northwest Maui. Steve was buckled into the right front seat beside the pilot, a hungry-looking, hound-faced ex-Southerner whose close-cropped sideburns showed white below his Atlanta Braves baseball cap. His name was Barton. Steve wasn't sure whether that was his first or last name. The three-person bench seat in the rear of the small cabin was empty on this hastily arranged private charter.

The chopper nosed down, picked up speed and began to skirt the heavily overgrown north slopes of the West Maui Mountains. Barton didn't seem to want to fly higher than eight hundred feet. He shouted something unintelligible into the whine and roar of the jet-driven rotor, then motioned to Steve to put on the padded headset with its little stalk mike.

"We'll cut across Kahului Bay to Pauwela Point, then pick up the road there," Barton's metallic voice informed him. "The Hana Highway is pretty open to Pauwela, then it starts to get rough. We'll cover it east from there, okay?"

"If you think that's the way to handle it."

"It's your two hundred dollars, ol' buddy."

The return drive from Hana hadn't been any more revealing than the trip out to that remote town. But winding through Hana's side streets, Steve had been struck with the realization that from the air he would gain an entirely different perspective. Back at Kahului Airport, he had learned that Maui offered several helicopter services, none of them based at the airport.

The first he'd called was booked through to Monday. The next could provide an hour's charter for $200 tomorrow morning, Sunday, and could pick him up at Kahului. Or he could get aboard at the pad near the Kapalua golf course near Napili in West Maui. Since it was obvious he'd have to stay the night, Steve opted for the latter, consulted his map, made a further call, and reserved a room at the Royal Lahaina on the Kaanapali Coast, only five or so miles south of Napili.

On the map, the drive looked like a short pull. It turned out to be thirty miles, first a straight cut through a valley of cane fields with Haleakala's towering mass to his left, the West Mauis looming on his right. Then a winding ramble along the sea's edge, an inland skirting of the old whaling town of Lahaina, and a search for the road to the hotel, not easy because no advertising signs appeared anywhere along the Kaanapali stretch of the highway.

When he was at last settled in one of the Royal Lahaina's oceanview rooms, he realized he had subconsciously opted for the long drive here to help offset his growing impression that he was on a self-inflicted mission of futility.

That changed abruptly as he watched the local TV news, initially as a time killer. Then he jerked forward on the bed.

Walter Van Hayden. *Van Hayden!* Had he heard that right?

Found at the Garvin estate just south of Hana, floating face-down in the swimming pool. An old man, swimming alone. And apparently he'd had a leg cramp or perhaps some kind of seizure and had drowned. Van Hayden, a prominent Phoenix attorney, now retired, was a friend of Leonard Garvin, CEO and chairman of Garvin Industries, a conglomerate built around the heavy construction business. Van Hayden had been using Garvin's home for a brief Hawaiian vacation. The body had been discovered at noon today by a Hana landscaper who was under contract to maintain the estate's lawn and plantings. "Indications are that the body had been in the pool for several days," the perfectly coiffed TV anchorman concluded, and he switched into a piece about increased tourism on Oahu.

Thus the sirens in Hana today, Steve realized. Van Hayden had been here on Maui. Jim had been here. Van Hayden must have called him to arrange a meet at what he'd believed to be a necessarily remote, secure location. Van Hayden had drowned; Jim had disappeared. Coincidence? Coincidence, hell!

Steve was up early and out of there without breakfast. The charter was set for eight o'clock when the blaze of the ascending sun would be full on the slopes below the Hana Highway.

Now the Jetranger banked around the last of the receding West Maui foothills, leveled into a southeastern heading, and began to cross Kahului Bay. The water looked like hardened steel. Three miles to his right, Steve watched the low buildings of the town of Kahului drift past, then the flat expanse of the airport. They made landfall a few minutes later, and drummed across the ragged, froth-edged lava outcrops of Haleakala's skirt.

Barton adjusted his collective lever and cyclic stick. The chopper nosed down in a long, concave arc to level out a few hundred feet above and seaward of the highway's kinky, gray ribbon.

"I'll keep this position relative to the road all the way to Hana," Barton's headset voice crackled. "You want a closer look anywhere along the line, you give me the word, right?"

Steve adjusted the binoculars he'd bought last night in the hotel's arcade gift shop. No better than four-power, but the focus was sharp. He nodded, and they began the eastward sweep along the Hana Highway.

The rain forest below the road's thin cut flowed past in a river of undulating green. Hopeless, Steve decided after fifteen fruitless minutes. But what was the alternative?

"Honomanu coming up," Barton announced. "The road turns into a real snake here."

It did indeed: swept high around an escarpment, cut deeply inward only to swing back oceanward in a near 180-degree hairpin, then S-curved around a promontory that Barton identified as Kalaloa Point.

"Just about halfway to Hana, now. Another twenty minutes at this airspeed—"

"Hold it!" Steve had caught a flash of light beneath the heavy foliage some forty yards upslope of the water's edge. Or thought he had. But it could have been the morning sun's reflection on pooled dew. Or its glint on an imperfection in the helicopter's windshield.

Barton pulled his chopper around in a tight 270-degree turn that took them out over the water briefly, then straight in.

"Here?"

Steve pointed to his right. "A few hundred feet that way."

The Bell howled sideways, hovered. Steve swept the forest with his inadequate binoculars.

Nothing.

Then . . . a tiny glimpse of white, almost obliterated by the dense canopy.

"Can you take us low enough to put our rotor wash down there?"

Barton shrugged. He took the chopper down gingerly until they were less than a hundred feet above the trees Steve had indicated. The slope of the mountain filled the windshield, a massive, green barrier.

Another flash of white! Steve adjusted the binoculars. Jesus! He saw it, the crumpled wreckage of a car. Then the chopper began to drift backward, away from the green-upholstered cliff face. Under the baseball cap, Barton's high forehead glistened.

"A touch close there, ol' buddy. You see what you wanted to see? You actually found it?"

"Kalaloa Point, you said this is? Any way we can get down there?"

"You kidding? You couldn't land a model airplane down there. Best bet's a boat. You finished here, let's get on back."

The boat was a Boston Whaler, unexciting but unsinkable and rock-steady. It was owned by the heaviest of the three cops aboard, Sergeant Holo himself. The others were Officer Miyamoto, who looked as if he were made mostly out of bronze cables, and Officer Phillips, a redheaded, heavy-boned man who had a severe sunburn that was peeling above his open collar. They wore long-sleeved khaki shirts, whipcord slacks, and Maui County Police baseball caps, and they didn't look much like TV or movie police. All three were under thirty.

From the helipad, Steve had driven to the Lahaina courthouse, headquarters of Maui's police force, ten miles down the coastline. Holo didn't try to hide his good-natured skepticism. "You want us to check out something you think you saw through those trees? That's rain forest, man. Hana gets seventy inches of rain a year. You know what it's like to go into that?" But he checked a chart he unearthed from a brimming desk drawer and pondered. "No record of an accident in that area. If you did see something, it's new to us."

"I have reason to believe my brother had an appointment to see Walter Van Hayden in Hana." Steve watched Holo's impassive face.

"Van Hayden? The old man in the pool?" Now Holo was

intrigued, and he wouldn't mind a boat ride on a slow day. He said that. Officers Miyamoto and Phillips seemed less eager.

"You know what we're going to be into when we get off the boat, Sarge?" the redheaded cop asked. Rhetorically, Steve realized, because they all knew a climb up more than a hundred feet of densely overgrown lava spill was not an ideal way to spend a clear, warm Maui morning.

Holo's personal Boston Whaler was made available for police work when it was needed. The four of them rode in his black Ford Bronco from the courthouse to his small home on a Lahaina side street where the boat on its trailer was hooked to the Bronco's hitch. Then Holo drove them out of Lahaina, down the coast highway, northward up Maui's central valley to Kahului, and an hour out the Hana Highway.

At Kalaloa Point, he pulled the rig to the left side of the road.

"Down there?"

Steve nodded. "Down there."

"I don't see a thing." Holo twisted around. "You guys?"

Phillips, seated nearest the edge, shook his head morosely. "Nothing but leaves and trees, Sarge."

Holo put the five-speed back in gear and veered back into the right lane. A few minutes later, he swung left into a turnoff that led steeply down into the tiny village of Keanae.

Here they launched the open Whaler in a cove. With Holo at the helm of his boat, now in official police service, they nosed out of the protected little harbor, then pitched and plunged straight seaward through moderate swells. A quarter mile out, Holo brought the bow to a west heading. Ten minutes later, they reached a position two hundred yards off Kalaloa Point.

Phillips thumbed up the bill of his baseball cap and peered toward shore. "A little cove in there, Sarge."

"Honomanu Bay," Holo said.

"Looks accessible enough, don't it?"

Holo spun the wheel hard aport. The open boat heeled over, nosed shoreward.

The east side of the bay was protected from incoming swells, but it had no beach. They anchored several yards from the dark lava strip between sea and tree line, and walked ashore in waist-deep water with wallets—and in the case of the three officers—gunbelts held high.

"Now exactly where, sir," asked Sergeant Holo when they stood dripping on dry lava, "did you think you spotted that wreck?"

From the ground, everything looked different, hugely out of scale. Steve forced himself to recall how this promontory had appeared from the air. Two-lobed, with the glimpse of twisted white metal above the second one.

He pointed. "Just above that other outcrop, a quarter mile down."

Like jagged glass, the lava began to cut into the rubber soles of his watersoaked sports shoes. Be a hell of a thing to trip and fall here. The sea, just twenty feet to their left, crumped into the lava strand. It smelled of fresh salt, but rolling out of the rain forest fringe upslope less than fifty feet to the right came the odor of sweet rot.

They worked along the rough lava single file, Holo in the lead, Miyamoto short-striding behind him, Steve next, with the rawboned Phillips in the rear. Holo kept looking back to check his anchored boat.

Then they were beyond sight of the Whaler, as isolated as they would have been on a deserted island. Steve heard only the crump and wash of waves; saw only sky, sea, the lava stretch, then the dense, alien upholstery of jungle that soared almost vertically upward before it sloped back out of their line of vision.

Where the mountain's hemline jutted seaward a second time, Holo stopped.

"Here?" he demanded of Steve. "Above this place is where you think you saw something?"

Steve nodded. "Here." He wished he felt as certain as he managed to sound. The whole perspective was different from what he had seen from Barton's helicopter. He felt dwarfed by the awesome rise of the mountain.

Holo shrugged, then led them across the lava to push up into the rain forest's humid clasp.

At first, the climb wasn't as difficult as Steve had expected; only moderately steep, and through waist-high palmettos, fragrant, broadleafed plumeria, a stand of yellow shower trees, then a tangle of snakelike vines as the slope abruptly steepened.

The undergrowth thinned as the sky was blotted out by the dense canopy of trees competing to reach sunlight. Steve's shoe slithered along a rotted branch, and he smelled the musty odor of decay.

They struggled upward for ten minutes, and made slow progress through a stand of black; moisture-laden trunks and straggly vines that clung to their legs like slippery wires.

Holo led the way blindly, but with a determination that Steve suspected was aimed toward proving him a crazy haole, a mule-headed white man who had no idea what he'd seen, or thought he'd seen in this misery of a jungle. The Japanese cop worked his way upward off to the left. Steve caught only glimpses of his khaki shirt along the soaring tree boles. Phillips was close behind, positioning himself, perhaps, to catch the clumsy mainlander when he finally made one misstep too many and plunged backward downslope.

Sweat soaked Steve's open-collared sports shirt and began to seep beneath the belt of his gray slacks. His white mesh shoes were black with the pulpy detritus of the forest floor. He had dressed as if he were going to the golf course, and he knew he must look like an ass in front of these seasoned Maui cops.

This whole thing—

Ten paces ahead, Sergeant Holo had halted. He swung his head with its curly black crown left, then right; pushed upslope three more paces, stopped again. Holo raised his chin. He sniffed the stagnant jungle air.

Then the smell hit Steve. The penetrating, sickly, rancid odor of death. He lurched upward an enervating ten yards, caught up with Holo, followed the sergeant's gaze. Through the crowding trees above them and to the right, he saw stark white metal among the black trunks and dull green drapery of trailing lianas.

God.

Miyamoto and Phillips tied their handkerchiefs across their faces. Steve held his tight against his nose. It didn't help much. Holo seemed impervious to the sickening stench as he scrambled upward, much faster now.

The car had crashed straight down. That was obvious from its compaction and from the naked tear along the branch of an African tulip tree directly above it where the bark had been stripped by the plunging steel. Steve's hands began to shake. He had trouble securing holds on saplings and underbrush branches. His legs threatened to splay out from under him.

He had almost reached the shattered car when Holo reappeared around its far side. The cop held out his arms in a blocking gesture. His face had an oddly putty-like appearance.

"You do not want to see this, Mr. Gammon."

Steve started to move past him.

"Believe me, sir. The driver has no head."

"Oh, Christ!"

Holo motioned Miyamoto and Phillips left and right, saying nothing, but Steve knew what they were searching for.

"Stay here, Mr. Gammon. Please."

Steve squatted on the spongy forest floor, his head hammering now. Maybe . . . maybe it wasn't Jim, after all. He'd seen white cars in the rental lots, a lot of white cars. A lot of Nissans.

Holo smashed that thin hope, having accomplished the grisly task of working around the decomposing, headless body and extracting ID.

"I am afraid it is your brother, Mr. Gammon. Driver's license, credit cards, insurance and AAA cards. All James J. Gammon."

Phillips and Miyamoto returned from their own ghastly little assignment. They shook their heads in unison.

"We will send in a recovery team," Holo decided, to his officers' instant and obvious relief. "We are not equipped, Mr. Gammon." Then he said with surprising gentleness, "I must apologize. I had thought we would find nothing here. I apologize."

The climb back down was no easier.

5.

Georgie Prescott was having a lousy time. Gammon's brother had started off being most obliging. He'd stopped at the Honolulu terminal baggage claim long enough for Prescott to take the chance and buy his aloha shirt. Then Gammon had boarded a clearly marked courtesy van from a hotel near the airport, and Prescott had followed in a taxi. Gammon had checked in; Prescott had checked in.

There was no practical way to cover Gammon if the man decided to leave the hotel during the night, and by then, the hour was past 9:00. Prescott left a call request for 5:30 A.M., and went to bed.

In the lobby the next morning, he read almost through Honolulu's morning paper before Gammon appeared to have a quick breakfast, still under Prescott's covert surveillance. Then Gammon checked out and took the van back to the airport. The Inter Island Terminal, this time. A flight to Maui. Prescott didn't like the limited number of passengers, but what choice did he have?

At Kahului, he was pleased that Gammon rented a car. He rented one himself. And he tailed Gammon to Hana. When he passed Kalaloa Point, though he didn't know its name, he recognized the location where Kolker had shoved their rented Chevy's bumper tight against the Nissan and bulldozed it across the left lane into empty air. He didn't feel any particular emotion here. He just recognized the place, and was pleased that Gammon drove right on past.

In Hana, he played an interesting game with Gammon, first wondering what in hell the man was up to, then realizing Gammon was covering the entire town in hope of turning up his brother's missing Nissan. He found a degree of humor in that.

Prescott slipped up only once that he was aware of. That was when he found Gammon's Toyota coming straight at him after a particularly tricky sequence of side street turns. Kolker might have called the second incident a slip-up, too, but Kolker wasn't on this assignment, and what better way to maintain surveillance on somebody at an isolated restaurant than waiting among the cars in the parking lot? It was just bad luck that he'd put the Plymouth in the front row, but where else would you park for a quick takeoff. It was bad luck compounded when he was held up—but only a few seconds—by the sudden appearance of the police car and ambulance hauling ass past the restaurant exit.

After that, the assignment hadn't been so easy. He had tailed Gammon back to Kahului airport, where the man had confused him. Gammon had used a pay phone, made one call, then had driven down the valley that divided the island, turned west and rolled on out to the Royal Lahaina resort. Pretty fancy digs. Prescott smiled at the pending inevitable prune-mouth reaction of the OmniSecure accountant on the FRET-SAW contract when he would see the kinds of places where Prescott was being forced to stay on the organization's "Edward Johnson" MasterCard.

The early-in-the-lobby technique had worked even better at the Royal Lahaina because the place had a much bigger lobby. This time, though, his time-killing perusal of the morning paper gave him a jolt. They'd found Van Hayden, afloat in

Garvin's pool since last Tuesday. Some swim, old man. They had to find him sometime, but Prescott hadn't expected to be back here when they did.

At 7:45, he had tailed Gammon's Toyota to the helicopter pad near the golf course. Then he lost him, of course. How do you tail a guy aboard a chartered helicopter?

Prescott took the only practical alternative. He waited in the parking area near the helipad, cooking his gizzard because the Plymouth was low on gas, and he didn't want to burn it up using the engine to run the A/C.

He sat out there for more than an hour. Hell of a job for a graduate—no, that wasn't quite true—for an attendee of one of New England's hottest prep schools. He'd almost made it; would have made it if he hadn't been nailed in the basement of the Science Building a panting half minute into his roommate's date from Miss Porter's School, and just beginning to get the rhythm. Something of a feat standing up, because she was only five feet three. The watchman's six-volt Eveready had instantly shrunk him to a wizened little carrot, and she had laughed. *Laughed!* The bitch knew she was immune. She couldn't get kicked out of someone else's school, but he was off Bolton Academy's roster in forty-eight hours.

He didn't return home to Marblehead. Never went back there. He couldn't face his parents' outrage, particularly his uptight mother's sure-to-be-acid reaction. The girl had been the daughter of a long-time family friend; a state senator's daughter, for God's sake. That's what had made him so eager to get into her tights. He'd discovered that he loved risk, but he couldn't stand abasement. Which was why he had drifted into the not-so-licit activities of OmniSecure though he still could not face his parents.

He'd had a lot of girls since that first abortive stab in Bolton's Science Building. He took them fast and hard and found their frequent gasps of pain stimulating. At first, he'd thought the sex got him off. Then he realized inflicting the pain did it. Without it, he had problems in bed.

OmniSecure was just what its name described: all security needs met. He wasn't exactly surprised the first time he'd been assigned what the government guys called wet-work. He didn't know who the man in the black raincoat was, only that their client wanted him dead. Prescott wasn't driving. He was on the passenger side. Youmans was driving. Jake Youmans caught the man ten feet off the curb at M Street and Twenty-second just after he'd rushed out of the Washington Marriott, panicked into the open by a carefully worded OmniSecure phone call. A rainy night in D.C. The man flew thirty feet straight ahead. When their wheels bumped over the crumpled body, Prescott felt a voluptuous gathering between his thighs. So this was how it was to be.

Gammon's chopper reappeared in fifty-seven minutes. Then Prescott tailed him to the Lahaina courthouse where Gammon stayed awhile. Next, things got tougher. Gammon came out with three cops and got in a Bronco with them. Prescott followed the Bronco, wishing now he'd rented a darker-colored car. White had seemed okay because so many cars on Maui were white. But it wasn't a color that exactly faded into the scenery.

The Bronco pulled into a house on a Lahaina side street so abruptly that Prescott had to drive right on past. He circled the long block slowly. When he turned back into Wainee Street, the Bronco was bumping out the dirt driveway, towing a boat on a trailer.

Easy tailing now. East on 30 to its left turn back up the valley, then east again on 36. The goddamned Hana Highway!

He stayed well behind, out of the Bronco's line of sight most of the time, with only an occasional confirmatory glimpse. After all, where could they go? As he passed it again, he recognized the sheer drop where he and Kolker had shoved Gammon's brother over the side.

Then he lost them. Son of a bitch! They had to have turned down the side road to Keanae. But he couldn't follow them down there, not down that short dead-end road to the water's edge. He stopped high up on the main road. They had to be launching the boat there.

Had Gammon seen something from the helicopter? Kolker and I, Prescott assured himself, hadn't been able to spot a damned thing from up here after the Nissan had banged into the jungle. But from the air . . .

He didn't like the scenario his racing brain was reconstructing, but his assignment was passive: watch and report. He turned around and backtracked to the point where the Nissan had gone over, parked the Plymouth well back from the road's seaward edge, stood where he could see downward without exposing more than his head to observation from below. And waited.

A few minutes later, the boat nosed into view around a promontory, cutting a white V a quarter mile offshore. Then it heeled landward to plow across the surf line and drift to a stop in a small bay directly below Prescott's position. They anchored there, waded ashore, walked back along the lava, the four of them in single file. Then they cut across the lava and pushed into the rain forest. They knew. They'd entered the bush at a point that would take them straight to the Nissan if they worked directly uphill. Yeah, they knew, all right.

Prescott got back in the Plymouth and returned to Lahaina. He parked in a public lot and took a table on the veranda of the old whaling village's restored Pioneer Inn. Watched the world go by, or this little corner of it. Killed time with two beers. Was tempted by a pair of girls in hot pants, one of them a not-so-bad ash blonde who looked back at him as they walked toward the wharf. Damn, he'd like to ram it to her dry and hear her squeal . . . But he was low profiling here. Waiting. He could see the courthouse in the next block, beyond a huge tropical tree that occupied most of the grounds and had dropped dozens of secondary trunks down from its giant limbs.

The Bronco returned nearly five hours later, after Prescott had walked every street in the downtown section that had kept him in view of the courthouse. This seemed one of the longest afternoons of his life. The Bronco came back, but minus the boat and trailer, which they must have returned to the Wainee Street house.

Gammon stayed in the courthouse for nearly another hour, while Prescott felt more and more conspicuous. Thank God for the heavy tourist traffic. Then Gammon came out alone, walked to a nearby parking area and got in his rented Toyota. Prescott fast-walked to the more distant Plymouth, almost lost Gammon in the slow-moving vehicular crush on Front Street, then tailed him back to Kahului Airport.

. . . And lost him in the dumbest way a tail ever lost his subject. Prescott had left the Plymouth in the rental car return lot, crossed the public parking area to the check-in counter, and now he ran into the prize nitpicker of all time, a Chinese dish with gorgeous almond eyes and a smile that never left her perfect oval face. But she turned out to be a royal pain in the bunger.

"You forget to write down the mileage, sir."

Two counters down, Gammon had finished his own check-in, and he walked right past Prescott into the terminal. Prescott felt like jumping up and down in frustration.

"I must have the mileage figure, sir." Her teeth were perfect and white as fresh coconut. He wanted to reach out, grab her by her slender throat and slam her lovely face down on the counter.

"Sir?"

Shit! He raced back to the Plymouth, squinted at the odometer reading, dashed back across the parking lot to the Ming princess.

"Three thousand and forty-five, damn it!"

The terminal was a madhouse. No Gammon anywhere. Prescott had lost him.

Accidental death? "The Nissan's rear bumper had been bent in a shallow V. If the car had crashed straight down, how—"

"It could have turned in the air, Mr. Gammon. That was a four-hundred-foot drop. It may have rotated during the fall, first struck its rear bumper at the top of the tree, then cartwheeled to hit the ground nose first."

Sergeant Holo had been impressively articulate, his precise diction having been honed, Steve had been told by Officer Miyamoto, at UCLA.

The autopsy had shown no alcohol content in the blood, but the length of time between the time of death and the date of the autopsy made that less than 100 percent accurate. The medical examiner carefully inserted such a caveat in his report, and accidental death in a single car mishap on a dangerous road was his official finding. Time of death was set "several days" previous to the body's discovery.

That was established in Maui. The cremation, at Marcie Gammon's phoned request, was done in Honolulu. Now Steve flew back to the mainland with Jim's ashes in a dark green plastic container the size and shape of a cereal box. Steve was exhausted—by the ordeal itself, but equally drained by the phone call to Marcie. She requested the cremation, wired permission to the Honolulu funeral director, and now Steve sat morosely over the cargo hold which held in its cold darkness his suitcase and what was left of his brother.

"He was visiting Hawaii alone, Mr. Gammon?" Holo had asked.

"I believe he was here to meet Mr. Van Hayden in Hana. The man who drowned." He outlined the FRETSAW connection.

Sergeant Holo's wide brown face had taken on new interest. He leaned forward, arms flat on his desk in his barren Lahaina courthouse office.

"That is a curious coincidence." Holo looked as if he didn't quite know what to make of it. "Did your brother tell you he was here to meet Mr. Van Hayden?"

"No, but phone memos in Washington indicated that Van Hayden tried to reach Jim twice in his office on Friday, May first. I think he finally got in touch with Jim at home on Saturday, and on Monday, Jim left suddenly for Hawaii."

Holo fiddled with a pencil. "Interesting. We will continue our investigation, of course."

Two chances of that at the Hawaiian end, Steve was certain. Fat and slim. He was just as sure now that the key to Jim's death lay well hidden, five thousand miles eastward, in the formal yet subliminally temporary FRETSAW headquarters near Dupont Circle. And the key also lay with Van Hayden, now beyond reach.

Or was he? Might not a brief stop in Phoenix be a logical next move?

After a fifty-minute plane change at Los Angeles International, he was headed there, not at all sure of what he would or could do next. He had solved the manner of Jim's disappearance; had found Jim's mutilated body at the foot of a towering Maui cliff. But that had only raised more questions.

Van Hayden had died about the same time. A chilling thought struck Steve like a needle in the heart. Was it possible that Jim had killed the old man, was racing back to Kahului Airport, and had misjudged the Kalaloa Point curve? He would have been on the outside lane on the return trip, the outside lane of a sharp left turn around the mountain's shoulder.

No! Steve refused to accept that. The odometer reading, Holo's report had said, had indicated Jim had driven not quite 30 miles, the distance from Kahului to Kalaloa Point. "It could have been damaged by the impact," Holo had speculated, "knocked to an inaccurate setting."

Knocked back to the exact distance from Kahului to the crash site? No, Jim had been headed toward Hana, not away. Somebody got to him. Somebody got to Van Hayden.

Why?

The 727 from Los Angeles whistled him into Phoenix's Sky Harbor in mid-morning. Steve felt grubby and bone tired, though he had managed a few hours' sleep on the

Honolulu–L.A. leg. He shaved at Sky Harbor, then found a phone. If the man had an unlisted number, where would he go from here?

But there it was: *Van Hayden, Walter,* in Scottsdale. Plus the law firm of Van Hayden and MacIlvane, Phoenix. Steve slipped in the coins and dialed the residence. He had no idea what to expect, but the totally in-control female voice was something of a surprise.

"Mrs. Van Hayden?"

"This is Mrs. Lester Terhune, Mr. Van Hayden's daughter, Lillian. And you are—?"

"Steve Gammon, Mrs. Terhune. My sympathies on the death of your father." God, he hoped she'd heard by now.

"Thank you." There was a lot of starchy defensiveness out there in Scottsdale.

"I'm calling, Mrs. Terhune, because of what may be no more than a coincidence. My brother, James Gammon, died in an automobile accident on his way to Hana, apparently the same day your father drowned."

"You have my sympathies, Mr. Gammon, but I fail to see a connection."

"Jim worked for a foundation in Washington, the Freedom Through Specialized Awareness Foundation. They call themselves FRETSAW, for short. Your father, Mrs. Terhune, was a member of that foundation's Advisory Council."

Now came a lengthy pause out of Scottsdale. Then she said, "I've just arrived here from Minneapolis to close down the house. Father had lived here alone these five years since Mother died. I'm afraid I don't know a thing about Father's business or personal affairs. We haven't been particularly close since I married." A hard little burr had crept into her voice. Evidently, Van Hayden hadn't been overly charmed by one Lester Terhune's making off with his daughter.

"Is there anyone in Phoenix who might have been, well, close to him?"

"Father did become something of a recluse after he retired,

I'm afraid. But he did maintain contact with his old law firm, Van Hayden and MacIlvane. His name meant something in this area. Arthur MacIlvane has kept it on the door since Father retired in 1982."

Steve next dialed the law firm, got past the receptionist to catch Arthur MacIlvane on his way to an early lunch.

"Look, Mr. Gammon, I've got an appointment here at one-thirty. Can't we make it some other day?" MacIlvane had the voice of a self-pampering man who didn't like his day restructured. "What is so important that we can't discuss it another time?"

"Try this, Mr. MacIlvane. Last week, my brother was driving to Hana to see Mr. Van Hayden. They both had connections with a particular Washington foundation. They both died. Does that give you more of a sense of urgency?"

"You have a compelling way of stating facts, Mr. Gammon. If those are facts."

"That's what I'm trying to establish. That's why I've stopped here in Phoenix on my way back to Washington."

MacIlvane cleared his throat. "Be here at one. Be out of here at one-thirty. Agreed?"

Steve entrusted his suitcase—and the mortal remains of Jim Gammon—to a coin locker, had a quick ham and cheese at the airport restaurant, took a taxi north on Twenty-fourth to Thomas, then a short distance west on Thomas. The building was four stories of precast, sandstone-finished concrete.

The Van Hayden and MacIlvane law offices occupied a ground floor suite in the front, to the left of the plate glass entrance. The air-conditioning was an instant escape from the furnace of desert sun without a hint of cloud in the blue that canopied the broad valley in which Phoenix was an irrigated green anomaly.

MacIlvane's receptionist wore a multicolored high fashion interpretation of native dress. But she wasn't Indian. She was bleached blonde, maybe from the sun, maybe from a bottle, with her mane gathered behind her head by a beaded clip.

"Mr. Cannon?"

"Gammon."

She bounced up and ushered him through a door at the end of a short corridor.

MacIlvane glanced pointedly at his watch before he stood, reached across his pickled oak desk to shake hands briefly, then gestured Steve to a chair. An uncomfortably hard one calculated, Steve decided, to encourage short meetings. Arthur MacIlvane was an A type. Medium height and build, with his carefully barbered, graying hair low over his oversized ears. Matching gray eyes were surprisingly close-set, but what was more arresting was MacIlvane's constantly twitching mouth. The thin lips worked even when he wasn't talking.

"Poor Walter's accident has been a real shock to me, Mr. Gammon, a personal loss, though his participation in the affairs of the firm has been understandably minimal since his official retirement several years ago." MacIlvane's lips worked soundlessly for a moment. "A personal loss," he repeated. "Walter was a friend."

"Does the name FRETSAW mean anything to you, Mr. MacIlvane?"

The lawyer's mouth twitched, as if he were trying to get a firm grip on syllables before trying them out. Steve wondered if the man was a stutterer who had to concentrate to overcome what would be a hell of a liability for an attorney.

"FRETSAW?"

"It's the acronym for a Washington organization called the Freedom Through Specialized Awareness Foundation."

"Awkward title."

Steve agreed. "The kind of thing you end up with when you want a snappy acronym. Do you recall ever hearing Mr. Van Hayden refer to it? He seems to have been a member of some sort of FRETSAW advisory group."

"He was a member of a number of boards." MacIlvane's lips twiddled with unspoken words. "That's the kind of thing an influential man gets into when he has retired but still wants to be active. Are you aware of what this F-FRETSAW organization's aims are?"

"Awareness campaigns, they told me. Keep our guard up against the Red Menace. That sort of thing."

"I can sympathize with 'that sort of thing,' Mr. Gammon. Walter surely could, and did. He supported a number of conservative causes. Responsibly conservative, not nuke-them-before-they-nuke-us nonsense, you understand. He was a fine man, concerned for his country."

"He lived alone in Scottsdale?"

"Yes, since Phyllis—Mrs. Van Hayden—died five years ago. Tragic thing. Lung cancer. Cut the ground right out from under him. That was when he began to devote a lot of time to his conservative views. At that point, he'd been retired from the firm almost ten years, but we kept in pretty close touch, particularly after Phyllis passed away."

"When was the last time you saw him?"

MacIlvane glanced at his watch again. "Two weeks ago."

"Did he seem upset or agitated?"

The lawyer's thin eyebrows hitched upward, and he cleared his throat twice. "Usually I'm the one asking the questions, Mr. Gammon. I'm not sure I like this."

"I've just lost a brother, MacIlvane, and I don't like that at all. Both he and Van Hayden were connected with FRETSAW. They both went to Maui, they both died."

"But not together. There was only one body in the pool."

"That's correct. Jim died in a car crash, on his way, I'm convinced, to see your old law partner."

"But you can't prove that."

"Circumstantially it's pretty obvious." Steve filled him in on the phone messages in Jim's desk, and Jim's reaction to the Saturday phone call. "And you haven't answered my question about Van Hayden's state of mind when you saw him two weeks ago."

"Your question?"

"Did he seem agitated about something?"

MacIlvane cleared his throat again. "No, not that I particularly noticed. What do you hope to get from me, Mr. Gammon?"

"Some sort of indication of what Van Hayden had on his mind. Think back, will you? It was only a week after your meeting that he was drowned."

"*Was* drowned? I thought it was an accident."

"Maybe that's what we're supposed to think."

MacIlvane stared across the desk. Then he planted his elbows on the polished oak, rested his temples on his fingertips, and fixed his eyes downward. A picture of a man searching his memory. "We met for lunch at Ernesto's Back Street over on Indian School Road. I remember I had the antipasto. Walter ordered what he always ordered at Ernesto's, veal scallopini. Now just what in hell did we talk about?"

"FRETSAW?"

MacIlvane tapped his temples with bunched fingertips. "How many times have I asked a witness this kind of question? 'What were you doing at noon on April twenty-sixth?' That's when it was. And he had a problem."

"What kind of problem?"

"A two-margarita problem, one more than usual. I recall, I said, 'You're doubling up on the cactus juice, Walter. Anything wrong?' I expected to get a smile with that, but he just stared at me. Made me feel uncomfortable. Then he said—I remember it now—he said, 'It's the IRS boys, Mac.' He always called me Mac. 'They're all over last year's return. They're driving me nuts.' "

Steve's eyes were riveted on the balding top of Arthur MacIlvane's downtilted head. The throat clearing, the lip twitching, now this overdone concentration bit . . . Arthur MacIlvane, Steve was becoming convinced, was a liar.

"And you said . . ." he prompted.

MacIlvane looked up. "I said, 'You have an accountant. Let him do the sweating. Why don't you get away for a while?' And that's when he decided to call Len Garvin and see if he could use Len's place on Maui for a few days. For R and R. Tax problems really got to Walter."

Nice try, Steve thought. But not very convincing to this jury, Arthur MacIlvane.

"My God," the attorney said, his face showing shock. "I was the one who recommended his going to Maui. He drowned there, and I'll always have that accident on my conscience."

"I don't think it was an accident, MacIlvane."

"What the hell are you saying? That someone killed him?"

"Because of what he knew."

"God in Heaven, what could he possibly have known that could have gotten him killed?"

"That, MacIlvane, is what I'm trying to find out."

Arthur MacIlvane stared at his desktop for a long time after Gammon left. *"What do you do when you find out something you had real faith in turns out to be something else?"* Those had been Walter's exact words at lunch, not the song and dance about tax problems he had just sold to Gammon. He hadn't been able to get Walter to expand on that provocative statement, and he hadn't tied it to FRETSAW until just a few minutes ago. Walter had supported a number of causes; he could have been concerned about any of them, MacIlvane supposed. Yet the coincidence on Maui was hard to overlook.

His mouth worked without sound. What in Christ's name could Walter have stumbled upon? MacIlvane glanced at his watch one more time. He had only a few minutes before he must leave. He reached for his phone, hesitated, then he punched the button for his private outside line that bypassed the call director at Hannah's reception station. He tapped in a 202 area code. It was only mid-morning there.

"Arthur MacIlvane here," he told the answering voice. "I just had a visit from the brother of one of your people." He summarized the encounter with a surprising economy of words for a lawyer.

"Interesting," said the voice at the other end.

"What in hell are we into?"

"Coincidence, Arthur. Sheer coincidence, I assure you. Think no more about it."

"I have a reputation to worry about, damn it." MacIlvane's lips worked furiously. "I don't want to be tied into anything like what Gammon was hinting at." He realized his phrasing was deteriorating under stress, and he struggled for control.

"And what was he hinting at, Arthur? Walter Van Hayden drowned, an old, infirm man swimming alone."

The receiver was greasy in MacIlvane's grip. "What about the other one?"

"Gammon's brother? What about him?"

"What was he doing there?"

"Why, I have no idea, Arthur. No one knows why he was there, you understand? It will simply fade away."

"I'm not so sure of that. I'm not so sure I want to continue to be—"

"Part of FRETSAW? Nothing has changed, Arthur. There's still the overt and the covert, and you have always been aware of that. Nothing has changed."

"Except that this Gammon isn't about to let his brother's death—and Walter's—simply fade away."

"Don't sweat it, Arthur. Is Gammon staying in Phoenix?"

"He said he was on his way back to Washington today."

"I see. Well, you knew a project of this nature was not going to be an unimperiled ride from time to time, but there's nothing for you to worry about. Stand fast in the faith, Arthur." He clicked off.

MacIlvane replaced his phone with jittery fingers. All he had done for FRETSAW was write a hefty annual check. What in hell had that gotten him into? My God, Walter, why didn't I listen to you?

Just off Dupont Circle, Horace Buttonwood cradled his own handset, and fingered his neat beard with a slow, reflective downstroke. Then he picked up the phone again.

"Miss Cortland, get me Mr. Kolker at OmniSecure."

* * *

"Asshole!" Milo Kolker shouted. His voice echoed in his rugless OmniSecure office, and Georgie Prescott felt his guts curdle. "You *lost* him. You got any idea what that makes us look like?"

Then Prescott's bowels began to harden again. Who did this public-school-educated, brain-limited son of a bitch think he was talking to?

"*You* try to keep a tail on a subject who switches from a car to a chopper to a boat, goddamn it. What was I supposed to do, grow wings and flippers? How fast could you have gotten *your* ass into another chopper and a second boat—especially the boat. They picked it up in somebody's backyard, for Christsake, not at a marina. Then they towed it across Maui, and launched it at some godforsaken little town along the Hana Highway. How was I supposed to get hold of a boat there to follow them? I would have stood out like a hard-on at a nudist camp. Besides, I watched them from the road. They found Gammon's body, all right. No doubt about that."

He hoped Kolker remembered it had been Kolker's idea to bulldoze Gammon's Nissan off the highway and down the cliff where he didn't expect it to be found. Across the squatty man's desk in the Eye Street headquarters of OmniSecure, he carefully watched Kolker's expression. No matter how Prescott explained himself to his boss, it always came out sounding defensive.

"Well, shit, Georgie." Kolker ran plump fingers through his outdated gray military whiffle and waited. Now it was his silence that was unnerving.

"I wasn't supposed to terminate him," Prescott pointed out. "I was only supposed to observe and report." He dug out a flat box of Sherman's Amigos and lit one of the skinny, four-inch, brown cigars with his gold Ronson. He'd meant that as a casual move, but his fingers spoiled it. They shook, something Kolker was sure not to miss.

"So, okay, Georgie, we know he went to Hana, cased the town—presumably for his brother's rented car, drove back to

Kahului, made a phone call, spent the night on the Kaanapali Coast—"

"At the Royal Lahaina."

"—then rented the chopper."

"The next day. I picked him up early in the lobby."

"Yeah, Georgie, then you lost him."

"But I buttoned on again when he got back, surveilled him from there—"

"Surveilled. Uh huh. Then he's gone again."

"No problem. He was looking for the Nissan."

"And *found* it." Kolker slapped his hand hard on the Honolulu paper Prescott had brought back to Washington. "No problem, my ass. Where did he go after you lost him that last time at Kahului Airport. Lost him at an airport, for God's sake! A frigging airport is stationary, Georgie, not flying off through the air like a chopper, or bouncing away over the waves like a boat. You lost him, dumb-ass, in an airport crowd."

Prescott was silent. He surely didn't want to tell Kolker he'd forgotten to note his rental mileage, and lost Gammon when he'd gone back to get it off the odometer.

"The man was flying home, that's all."

"We've had a subcontract watch on his house in Fort Myers, and we've had an OmniSecure man staked out at his brother's Connecticut Avenue place since you called in you lost him. Gammon hasn't shown up at either place, Georgie."

"It takes time to fly in from Hawaii."

"You're here."

Prescott had no answer for that.

"It means one of two things, Georgie. Either he's gone somewhere else, or he's stopped along the way. Now why should he have done that?"

"I don't know."

"I don't know either. I do know the odds point to his coming back here to D.C."

"You think so? Why?"

"To console the widow, Georgie. That's what I'd do if I was

her brother-in-law. Especially *her* brother-in-law." Kolker jammed his hands in the pockets of his gray slacks. Prescott thought he looked like a boxer-turned-insurance-man in his charcoal suit.

Kolker sighed and sat on the edge of his battered wooden desk. He loomed over Prescott's low chair. "Okay, Georgie. You've had your lumps. I'm only trying to sharpen you up, you understand?"

Prescott did not understand at all.

"The client found him for us. Gammon stopped off in Phoenix, talked with Van Hayden's law partner, then headed back here."

Prescott stared up at him, then forced his voice steady. "I told you." Jesus, Kolker had been playing with him!

Kolker shook his head as if he was exasperated by an erring puppy. "Yeah, you told me. Now get your butt over to the Crossmoor Arms on Connecticut. Relieve Olshinsky. He's been there all night. And, Georgie, for God's sake, avoid an exposed mode, and you report in when Gammon shows, you hear?"

"Yeah, Kolker." Prescott's confidence was flooding back. "I'll call in." You bet your ass I'll call in. Prescott was up to here with the problems Gammon was giving him.

6.

The memorial service in the nondenominational chapel of the Bethesda funeral home was brief, impersonal as the functional chapel itself, and surprisingly well attended—by FRETSAW people, Steve realized. He didn't know how to react to that. Afterward, in the dwindling crowd in the funeral home's drizzle-glistened parking area, bespectacled Becky Rossmyer offered her condolences with a handclasp that seemed to Steve an attempt to convey something more than sympathy.

Horace Buttonwood nodded his pro forma respects from twenty feet distant. The blonde Miss Cortland, to Steve's surprise, softly laid her hand on his arm and just as softly said, "We are all so sorry." Her skirt of respectfully dark green suede was taut across her lush hips. Several Foundation people Steve hadn't met expressed condolences, then the knot of people unraveled into the surrounding cars. It was over, the departures accelerated by the fine, misty rain.

"The ashes?" the slim, little funeral director had asked just before the service began.

"The ashes?" Marcie repeated hollowly.

"Mmm, yes, Mrs. Gammon. Their disposition."

She looked confused.

"Hold them here," Steve had said into her silence. "We'll let you know shortly."

Now he drove her back to the Crossmoor Arms, not knowing how to say it. Then she said it for him.

"Do you really think somebody . . . that he was purposely killed, Steve?"

"That's what I intend to find out. And if he was, if Van Hayden was, it could be dangerous to you. That's why I'd better get myself a discreet place to stay while I'm in Washington. I don't want to expose you to whatever the hell it is that FRETSAW is really up to."

"Please, Steve, I don't want to be in an empty apartment just now. I really don't." Huddled in the seat beside him, she looked like a bereft little girl staring unseeing through the windshield at the increasing rainfall.

"Marcie, I don't think that's a good idea."

"Please," she said so softly that he could barely hear her, almost as if she were talking to herself.

Back in the apartment she made a pretty fair sausage omelet, he told her, as he added to their plates the prefab French fries he had heated on a cookie sheet in the oven. They ate at the kitchen table.

"You ever talk with Buttonwood?" he asked.

"Once, at some fund-raising cocktail party FRETSAW was sponsoring at the Washington Hilton. I thought he was kind of once-removed."

"Once-removed?"

She took a sip of coffee. "As if he were talking to me on one level, but thinking on another."

"Check."

"None of this proves anything, does it?"

"Afraid not, Marcie. But I'm not going to let it rest here."

She began to collect the dishes. "You be careful, Steve."

"I'm going to try something tomorrow."

"Steve, I know how you feel. I feel the same way about what's happened to Jim. But maybe you should . . . I mean, if there was anything suspicious about Jim's death, wouldn't the police have—"

"You think I'm off on some sort of wild tear on this thing?"

"I don't know what to think, Steve. I'm so tired, so depressed." She did look exhausted. "You're going back there, aren't you?"

"To the Foundation for more stonewalling? Not quite."

"What's that mean?"

"It means I'm going to try it another way."

"I don't think it's a good idea for us to meet so near the Foundation offices." Becky Rossmyer's voice was sleep fuzzed. He'd caught her at home—the only Rossmyer in the book—before she left for work.

"A restaurant further away, then. I'll pick you up."

"I've got only an hour."

"Tell them you're sick. Get the afternoon off."

She hesitated.

"Becky, there's something going on at FRETSAW that I think has gotten two people killed. One of them was a man I think you admired very much."

She sighed, hesitated, then she said, "All right. I'll be at the southeast corner of Twentieth and N streets at twelve-fifteen."

Northwest Washington traffic was heavy this overcast Tuesday afternoon. Steve was two minutes late. She wasn't there.

He drove through the intersection, merged into New Hampshire's traffic for a block, swung hard right at Dupont Circle to head south on Nineteenth, then west on M, and back up Twentieth's one-way northbound traffic flow.

He spotted her this time, a tiny figure at the curb, in a tan skirt, white blouse, and tan cardigan, with an oversized brown suede purse hanging from her shoulder. He guided the Buick to the right-hand curb, reached across to open the passenger door. She slipped in.

"Sorry. I must have missed you on my first pass."

She hunched down in the seat. "Let's get out of here."

He edged the car back into traffic, swung smoothly around Dupont Circle again, pulled into northbound Connecticut, and merged into the outbound traffic coming up the ramp from the underpass.

She hadn't said a word for five blocks.

"What is it, Becky?"

"I'm not good at lying."

"You had trouble getting out of there?"

"I told Alix I was feeling nauseous. I hope she believed me."

"Alix?"

"Alix Cortland, Mr. Buttonwood's executive assistant. She's also personnel director for the administrative assistants—us secretaries."

They crossed the long bridge over Rock Creek Park and passed the National Zoo.

"So if she okayed your getting out of there this afternoon, what's the problem?"

"Maybe I am overreacting. Where are we going?"

"We'll pick a restaurant at random outside the Beltway, somewhere nobody from the Foundation is likely to be. That's what you're really worried about, isn't it?"

"Maybe it's stupid to think this way."

"I'm assuming it's stupid not to think this way."

"You're making me feel better and worse at the same time," she said.

They settled on the Olive Grove, a modest Greek restaurant in a nondescript business block at the outskirts of Wheaton, and both ordered a Greek salad. This wasn't going to be a big appetite meeting.

"Maybe you were telling Alix Cortland the truth."

"Don't I wish." She poured cream into her iced coffee and stared into the intricate, descending swirls. She looked away, then up at him. Her eyes brimmed. "He was such a nice man to work for. A nice man." Her voice faltered. "I'm so sorry about the accident."

"Becky, I think they killed him."

With her glass halfway to her lips, she froze. "The Foundation? God, I can't believe that. *Why?*"

"Why are you so uptight working there? You told me the atmosphere was upsetting. Is it more than that?"

"No." She tasted the coffee, put it down to add a half teaspoon of sugar. "Yes." She stirred the coffee absently. "It's the secrecy. They never have staff meetings. Everyone is compartmented in his or her own little bailiwick."

"Officewise?"

"Assignmentwise."

"Isn't it that way with a lot of organizations? A need-to-know policy for everyone?"

"In a fund-raising organization? Oh, I don't think so."

"Something's going on there. I couldn't get to Pope at all. Buttonwood was a playback for the party line. I assume Pope would be, too. He probably wrote it. So I feel that I'm up against a blank wall. But there has to be a crack in it somewhere. No doubt the seven trustees all sing the same tune, or they wouldn't be trustees. And I presume they'd promptly report to Pope or Buttonwood anything I asked."

"You sound suspicious of everybody."

"I am beginning to develop a degree of paranoia. I'd rather not go at the trustees. But what about members of the Advisory Council, the people who kick in ten thou and up? They certainly aren't handpicked. You said they never meet, but I wonder how much they are told about the Foundation's activities. They've got to be told something fairly arresting to cut loose major money like that."

"I hope you'll forget that you learned about the Advisory Council from me, Mr. Gammon."

"Steve."

"Steve. I don't think I'm even supposed to know about the Advisory Council."

Their salads arrived, and Steve and Becky fell silent while the aproned, middle-aged waiter set the plates in place, plunked down a platter of thick-crusted slabs of white bread, nodded in self-satisfaction, then finally left them on their own again.

Becky nibbled one of the tart, black olives. Behind her oversized glasses, her eyes were on his. "Steve, please?"

He nodded. "But how did you find out about it?"

"Alix."

"Buttonwood's assistant, she tells you stuff like that?"

"She doesn't like him much. He's arrogant and unfeeling and treats her like . . . an ordinary secretary."

"So why does she stay on, if she feels that way?"

"The money, I guess. That's why a lot of us stay. Except I stayed because of Mr. Gammon, too." Her eyes clouded again.

"You more than liked him, didn't you, Becky?"

"Yes." She didn't look up. "But it was never more than an at-work thing. I never saw him outside the building. I think it happens a lot. I felt a lift every time your brother talked to me. It wasn't love in the usual sense. There was no way I could be unfaithful to my husband. But there was something there." She shook her head. "Oh, I sound so terribly adolescent talking about it."

"I think I understand." Did Erica Brindell ever feel that way about him? He switched off this unsettling subject. "How far do you think Alix Cortland might be willing to go?"

"With what?"

"In disclosing what she knows about Foundation business."

Now Becky looked as if she didn't want to go any further with this herself.

"I don't mean with you as a go-between, Becky. That just might be dangerous. I want to talk with her myself."

"But then she'll know I've told you—"

"Not if we go to basics. Tell her I was smitten with her when I visited the Foundation. Tell her I want to meet her socially."

"I'm not so sure she'll go for that."

"She's not married or engaged, is she? I didn't see any ring."

"No, she's just like a lot of attractive women: she has a defensive reflex. I guess it starts early, when you're the junior high glamour queen, and the boys begin to get aggressive about it. I never had that problem. I was the class mouse, but I'll bet Alix was even a beautiful baby."

"All I'm asking is that you pave the way a little, so I won't look as if I'm coming totally out of the blue. Will you do that much, Becky? For me. Hell, for Jim." Dirty pool, Gammon.

She knew it. "You aren't exactly playing fair with me, are you? Doesn't this make us co-conspirators?"

"I hope it makes us the good guys, Becky. I have a gut feeling that the Foundation people are the conspirators."

Steve had noticed the maroon Camaro when he'd pulled out of the Crossmoor Arms garage this morning. When he returned, there it was again, parked a half block east of the cross street's intersection with Connecticut. It was pulled beneath the sidewalk maples, but not so far, Steve noted, as to obscure the driver's view of the front windows of Marcie Gammon's fourth floor apartment.

A parked car on that side street wasn't necessarily significant, but what was arresting was the fact that somebody had been sitting in it this morning, and was still in it now. An all-day vigil?

Or had the Camaro been on his tail and just now returned?

If its driver had indeed been following him, then that driver presumably knew where he was staying, could have assumed he was headed back here from his meeting with Becky Rossmyer, and could easily have broken off a few blocks north to reposition himself to continue his surveillance of Marcie's apartment.

Steve had told Becky that he felt a growing sense of paranoia. Hell, the impression that the Camaro's driver was watching, even following him had to be only that—an impression. Like the business of the blue, white, and yellow aloha shirts in Hana, twice at Kahului Airport . . . and hadn't he seen the same kind of shirt in the Royal Lahaina's lobby the morning of the helicopter charter? Talk about paranoia. There had to be hundreds of shirts like that for sale all over Hawaii.

Or was he being incredibly stupid? Up to now, he had just gotten the impression that FRETSAW was not as benign an organization as Horace Buttonwood had painted it. That gut feeling had been reinforced by Becky Rossmyer's attitude, though she hadn't given him any specific reasons for her own unease.

Had the Camaro's driver seen him pick up Becky today? Had he tailed them to Wheaton, watched them enter the Olive Grove? Steve had talked Becky into that meeting. What might he have exposed her to now?

If he had been followed, here and in Hawaii, and if he was being followed now, couldn't that be a chilling confirmation that FRETSAW was more than a money funnel for a political viewpoint? What in hell could it be involved in that had precipitated the deaths of two of its people?

What had Van Hayden found out?

Steve parked beneath the Crossmoor Arms without difficulty. The attendant knew him now, even gave him a lackadaisical wave as Steve walked to the elevator. Marcie's car was back in its assigned space. She was home from her morning appointments with Jim's lawyer and his broker.

He used the spare key she had given him, and found her at the kitchen table poring over legal papers.

"Can you believe all this?" she said without looking up. "Jim's will made me coexecutor along with his lawyer, and I've got all this stuff to read and sign."

"That's the least of your worries, Marcie. Let me show you something." He led her to the small living room in the front of the apartment. "Stay back from the window."

"What in the world . . . ?" She wore a bemused smile.

"See that car over there on the side street, the Camaro?"

"The maroon car?"

"He was there when I left this morning. He could have followed me, and he's back there again."

"That's crazy. Why would anyone want to do that?"

"You tell me. And I don't think it's the first time." Steve told her the number of times he'd noticed the same kind of shirt in Hawaii. "Probably the *same* shirt, now that I think back. I've been dense as hell about all this."

"Not so dense, Steve, or you would never have found Jim's body."

"Naive, then. These bastards have known every move I've made."

"If you're right about being followed. And you're not really sure."

"Just the same, I think I'd better move out of here. My staying ties you in with what I'm doing."

She laid her fingers on his arm. "Steve, I'd rather you'd stay. I'd feel a lot safer."

"It would be like asking the tethered goat into your hut. And we don't know how far these tigers are willing to go."

"Don't you think I'm at risk anyway? If you're right, they killed Jim for something he knew. Won't they have to assume that he could have told me?"

"You're going too fast, Marcie. I think they killed him to prevent his learning whatever Van Hayden was going to tell him. I was the one who went to Hawaii and found his body. Now they have to be wondering if I've made the connection, wondering what else I've uncovered. They're worried about me, not you. But if I stay here, you will be implicated just as surely as if you had been on Maui yourself."

They walked back to the kitchen, then she turned to face him. "Stay, Steve. Please."

Which was the greater risk now? To remain here with her and surely involve her—in FRETSAW's view—in something that had already cost lives? Or to leave her here alone and possibly already implicated, as far as FRETSAW was concerned?

"You'll keep the door locked all the time. You'll let nobody in you don't know, and nobody in from FRETSAW, even if you do know him." Paranoia, or common sense? Or naive idiocy?

Her face brightened. "Does that mean you'll stay?"

"As long as I'm in Washington. But I mean it: you keep that door locked."

At 9:00 the next morning, he called the information desk at the Library of Congress. Did they have any information on an organization called the Freedom Through Specialized Awareness Foundation?

"It should be listed in *The Foundation Directory,* sir. Just a minute." She had the eager voice of a young woman eager to cooperate. When she came back on the line, she summarized the listing for him. "Established in 1985. Richardson Pope, president; Horace Buttonwood, executive director. Reported annual income from public subscription: $2 million . . . Disbursements reported last year were $1.5 million. Balance is assigned to operating expenses . . . Primary area of interest: informing the public on democratic ideals."

Not a hell of a lot of help there. "Do you know how the *Directory* gets its data?"

He heard her scrabbling through pages, then she said, "Apparently from the organizations themselves, sir."

Stonewalled again, this time on paper. The meager data on FRETSAW had been supplied by FRETSAW. All right, there was another possibility.

But *The Washington Post*'s library had nothing at all on FRETSAW, Pope, or Buttonwood. Talk about low profile. Then he had yet another idea, and had the paper's librarian transfer him to the advertising department.

"Freedom Through Specialized Awareness? Some sort of foundation, you said?" The man in Advertising sounded as if he wanted to be doing something else. "Hang on." He came back two full minutes later. "Yeah, their agency placed a couple of full pages with us. One in September 1986. Another this January."

"Who's their agency?"

"Kinnon & Fields, out in Bethesda."

Steve found their number in Marcie's Maryland suburban phone book.

"The FRETSAW account?" This voice was little-girl soft. Hesitant. "Just a minute, I'll transfer you to Mr. Hollis. He's the account executive for the FRETSAW ads."

Hollis wasn't hesitant at all. He sounded like a prosecuting attorney. "What they spend on that account is their business, Mr. Mifflin." Steve had decided the fewer references to the name Gammon, the better. "Who did you say you were with?"

"I didn't. My group prefers to remain anonymous until we can find a Washington area ad agency capable of handling a nonprofit foundation account in excess of a million."

With a derisive little laugh, Hollis relented. "Hell, Mifflin, just between us, the FRETSAW account hits a mill plus. No problem handling your people. No problem whatever."

So Hollis of Kinnon & Fields had neatly corroborated *The Foundation Directory*'s disbursement listings for FRETSAW. I haven't made any real progress at all, Steve realized.

Except in one important area. He had crossed a line, the line between straight research and deception. "Mifflin" had found it easy to lie to Hollis, but not altogether easy to live with after he hung up. I'm an aboveboard development consultant, not a detective, Steve told himself. Yet he was willing to be damned near anything to get to the bottom of whatever had led to Jim's death. He'd had only limited and long-ago military training and experience in what he was doing. That couldn't matter. He was intelligent, resourceful, and driven by smoldering anger that would not be tempered until he found what FRETSAW's real purpose was. And, damn it, tore it apart.

FRETSAW had killed Jim. He was convinced of that. It had killed Van Hayden. It had put Blue-Yellow-White Shirt on him in Hawaii. It had a maroon Camaro's driver watching him across Connecticut Avenue.

And what did he have? He had Becky Rossmyer.

She called at 12:30 from a booth on Twentieth Street, she told him. "I'm on lunch hour. Only have a minute."

He heard traffic in the background. She had to be using one of those damned phone cowls on a stumpy post. Whatever happened to real phone booths and privacy?

"I talked to Alix," she said. "Told her you'd found her really attractive, that you want to see her, but you're hesitant about appearing too forward."

"Sounds mighty thin now, doesn't it? What was her reaction?"

"I think she liked that. She's had it with frontal approaches."

"How do you think she'll respond if I call her this afternoon?"

"Not at FRETSAW! They hate personal calls. For all I know, they might even monitor them. Get in touch with her at home, after work." Becky gave him the number. "Remember, you're a shy guy. I paved the way. Don't rip up the pavement. She'll be home around six."

He spent much of the afternoon, as he had the morning, on the spare room's telephone. Marcie had left at noon for a lunch with the publisher of a Washington-based interior design magazine. "The article he wants me to work on will bring in only eight cents a word, but I've got to be busy, Steve. Work or fall apart."

She had dressed in a gray skirt and jacket over a white blouse with a tiny blue string tie. Russet hair loosely curled, those lovely satin lips a pearl blush. Her light blue briefcase looked out of place. When she left, she kissed him lightly on top of the head at he sat at Jim's—now her—desk in the bedroom-office using the phone. That was a fleeting little tenderness, as if she were conscious of the possibility even that might lead to more. He didn't want that to happen. Didn't want, or shouldn't want? They weren't the same thing.

"There are sandwich makings in the fridge," she called from the door. Then she was gone.

He slapped his hand on the desktop. Damn! He should have insisted that she stay here. God only knew where FRETSAW had positioned her in this thing. But she had told him in no uncertain terms that she wasn't going to "drop out and hole up. I *will* keep the door bolted when I'm here alone. And

I *will* be careful at all times." A little tone of mockery had crept into her voice. "But I'm not going to be afraid to go out in broad daylight and talk with a publisher in a crowded restaurant."

Steve walked down the apartment's short hall and into the front room to watch the Camaro. In a few minutes, Marcie's powder-blue Honda emerged from the building's access drive, and turned onto Connecticut.

Beneath its thin screen of maple leaves on the cross street, the Camaro stayed in place. That appeared to settle the question. They were after him, not her. Yet.

Now he tried to get lines on Pope and Buttonwood, not as FRETSAW officers, but as individuals.

None of the papers—the *Post,* the *Times,* none of the suburban weeklies—had a thing on either man. In a city that teemed with publicity seekers, these were two anomalies.

He called the Library of Congress again. No, neither man was listed in *Who's Who* or its less prestigious companion volume, *Who's Who in the East.*

How did reporters get a line on people who hadn't left readily accessible trails? Asked them, Steve realized, but that seemed less than advisable in this situation.

Six o'clock was a long time coming. On impulse, he used his AT&T credit card to call the number he'd kept for Van Hayden's Scottsdale residence. The daughter was still on the scene, but, no, she hadn't found anything in her father's effects that she thought would be helpful.

"Only some canceled checks made out to the Foundation, a pet charity of his, judging from the size of them." There was a touch of bitterness in Lillian Terhune's voice. "Ten thousand last year and the year before, and fifteen so far this year."

His fee for Advisory Council status. Van Hayden had probably been good for fifteen or more Gs the rest of his life, and if they'd played him right, FRETSAW would have been named in his will.

Maybe it was.

"No, Mr. Gammon. He left various amounts to a number of charities and causes, but not to that particular foundation. Not in the final will."

"His final will?"

"He had left that group a substantial sum in the original draft of his most recent will, but he drew up a codicil just a week before he died, and the codicil canceled the bequest to the Freedom Through Specialized Awareness Foundation."

They'd gotten to him. Jim had gotten to him. Planned giving was Jim's specialty. Reasonable assumption: Jim had gotten to know him quite well, had convinced Van Hayden to put the Foundation in the old man's will.

Then Van Hayden must have learned something that prompted him to add a codicil that eliminated the Foundation. He'd not only done that; he'd also contacted Jim and asked the man he'd known best at FRETSAW to meet him in Hawaii, asked him to do that abruptly, urgently. Apparently Van Hayden had learned something so sensitive that he had wanted to isolate both of them while he disclosed whatever it was.

Not a bad theory. All the evidence was circumstantial, but coincidental circumstances were all he had to go on. Steve paced the small room, hands plunged in his pockets absently jingling change. He strode to the front windows overlooking Connecticut Avenue.

The afternoon overcast had lowered to melt into light, persistent rain. The Camaro was still there, its driver visible as a shadow behind his wet windshield. Steve paced to the kitchen, made a fresh pot of coffee.

Marcie returned at 5:00, burdened with briefcase and a damp and lumpy bag from a stationery store.

"How'd it go?"

"Fine. He wants me to turn out two articles, not just one. Maybe more than two."

"Sounds like a lot of words for eight cents per. You want some coffee? I've got a fresh pot going." He felt oddly like a housebound husband welcoming home his working wife. Even experienced a little guilt twinge, maybe because the rain had frizzled her hair and given her a distraught look.

"Okay. Let me put this stuff in my bedroom first."

"You do your writing in the bedroom? Put it in the spare room."

"That's Jim's desk."

"No, Marcie, it's your desk now."

She put the bag and briefcase on a kitchen chair. "I'd better get out of these damp things and start supper."

"Not for me, thanks. If I'm lucky, I'll have a dinner date." He felt another pang of unwarranted guilt.

"A date?"

"Line of duty."

When she returned, now in her apple-green housecoat, he set out two cups and poured the steaming coffee. She sat across from him at the kitchen table, added sugar only, tasted and nodded. They sat in silence, and he was aware of an awkward tension.

She said abruptly, "I thought you were worried about my being here alone, and now you say you could be going out tonight." That sounded remarkably possessive until he saw her pixie smile.

"You crossed right in front of that Camaro. It stayed put. It's a reasonable assumption that he's interested in me, not you." He glanced at the clock over the sink. "Duty calls."

He sat at the spare room desk to dial, wondering how convincing an actor he was about to be. Three rings. He was a few minutes early. She might not yet be—

"Miss Cortland? This is Steven Gammon. We met at the Foundation a few days ago, and you were kind enough to attend my brother's memorial service. I want to thank you for that."

"Yes, Mr. Gammon?" Her voice was low and controlled, and she wasn't giving him any help.

"I realize this is awfully short notice, but I wonder if we

might have dinner together this evening?" That was putting it on the line, but if Becky Rossmyer had been adept at her purposeful girl talk, he shouldn't have to spend too much time on this verbal dancing.

"You don't give much notice, Mr. Gammon."

"My apologies for that, but I'm in town for just a short time. And, sure, this is an impulse call. I'm kind of surprised at myself, to be honest about it."

Her silence thundered.

"Look, I'm a divorced man, not on the make. I'm in town because of my brother's death, feeling low as hell, tired of meals alone, and I met a beautiful woman. That's all there is to it, Miss Cortland."

"Alix," she said. An easing of resistance. "I like seafood." A sale.

7.

He made a reservation at Jean Louis, picked her up at her North Sixteenth Street apartment precisely at 7:00, turned the Buick over to valet parking at the Watergate at 7:25. That had not been easy.

When he had pulled out of the Crossmoor Arms service drive, he kept his eyes on the rear-view. Nothing. Had he been wildly wrong about the Camaro?

After he drove a full block south, there it was. Suspicions confirmed, Gammon. He was being watched. He was being followed.

And he was leading the Camaro and its driver straight to Alix Cortland.

This would not do at all. There had to be a way to shake the other car without a tire-screeching and possibly fruitless attempt at evasion through Washington's rain-slicked streets. And Steve wasn't so sure he wanted to reveal that he had detected the tail. Let him continue to be visible where *he* could be watched—and avoided.

But how?

Steve rolled the Buick down Connecticut's broad, tree-lined, slick pavement through moderate evening traffic. Where could he pull in, lose the Camaro without appearing to, then pull out again, and take a cross street to Sixteenth?

Then, past the bridge over Rock Creek, he saw it, a multilevel parking garage, its green neon beckoning arrow hazy behind the drizzle.

He pulled around a slow-moving Ryder truck, cut abruptly across in front of it, and rocked the Buick to a stop at the automatic dispenser just long enough to yank out the pasteboard parking ticket. The little orange barrier lifted. He gunned the car up the ramp and began the left-hand ascending spiral.

If the Camaro's driver had seen him veer into the garage, then he would be at the entrance now, hurriedly snatching his ticket. Or had he watched Steve swing around the truck, and assumed he was still moving southward down Connecticut?

Steve rolled down the driver's window, slowed the car and listened. A level below, he heard the squeal of tires. Bastard!

He had noted with dismay that the garage's exit ramp was not a separate one, as he had hoped. Descending cars used this ramp's well-marked inside lane. His idea of a quick crossover to a separate exit ramp was useless. And the pursuing Camaro was forcing him even higher to an inevitable dead end on the garage roof.

Then he saw the van, an old, yellow Plymouth Voyager, the long version produced before Chrysler came out with the stubby Voyager minivan. He held his breath. Yes, by God! On the far side, the space was empty. He whipped the little Buick Skyhawk close behind the hulking van, snapped off the lights and ducked below seat-back level.

The Camaro was not quite fifteen seconds behind him, though now the driver had slowed his charge up the ramp. It was likely, Steve reasoned, that he realized he was about to find his subject in the act of parking. He no doubt planned to drive on past, park the Camaro just beyond the next obscuring turn, then follow on foot.

Steve had two advantages. He knew he was being followed,

and he wasn't going to do what he assumed the other driver expected.

The Camaro rolled past, its lights flashing across the Buick's ceiling. Steve edged up to window level, watched the tail lights disappear around the ramp's next turn, smelled harsh exhaust.

He twisted the Buick's ignition key, backed quietly without turning on the lights, let the upgrade of the ramp stop his reverse arc so the brake lights wouldn't flare. Then he coasted silently back down.

Where the ramp forked to the exit booth, he pulled two dollars out of his wallet and handed them through the window to the black attendant.

"Keep the change. The Washington Hilton is down to the right, isn't it?"

"You got it, man."

That should give the Camaro's driver something to work on, should he have the foresight to ask at the booth. Steve swung the Buick down Connecticut, passing the Washington Hilton's curved hillside rampart, then cut past its parking garage entrance on T Street, jogged left, then right at Florida, and followed T Street three more blocks to head north on Sixteenth.

On the roof of the parking garage, Georgie Prescott slammed the Camaro's steering wheel with his palm. How could he have blown Gammon's trail *again?* The guy was no pro. In fact, he couldn't know Prescott was on his trail. Prescott *was* a pro. Yet Gammon had somehow disappeared in this damned garage.

He could hear Kolker now. *"You lost him in a parking garage? Jesus, Georgie!"*

Prescott hadn't been fifteen seconds behind Gammon's blue Skyhawk when the man had entered the garage. He'd followed Gammon up the ramp only two turns behind. Yet when Prescott reached the fifth and final level, no Buick. No Gammon. Nothing up here on the roof but empty slots, open to the rain that sifted through his headlight glare. Plenty of space up here . . .

Plenty of spaces on the way up, too. That had to be it. Gammon must have pulled into one of them, snapped off his lights and watched the Camaro gun right on past.

Which meant the guy was on to him. He sure hadn't acted like that today, although Prescott had wondered about it when Gammon did all that winding around N and M and Twentieth. Then he realized the subject was looking for someone. And found her. Little thing, dark hair, tan skirt and sweater. Too far away for him to get a good look at her face.

He had tailed Gammon and the girl way the hell out to Wheaton, to a Greek restaurant. He faced a judgment call there. Should he go in, or park where he could see the place and wait for them to come out? If the restaurant wasn't crowded, and it sure didn't look as if it would be this wet, early afternoon, he would be putting himself in an exposed mode, as Kolker liked to say.

They were in there an hour while Prescott tried to ignore hunger pangs, and the fact that he mightily had to piss. He had a cardboard drink container for that, but this was a busy thoroughfare with some sidewalk traffic, too, despite the rain.

When they finally came out, he waited until the Skyhawk rolled past. Then he pulled out and followed them through Wheaton, trailing not quite a block behind with three cars between as a screen. Then Gammon had turned south on 97, swung right, into 390, just above the D.C. line, then followed it into Sixteenth Street. A half block south of P Street, Gammon pulled to the curb. The girl got out and transferred to a taxi that had just discharged a passenger in front of the National Wildlife Federation Building. Now two cars behind, Prescott got a better look at the girl as traffic compressed behind Gammon's Buick.

Then the subject moved out again, took a quarter of Scott Circle's circumference to emerge northwest on Massachusetts, stayed in Dupont Circle's outside lane to Connecticut, then accelerated north on Connecticut.

Back to the apartment building, Prescott was willing to bet.

Six minutes later, he pulled the Camaro off to the right, drove one residential block, then turned left to parallel Connecticut for three, emerging into the cross street just south of the Crossmoor Arms to park again under the familiar overhanging maples.

And here came Gammon, neatly predictable, rolling his Buick Skyhawk into the apartment's garage drive across the street.

Prescott checked the sidewalk behind him. Empty. At last, almost at the rupturing point, he used the drink container. Then he settled back, stomach growling, to wait. Always waiting. Hell of a job. Occasional bursts of action, spaced like sparse pearls, on a long, long string of waiting.

He played the Camaro's radio for a while, then turned it off because leaving it on too long would weaken the battery. Late in the afternoon, he ate one of the sandwiches he'd brought. Swiss on rye, wrapped in clinging clear plastic that was hard to peel off.

He thought about Deenie O'Hara. Al least, that was what she'd told him her name was. Short for Geraldine. Met her at the Channel Inn bar on Water Street along the northeast bank of the Washington Channel. She was a big-boned woman from West Virginia with bleached white hair done up in that kinky curl style. That wasn't all that was kinky . . .

Prescott shoved up in the Camaro's seat. The Buick nosed out of the service road and eased south on Connecticut. It crossed thirty yards in front of him. Time 6:47 P.M. He had twisted the Camaro's key, nosed out of the side street into light traffic, then trailed the Skyhawk down the main artery.

Now, literally blank-walled on the top floor of the parking garage, Georgie Prescott found himself giving Gammon a degree of grudging respect. But the guy hadn't evaporated; he had whipped in here, let Prescott race past him, and now he was no doubt on his way back down. Then out.

Prescott wheeled the Camaro around in a tight 180, and

began the descending spiral. At the attendant's booth, he handed over his ticket, paid the $1.50 minimum.

"You see which way that blue Skyhawk went out of here?"

"I didn't see no Skyhawk." The black face stared at him with eyebrows arched high. Prescott sighed, groped again for his wallet, handed the youth a five.

"Oh, *that* Skyhawk. Man say he looking for the Hilton."

"Which Hilton?"

"The Washington Hilton, man. He say the Washington Hilton."

Prescott was out of there in a screeching leap, narrowly missing an oncoming Capitol Cab. Three blocks down, he cut left into T Street, took his ticket at the Hilton's parking garage entrance, and began a systematic search for the blue Skyhawk. If he found it, what then?

He didn't have to be concerned about that. He didn't find it.

Her electric-blue cocktail sheath, form-fitting across her lush thighs in what appeared to be her consistent image, was as elegant as the restaurant's silken and mirrored decor. Alix Cortland draped her black velvet evening jacket over the back of her chair, touched her turned-under, shoulder-length cornsilk hair, and ordered a daiquiri and the Maine lobster with caviar butter. Steve opted for a martini and the Magret duck with dates and honey, and Volnay 1947 for the table. American Express was going to love this, a three-figure dinner check.

She had been ready when he buzzed her apartment door. In the car, they had talked weather and traffic. Now, in this secluded corner of the Watergate's increasingly crowded restaurant where he hoped no Foundation people were willing to invest a hundred bucks in a meal tonight, she rested her elbows on the tablecloth, laced her fingers beneath her chin, and smiled at him. A half smile, really; not of pleasure, but of curiosity.

"So, Mr. Steven Gammon, what are you after? My body or my brain?" Her piercing lavender eyes snapped challenge.

"Beg your pardon?" God, she was blunt.

"I want to know where I stand. If all this gastronomic splendor is to impress me, I'm impressed. But it won't buy anything."

"I told you I wasn't after anything more than a pleasant evening."

"Mr. Gammon—"

"Steve."

"Your brother is killed, Steve. You talk with Mr. Buttonwood. You deceive me into taking you to Jim Gammon's office without forewarning anyone. You charmed Becky. Now here we are, on very short notice, and you expect me to believe that you are wining and dining me in the very expensive, very exclusive Jean Louis just for the pleasure of being with me?"

"But you did agree to come." Whose side was she on?

She offered her Mona Lisa smile again. "Yes, I did." She dropped her arms and sat back as the waiter placed their drinks. Steve said nothing, even after the waiter had left. She seemed to want to talk, to exert some kind of superiority. Fine. He could provide her the silence she obviously wanted to fill.

"Our Mr. Buttonwood, how did he strike you?" she asked.

"Professionally unctious, but more concerned with FRETSAW's funding success than with its people."

One buckwheat-honey eyebrow arched upward. "That's very perceptive, Steve." She sipped her daiquiri. "Exactly what do you think happened to your brother?"

"I know what happened."

"I mean, did he fall asleep and drive over the edge, or was he helped over the edge?" She waited for him to take the cue. Was she here out of curiosity, or because she knew something she wanted him to know?

Or was she here on FRETSAW's behalf, to determine what kind of threat he might be to whatever FRETSAW's real mission might be?

He smiled to himself. It was remarkably easy to concoct a

half dozen scenarios for what could be nothing more than an expensive dinner with a blonde. All right, Alix Cortland of the luxuriant hips, this is a reaction test:

"I think he was killed to keep him from reaching Walter Van Hayden. And Van Hayden was killed to keep him from getting to anyone else."

After he'd said that, it struck him as a potentially huge mistake.

But even in the subdued glow from the recessed lights in the mirrored ceiling, he could see that she had paled. Was she that good an actress?

Where did she stand? He hadn't called her until nearly 6:00 this evening, and she was ready by 7:00. Even so, that had given her time to check with Buttonwood, to tell him Jim Gammon's brother was seeing her within the hour. And when the evening was over, she would be able to brief Buttonwood on exactly what Steve knew, where he planned to go from here.

She'd surely had time for that quick call. Hell, if she had set this up with Buttonwood right after Becky had talked with her this afternoon, she wouldn't have had to call him at all tonight.

"You think they both were murdered." She offered that not as a question, but as a statement, as if she were fixing his bitter opinion in her mind.

"What do you think, Alix?" This was like circling a wall, looking for a way in.

"I think it was strange that Mr. Buttonwood appeared so agitated before they were reported dead, then so in control afterward."

"Fascinating observation." Would she have said a thing like that if she were here under Buttonwood's guidance?

The halting conversation went on hold once more as the waiter arrived with his laden service tray. When he had finished rearranging the table and left them with the beautifully prepared lobster and the crisp duck in its fragrant honey sauce, she smiled again. "It's not my body, is it? That's something of a surprise, and I'm intrigued. Exactly what do you want?"

He began to work on the duck, then paused, met her pale eyes with their stiletto pupils. Took the plunge. "I want the roster of FRETSAW's Advisory Council." If he had read her wrong, God only knew what the consequences would be.

"The Advisory Council? Why?"

"Because I'm sure every member of the Board of Trustees would spout Buttonwood's company line. But the Advisory Council members apparently don't meet, presumably don't have much direct contact, probably don't get a concentrated company line briefing. Right?"

"They never meet. The whole thing is a device to attract major donors. They're called advisors only because they've contributed at least $10,000 a year. It's not a real council at all." She picked up her fork, then looked up at him. "You intend to talk to all twenty-two of them? What could they know?"

"Van Hayden knew something, and it was enough to drown him. How can I get the list? Surely it's on computer at FRETSAW. Who has access?"

She tasted a morsel of her lobster, first daintily dipping it in the caviar butter. "You're serious, aren't you?"

"Damned right. Who has access to the list besides Pope and Buttonwood? I'm sure they didn't enter it, and I doubt they maintain it. Who else has access?"

Alix Cortland's long, graceful fingers squeezed a half moon of lemon along the lobster tail's length. "One other person, Steve." She smiled at him. "I do."

"Logic told me. Next question. Can you get me a printout?"

"FRETSAW isn't exactly the Pentagon. It's possible."

"*Will* you get me that printout?"

"It could be risky."

"Why? You just said it's not the Pentagon."

"It's the atmosphere."

"So I understand."

She sipped the Volnay. "Oh, this is very nice."

"You haven't answered me."

She took three long swallows, then set down the crystal wine glass with elaborate care. "All right, I'll get you the printout."

That was a surprise. He'd thought he was being set up for a quid pro quo. "Why?"

That caught her off-guard. "What do you mean, why?"

"Why are you willing to risk your job—maybe more—for me? You don't owe me a thing. I have to wonder where you stand."

"I don't like working for a man who threatens employees . . . who threatens me, to be specific about it."

"Buttonwood has threatened you? How? For what?"

She sighed and put down her fork. "Oh, damn it! I shouldn't have come out with you at all. I knew Becky was setting me up, and I knew what you were trying to do."

"That I wanted the list?"

"Not that specifically. I knew you wanted to investigate FRETSAW."

"But here you are, Alix."

"I guess that tells me that I want this whole thing over with, doesn't it?"

He refilled her wine glass. "As the Russian lover said, 'Enough of this romance, let's get at it.' "

"That's not quite how he said it, but you're right. I can't have it both ways. It's really quite basic. Eighteen months ago, I did something incredibly stupid. I'd just moved to Washington and signed on with the Foundation after ending a distressing affair with a man in Delaware. In Wilmington, my hometown. And then I found myself pregnant. Pregnant without money for an abortion. Until one day, Mr. Buttonwood gave me a handful of checks and cash to deposit in the Foundation's account. He'd just gotten it out of that morning's response to one of our direct mail campaigns, and I assumed he hadn't totaled it."

Alix took a long, shaky pull at her wine. "I took out enough cash to pay for the abortion and some other expenses. And a week later, he confronted me with that. He had Xeroxed copies of all the checks and a statement of the cash amount, and had one of the mailroom clerks sign as a witness. So as soon as I gave him the deposit receipt, he knew what I'd done. He gave me a choice. A documented charge of grand larceny, or . . ."

"Or what?"

"One guess. He has his own personal blonde toy whenever he wants to play. We use my apartment."

Steve was silent, absorbing the impact of her words. Then he said, "Why don't you quit, disappear?"

She looked away. "I . . . can't. For two reasons. One is that I've been in trouble before, and he knows it. He found out when he checked my job application. I've got a record, Steve."

"A police record?"

"The man in Delaware—the one I had the affair with—he was manager of a jewelry store, and one night he went back after they'd closed, and he took $20,000 worth of emeralds."

"And you were with him?"

"I stayed in the car. I swear, I thought he was going back for some papers he'd forgotten. But I was arrested along with him. I was given probation. Now there's this thing with FRET-SAW. Mr. Buttonwood had me sign a statement about the money—a confession. I don't know where he keeps it, or even how many copies he made. But with that and the other thing, I'm hopelessly locked in, Steve."

"Sweet fellow, your employer. He set you up, and now—"

"Set me up?"

"Did he know you were pregnant and up against a financial wall?"

"He could have. I never thought of it that way. Why, that son of a bitch!"

"A son of a bitch and a blackmailer."

"And I'm a common thief. Birds of a feather in bed together."

"Let's see if I've got the big picture. Buttonwood's got a hold on you, and you're hoping I can bring him down." That was the quid pro quo.

She picked up the fork again, and twisted loose another pearl-white lobster morsel. "I said you were perceptive. Think about what I'm doing to keep him quiet, then imagine what I'm willing to do to get him out of my life for good."

"All I'm asking is that you get me a printout of the Advisory Council list."

"Is that really all?"

He lifted his wine glass to touch it to hers and nodded.

"You're good, you know that?" she said. "You've just asked me to betray my employer, and at the same time you've made me feel like a lady."

Jesus, back on the carpet again in Kolker's barren OmniSecure office. More accurately, back on the vinyl. The office had no carpet. It didn't have much of anything. Kolker's beat-up wooden desk, creaky wooden swivel chair, and a filing cabinet; all of it circa some passé dark oak era. A rock-hard visitor's chair to match. Not a picture on the institutional green walls. One narrow, metal-framed window with a bleak view of Eye Street, two floors down through the slats of the rickety wooden blind.

Kolker planted his right cheek on his desk corner and nodded at the visitor's chair.

"Sit, Georgie."

Prescott sat.

"You lost him *again?* In a parking garage? You are some frigging operator, Georgie."

"These are some frigging hours you've got me on, Kolker." He gave the name the same derisive inflection Kolker had given his.

"This is no nine-to-five romp. You want that, get a job with the feds. We're paying high, right?"

Prescott looked up at him.

"Right? I want to hear it."

"Right!"

"Goddamn right, right. So we expect results. I do, and so does the client, and so does the man downstairs. This is a war, Georgie. Us against Them. Anybody tries to disrupt what our side is doing is automatically one of Them. You grasp my meaning?"

Prescott nodded glumly.

"We're good, Georgie. We're the best. And we're surrounded by citizens who haven't got the slightest idea what this country is all about. You got a chance to do something about that, and what the hell have you done with it? Blown it in Hawaii, blown it here. What do you want me to say, Georgie?"

Prescott felt his blood cooking. Another ass-eating by this half-educated, weirdly idealistic, super-patriot spin-off. But confrontation with your boss—with this particular boss—did not pay off in anything good. Prescott liked this job; a lot of it, anyway. The idea that he was in the big-time security business. The moments of visceral excitement. And he sure liked the money.

"I've uncovered a number of facts we can use, Kolker."

"Try me."

Prescott also hated sitting several feet below Kolker in this dumb rock of a chair. He stood and took four paces to the window. Still raining this morning.

"The subject was observed to—"

"Cut the crap, Georgie."

"Gammon picked up a little black-haired woman at twelve-forty P.M. yesterday. Took her to the Olive Grove in—"

"What the hell's that?"

"A Greek restaurant in Wheaton. Stayed there about an hour, drove her back to D.C., and let her out near Sixteenth and P streets, where she transferred to a taxi."

"Who was she?"

"I don't know. I followed him, not her. That's the assignment, isn't it?"

"Did you get a look at her?"

"When she got in the taxi, yes. I was only a couple cars away. Short woman with big glasses."

"And black hair, you said." Kolker slid off the desk, strode to the filing cabinet, and yanked open the second drawer. He pulled out a thick looseleaf binder, and handed it to Prescott. "See if she's in there."

The black three-ring held four glassine pages of photos in pockets, each with a typed name underneath. He found the dark-haired woman on the third sheet, lower right-hand corner, and handed the binder back to Kolker. He tapped the photo with his forefinger. "Her."

" 'Rebecca Rossmyer,' " Kolker read. He replaced the binder in the file drawer, extracted a manila folder, and ran his finger down a listing in the folder.

"Well, you weren't a total loss, Georgie. She's—or she was—administrative assistant to James Gammon. Interesting connection, but what does it mean?"

"Maybe a little personal consoling," Prescott suggested. "Brotherly love? How should I know?"

Kolker grimaced. "Don't be so damned hair-trigger about everything. I was only asking retort . . . retor—"

"Rhetorically." That felt good.

"Yeah. They sure didn't pick a restaurant for bed benefits. They picked it for talk."

"My guess is they set it up there, then he went back to the apartment, got himself prettied up for their roll in the hay. He left around 6:30—"

" 'Around'?"

Prescott consulted his notebook. "Subject left the Crossmoor Arms at six-forty-one, drove south on Connecticut, cut into the Eljay Parking Garage just south of the Taft Bridge."

"That's where you lost him, right?"

"That's where he made me."

"Hell, Georgie, he made you before that. That's why he played garage tag. Be accurate."

Prescott clamped his teeth against the smart crack that threatened to come out anyway. Swallowed it. "Okay, before that. When I came back out, I asked the garage boy which way Gammon had gone. He told me the guy had asked the way to the Washington Hilton. I drove there immediately, checked the entire parking facility, but the subject's car wasn't there."

"Of course it wasn't. You were dancing to Gammon's tune, Georgie."

Prescott decided it would be politic to eat that one, too. "I returned to the apartment building, and waited there until Fabrizio relieved me at nine. Gammon didn't show."

"He showed at ten-thirty, according to Fabrizio's report."

"Who's on stakeout now? You told me to come straight here, so who's there now?"

"Hutchins. Not in a maroon Camaro. From here on in, that's out. Use a pool car."

"I hate the damned pool cars. You couldn't outrun a Yugo in any of them."

"You got any more hot iron in your garage?"

"No."

"Then use a pool car. You're back on station at noon, and for Christsake, don't keep parking in the same place. Hutchins is on Kanawha or Jocelyn in a dark green Chevette. Don't forget to let him know you're there."

Kolker sat back down on the edge of his desk, and tapped the manila folder on his knee. "Georgie, listen to me. This guy Gammon is turning out to be a lot smarter than you give him credit for. Don't underestimate him."

Her skirt felt impossibly confining. She was fighting pre-middle-age spread in the hip area, but that wasn't what made her feel impossibly girdle-bound at the moment. A bead of perspiration, cold as a sleet granule, inched erratically downward between Alix Cortland's breasts behind her bra.

Why this onset of the heebies? Buttonwood had gone to lunch ten minutes ago. There wasn't anyone left on this end of the second floor. The risk factor was nil. Yet her fingers trembled.

She punched her terminal's ON button, flexed her fingers in a vain attempt to rid them of nervous tremor, then tapped in the access code. The little plastic clicks sounded like pistol shots to her, yet shutting her door to the hall could invite curiosity from any of the phone bank people drifting in and out of their boiler rooms down the hall.

The CRT screen flashed an amber READY. She touched the square, gray PRINT button. The daisy wheel printer on the table beside her desk began its dry rip.

The paper scrolled upward in line-by-line jerks with agonizing slowness. Then her heart thumped. Footsteps. First far down the hall, then closer. Then right at her door. God, had Buttonwood forgotten something?

A beardless face peered into her office. Not Buttonwood, thank the Lord. A round, dried-apple face, with a Halloween pumpkin grin baring square teeth. Pathetic old Hank Loper. Actually not so old; he just had that kind of a face. Probably looked twenty-one when he reached puberty.

He handed her a sealed brown envelope, the daily take from the third floor mail operation.

"You fixed up for lunch?" he asked.

Loper, supervisor of the direct mail department, had a master's degree in English from the University of Maryland, and he knew exactly how that sounded. His little joke, a couple of times a month.

"I'm just having grapefruit."

"We'd make a peach of a pair," he said amiably, and he walked back down the hall to the stairs. Last month, she'd said she was just having a piece of leftover cheesecake, and he had told her, "Your gain is my loss." That, right after she had taken a close look at herself in her bathroom's full-length, and thought she had detected a noticeable broadening of outlook.

She had broken into wry laughter. A week before, in the invaded privacy of her own bedroom, Buttonwood had complained that he was putting on weight. Now here *she* was, widening out. My boss is really putting the pressure on, doctor. Life was just great.

And here had been Loper the Hoper, hanging over her printer while it grated out corporate treason. Had his beady little eyes been safely glued on her sweatered chest? When she'd realized how conveniently near the door the printer was, she had swiveled a few strategic degrees. The eyes had it, but in time?

She wasn't cut out for this. What was she cut out for? She'd laid her life story on the tablecloth at Jean Louis because she thought she could trust Steve Gammon, even get help from him. Now she was in a sweat because of what he had her doing. Buttonwood had her by the whatever-he-wanted; Steve was manipulating her neatly; and for all she knew, Hank Loper had gotten an eyeful of more than what he had come to see. One of her explicit duties was to safeguard the Advisory Council list, and Hank knew that.

How did a reasonably good-looking, passably bright blonde girl from Delaware get herself into this kind of bind?

The printer, thank heaven, abruptly ceased its data retching. She pulled the pastel-green-and-white-striped printout from its roller, ripped it free, then hurriedly folded the sheet and stuffed it in her purse.

Two floors below, in the small, climate-controlled room that contained the mainframe computer to which all of FRETSAW's desk terminals were connected, another printer made an automatic entry. None of the administrative or executive assistants had ever seen this room. They knew it existed, but as no more than necessary housing for the mainframe, the corporate computer's centralized brain. They were not aware of the little dot matrix recording printer that was wired into the incoming cable that centralized the keyed requests from every terminal in the building.

Usually silent during lunch hours, the printer came briefly to life just after midday on May 21:

1223-5-15. PTB STA 2.

That was all. It said a lot. Time, date. PTB was the access code Buttonwood had selected for the Advisory Council list. Barnum's initials. Station 2 was the terminal on Alix Cortland's desk.

8.

The maroon Camaro was not across the street, hadn't been there at all this morning. Steve found that no surprise.

"They know that I know I'm being followed," he had told Marcie last night. Now no car at all was pulled beneath the side street maples across Connecticut. Yet that was no relief. What had been done instead? If FRETSAW had been concerned enough about his activities to put a tail on him, they surely were not going to cancel surveillance just because he had spotted the tail.

The fact that it looked clear out there was no assurance that the Crossmoor Arms and its environs were free of FRETSAW's people.

He had made progress. Alix Cortland had called last night, and she had read him the Advisory Council list, which he had copied down in laborious longhand. Now he and Marcie shared scrambled eggs, toast and coffee, a brotherly-sisterly breakfast almost to the point of self-consciousness. That was another unexpected reaction.

But the self-consciousness was here every time he looked at her auburn hair and soft lips.

She put down her coffee cup. "Now what?"

"Now I'm going to work on that list."

Twenty-two names, addresses, and the donor history of each. The list showed that a lot of these people had kicked in more than the $10,000 minimum. The total take over the past twelve months was close to half a million. Jim had been pretty damned busy. Walter Van Hayden, late of Scottsdale—but not yet excised from the computer—had upped his ante to $15,000 this year, as his daughter had told Steve. Date received: April 2. After that, obviously, he had learned something highly disturbing.

"You're going to travel to"—she peered at his two notepaper sheets—"to Maine, California, Missouri, and a dozen other states?"

"By phone to them. But there are closer possibilities. This one, Burlington Claibourne, should be a lot more accessible."

"In Key West?"

"Read the whole entry. He's there from October through April. May to September, he's in Annapolis. From the marina address, I'd say he lives on a boat. Annapolis is what? Twenty-five miles from here?"

"Steve, I don't understand what you hope to get out of these people."

At the sink, he rinsed his cup then turned to lean against the counter, arms obstinately folded. "Van Hayden would hardly have called Jim to Maui to talk about a further donation, or to give his opinion of FRETSAW's ad campaigns. Something a hell of a lot more serious than that got them both killed. I'm betting that these major donors, at least some of them, haven't kicked in five figures just to finance newspaper ads."

"Granted all that, if there is something less than legit going on, why would any of the people on this list tell you about it?"

"Because, my perceptive sister-in-law, I'm not going to go at them as the vengeful brother of their late friendly fund-raiser. I'm a concerned fellow-traveler, consumed with eagerness to support the cause of Freedom Through Specialized Awareness. And I hope one of these sheared sheep will be kind enough to tell me just what in hell that cause really is."

"You're not going to them as Steve Gammon, obviously."

"Meet Henry Mifflin. Old U of Illinois classmate of mine. Never came back from Vietnam."

"I'm not sure I like this, Steve. If FRETSAW is concerned enough to have someone following you, what will they do if they catch you playing undercover agent with their blue-ribbon donors?"

"No problem, Marcie. They won't catch me."

Horace Buttonwood read the monitor printout entry again, gripping the white and pastel green sheet in both hands.

1223-5-15. PTB STA 2.

His own secretary—executive assistant—had ordered a printout of the Advisory Council list. Yesterday. During the time he had been absent from the office.

He lay down the sheet and drummed agitated fingers on his desktop. What in hell was she up to? His first impulse was to order Alix in here and put that question to her. Point-blank. Count on surprise to jolt it out of her.

Then he felt an unsettling wash of uneasiness. He controlled her, yet here she was dipping into confidential Foundation data on her own initiative. There was something hugely unsettling about this.

Another negative consideration was that if he were to rush out to her cubicle and hit her with it, she would realize her desk terminal was monitored. Then it wouldn't take her long to deduce that every FRETSAW terminal was similarly monitored. That knowledge, spread through the organization, would alter employee perceptions considerably. The long-term, even short-term effects of that could be seriously deleterious, to say the least.

But what shook Horace Buttonwood more deeply than the corporate ramifications of Alix Cortland's apparent deceit was the fact that if she were fired because of this, he stood a very good chance of losing the only woman to whom he had access on demand. The thought of no more throat-quickening interludes between Alix Cortland's pillowy thighs turned the fingers running down his beard icy cold.

Steve Gammon, goddamn him, had to be the initiator of this. Buttonwood's hand moved from his beard to the open folder of OmniSecure reports on his desk. Gammon had taken Rebecca Rossmyer to lunch, way out in Wheaton. Then OmniSecure's man had lost him—or Gammon had lost OmniSecure's man—the evening of the following day. Who had Gammon taken to dinner? Alix? It was logical to assume that it was Gammon for whom she had run out the Advisory Council list.

The bastard just wouldn't quit.

Buttonwood felt as if a pig of cold lead had just been hung between his shoulder blades. He had to take this to Pope. No way around that; no way at all, because Pope also received Showalter's reports, and Pope could be aware that no business was pending that would require an Advisory Council printout. He shoved back from his desk, jerked to his feet, strode to the door.

"I'll be down with Mr. Pope," he told Alix.

She half turned to look up at him. Was that anxiety in her piercing lavender eyes? She couldn't know that he knew. The monitor printout had come up here in the interoffice mail, but it was sealed daily by Showalter in the basement mainframe room and marked "Personal."

Buttonwood walked to the stairs at the far end of the hall with what he hoped looked like confident strides. He could feel her watching him. On the stairs, he took hold of the polished banister rail, a slippery grip. His palms were moist. Why was he so shaken every time he went to Pope? They were in this together, weren't they?

At the foot of the staircase, he nodded down the hall to Miss Simmons behind her reception desk, and walked back along the ground floor hallway, not so confidently now, his leather soles clacking on the polished parquet, then muffled by the Oriental runner after he turned the corner into the short cross corridor that led to Richardson Pope's office.

He tapped on the carved walnut door with hesitant knuckles. He was the executive director of FRETSAW, but why did he always feel like a supplicant when he came to this office?

"Yes?" The voice was muffled by the heavy door.

"Horace."

The door buzzed. It had a lock, electronically controlled from Pope's desk. Buttonwood pushed the door open.

The president's office was designed to put occasional big-league visitors at ease. It looked like a sumptuous living room. Earthtone Karastan carpet, tan grasscloth walls, mellow mahogany woodwork, bookcases along one side with elaborately leatherbound sets of Dickens, Thackeray, the Great Books of the Western World, all selected for effect, Buttonwood deduced. Pope didn't seem like much of a reader.

On the opposite wall hung a big Hudson River School panorama of the Palisades as that area had looked to the artist in the 1800s; a moody oil with shafts of sunlight trying to cut through cold mist at daybreak. Beneath it crouched a green leather sofa, wide enough to seat five. At its near end stood an ornate walnut circular conference table with four matching chairs.

There were no visitor's chairs near the imposing partners' desk that dominated the far end of the office. Its polished expanse was devoid of anything save a telephone and notepad, which always gave Buttonwood the defensive feeling that Pope was totally intent on what was being said. The man made frequent notes, or gave the impression he was doing so, and the brown Touchtone phone at his elbow seemed poised for an instant call to some source who might prove Buttonwood a liar. Such was the effect.

The overbearing impact of the sumptuous room, contrasted with the cleared-for-instant-action desk, was only a setting for the most intimidating feature of all: the physical presence of Richardson Pope.

He was totally bald; more than that, he was devoid of all hair. No eyebrows, not a hair on the backs of the big hands. The man had been baby-skin smooth since a childhood disease had denuded him at the age of fifteen, so his story went. That, Buttonwood had thought, was enough to make any teenager into a defensively arrogant adult. The fact that Pope had burgeoned to six feet four, and had a nose that hooked raptor-like over his perpetual scowl, made his hairless skull an object of considerable menace. His odd predeliction for suits in the beige to tan range, together with his tanned bald pate, made him look, Buttonwood felt, like a brooding block of sandstone.

The voice offered no relief, either: a guttural rumble. Pope invariably sounded to Buttonwood as if he were suffering from deep-seated pain. He looked pained now as, with his customary abrupt nod, he ordered Buttonwood to seat himself on the immense sofa.

Buttonwood cleared his throat of suddenly accumulating phlegm. He was a full fifteen feet from Pope's big beige leather swivel, and the distancing made conversation additionally difficult.

"We seem to have a complication," Buttonwood said carefully, "in regard to the Gammon situation."

Pope fixed Buttonwood with sand-colored eyes, folded his hands on his desktop, and said nothing at all.

Buttonwood's throat clogged again. He ground it clear. "Somehow, I believe he has gotten hold of the, ah, Advisory Council list."

Now Pope spoke, an ominous one-word rumble. " 'Somehow'?"

Oh, Christ. CYA time. "Through Miss Cortland's station, I'm afraid. That doesn't conclusively indicate that she keyed the request. That's just where the request originated."

"Who else knows the access code?"

"I do. And Showalter, of course."

"And you did not authorize the access?"

"I did not."

"Nor did Showalter, obviously, or you would never have learned about it, correct? Ergo, the list was called up by your executive assistant."

"It would seem so. And through interpretation of OmniSecure reports of Steven Gammon's activities, I have reason to believe she acquired the list for him."

Pope sat immobile. Sandstone. Only the eyes looked alive, and they would not leave Buttonwood's face. Didn't the man ever blink those seemingly lidless eyes?

Buttonwood's mouth went dry. "Obviously, I'll give Miss Cortland immediate notice."

Pope rumbled, "You will not."

"Not fire her?"

"That would immediately warn Gammon, would it not? And it would sever a clandestine in-house connection to Gammon that we are now aware of."

Buttonwood stroked his beard, realized he was doing it, and dropped his hand to the sofa arm. "Then what—"

"Gammon has the list," Pope said, more to himself than to Buttonwood, and as if Buttonwood hadn't spoken at all. "What will he do with that list? That is the concern. And the answer is obvious. Next question: what is to be our counteraction?"

Buttonwood was absorbed in Pope's oral thinking. He started when Pope abruptly said, "I asked you a question, Horace. What is to be our response?"

"I'll make that my first priority on today's agenda."

Pope snorted. "Don't waste our time. I'll tell you what our response will be."

And he told him.

Burlington Claiborne looked like a heavyweight who'd had the good sense to retire while his nose was just a touch flattened. His ample bronze hair showed silver only at the temples. His broad face was the color of walnut shell. The big arms that jutted below a white Brooks Brothers polo shirt had a wrestler's heft, but his pale blue duck slacks were rope-belted around a surprisingly slim waist for a middle-aged man. He wore an oversized chronometer on his left wrist that seemed affectedly ostentatious. Six muscular feet of yachtsman, yet he was almost unnoticed at first. What stunned Steve's searching eyes, as he eased Marcie's Honda along Compromise Street on the curiously Old World Annapolis waterfront, was the yacht.

It dwarfed its owner, not necessarily by its size, though it was far from a casual weekender. What diminished everything around it was its breath-grabbing sumptuousness.

Claiborne stood at the bow of his rakish vessel, both hands on the varnished hardwood rail, as Steve pulled into a parking slot he felt was far enough distant so that Claiborne could not make out his plate number. Steve was reasonably sure he hadn't been followed this time. Marcie had driven the Honda out of the Crossmoor Arms with Steve hunkered on the floor in the back. The FRETSAW people had shown no previous interest in Marcie. He counted on that. She drove to the Sheraton-Washington Hotel on Woodley just off Connecticut, a block north of the National Zoo, parked the Honda along the hotel's entrance drive, then—as he had instructed her—caught a taxi at the hotel entrance for her return to the apartment.

Steve watched Woodley Avenue for a full five minutes. Not a sign of a tail. He had moved into the driver's seat, twisted the key, swung the Honda back into Woodley, then down Connecticut to Massachusetts to emerge northeast on New York Avenue: Route 50 to Annapolis. Not a Camaro in sight.

Now Claiborne called over the rail, "Mr. Mifflin?" He had the throaty bark of a man who enjoyed being heeded.

"Mr. Claiborne?"

"Welcome aboard, sir." Claiborne lifted a hinged section of the teak railing to offer Steve access to the forward deck.

"Your call gave me an excellent excuse to escape a shopping trip," Claiborne said with enthusiasm. "I'd sooner talk world politics any day than prowl the commercial byways of Annapolis."

He led the way aft along the narrow portside deck to an entranceway.

"Rustie is a world-class shopper. Can't blame her. It's her release. How many women would live the year round on a boat without a generous amount of well-financed shore leave? Got to be frustrating for her, though. She can't buy anything large. No place to put it." He swung the doorway wide. "After you, sir."

The yacht's salon was a knockout; maybe eighteen feet by twenty-five, bigger than a lot of living rooms. Five-section, L-shaped conversation pit, a circular glass slab dining table with four ultramodern Swedish chairs, two upholstered barrel chairs, a bar with a twenty-six-inch color TV and built-in VCR. Hell, a whole stereo system at the big room's stern end. Peach carpeting, mahogany or teak veneer everywhere. A spiral staircase up, another down. The whole, outlandishly lavish ball of wax.

"Hell of a boat," Steve said.

"Isn't she a honey? Fifty-three feet of seagoing boat by Ocean Yachts. Got a full galley, and a guest stateroom and head forward. Up the spiral ladder there is the bridge, fully instrumented with ship-to-shore and ship-to-ship communications, including mobile phone. Two helm chairs, twin L-lounges up there, and an eleven-foot outboard on electric davits. You're standing over two more staterooms below, two full heads, and my pride and joy: twin Merlin V-12 diesels, 1100 horse each. Thirty knots with standard power. At twenty knots, she's got a range of 340 nautical miles. Named her *Take Over* because that's where the money for her came from—when Carl Icahn threatened to take over a company we had some bucks in, and the stock went through the roof."

He gestured toward the bar. "What are you drinking? Got no yardarm, so we never worry where the sun is."

"A small brandy?"

"Courvoisier okay?"

Claiborne, Steve noted when they sank into the yielding gray cushions of the conversation pit, seemed to be on lemonade. Low on alcohol, but high as a kite on his ocean-capable toy.

"All right, sir," Claiborne said, draping one impressive arm along the back of the sectional sofa and balancing the tumbler on his knee with his other hand, "what can I do you for?"

"Well, as I told you on the phone, I'm in a position to make a grant to the Foundation, but I'd like to know a bit more about it before I commit."

Claiborne nodded amiably. "How'd you hear about me?"

"Couple of months ago, I ran across a fellow named Gammon."

"Jim Gammon?"

"I think that's what his name was. Yes, Jim Gammon." My God, lying comes easy, Steve realized, when I really try. "He mentioned your name as a reference, and gave me your summer and winter addresses. Then I found myself in this area on business, and I was lucky enough to find you . . . in port."

Claiborne sipped his lemonade. "What business are you in, Mr. Mifflin?"

"Land development." Anything else could evolve into a trap, Steve thought, if Claiborne pressed for details.

"Good money in that these days. Made mine in the market before the '87 crash. Inherited the family Toyota dealership, sold out when Toyota got hot, then took a big bite of Chrysler back in '82—when everybody thought Iacocca was full of low octane. You could pick it up then for single digit peanuts. Then off she went, and here I am." He slipped his arm off the sofa back to roll his glass between his palms. "What's your concern about FRETSAW, Mr. Mifflin?"

"FRETSAW?"

"The acronym. Damned if I'll use that mouthful of a formal title. You've got some sort of hesitation about jumping in, or we wouldn't be talking."

"My problem is that I like what the Foundation stands for; I want to be part of that. But I'm looking for something that's a little more . . . active, if you understand what I mean." There's the bait, Burlington Claiborne. Now we'll see if the bobber goes under.

"More active," Claiborne sparred. "How much did Jim Gammon tell you?"

"He detailed the ad campaign objectives, but what I'm saying is that public information ads are one aspect. One passive aspect. But the way I see it, this country is drowning in advertising. You have to shout to be heard at all. I want to back something that does more than that."

Come on, Claiborne. I'm about to run out of generalities, and I have no idea where to go from here.

"You sound like our friend Ollie North." The bronze man smiled ingratiatingly.

"He had the right idea," Steve ventured, "but he sure wasn't slick on execution. The hostages stayed put, not a hell of a lot of funds got to the contras, and Iran ended up with weapons to use against us. That's not exactly the kind of thing I want to put my money into." Chew on that, Burlington.

Claiborne drained his lemonade and rolled the empty glass between his palms, elbows resting on his knees. "Suppose FRETSAW were a bit more involved than only placing ad schedules. Might your interest level be upnotched?"

"I'm not sure I follow you."

"How much of a commitment are you, ah, willing to consider?"

"Five figures—*if* I'm underwriting right-thinking people who will do this country some good. You understand my position?"

"Another brandy?"

"Thanks. Make it a short one."

Claiborne seemed to need a break for deliberation. When he returned from the bar to hand Steve the snifter, he smiled as he sank back into the sofa. "There is something satisfying about pulling strings that reach six thousand miles."

"I'm afraid I don't follow that, Mr. Claiborne."

"Burlington, please. An old family name I've been saddled with. And may I call you . . ."

"Henry."

"Well, Henry, have you ever heard of a man named Vladimir Shcherbitsky?"

Steve sipped the smooth Courvoisier. "Afraid not."

"But you have heard of the Ukraine." Claiborne flashed dazzling teeth with that little, good-natured put-down. "The breadbasket of the Soviet Union, and a large pain in Mikhail Gorbachev's revisionary ass." He paused, apparently for effect.

Steve raised his snifter. "To pains in Gorbachev's ass."

"Exactly. Shcherbitsky is the party leader in the Ukraine, a holdover Brezhnev hardliner. There is obvious friction between him and Moscow. The grizzled, entrenched Ukrainian traditionalist versus the new kid."

"But the new kid is in charge. Why doesn't he just boot this guy out?"

"The best guess is that he remembers Kazakhstan all too vividly. He dumped a Brezhnev buddy from his party post there in '86, and found himself with riots on his hands. He sure doesn't want that in the Ukraine. That's the second largest republic in the USSR. Fifty-one million people. So it's a standoff."

"All this is colorful background," Steve said, "but how does FRETSAW fit in?"

"Delicately, Henry. Very delicately. And totally behind the scenes. You understand?"

"I'm beginning to."

"You've got to give me your word that what I'm telling you is strictly between us. Agreed?"

"Agreed." What in hell was going on?

"FRETSAW began as a public information organization. It still uses that as a cover."

"A cover?"

"Let me finish, Henry. The advertising campaigns are a

screen for our taking on what could be termed targets of opportunity. Projects certain government agencies should be handling, but under the thumb of a gun-shy Congress . . ." He shrugged.

"And the Ukraine offers one of these opportunities?"

"Exactly. An uprising there surely would be put down by Moscow, but it would seriously damage the Soviet image worldwide; would weaken Gorbachev's hand everywhere the Soviets are making inroads. Nicaragua, Afghanistan, Angola—think of the effect on Soviet influence in those areas alone, were Gorby faced with a major upheaval in his second-largest republic!"

"And FRETSAW's part in all this?"

"An element of . . . support for Mr. Shcherbitsky."

"You're not telling me you want that hardline Russky to win, are you?"

"Oh, hell, no! There's no way he can. Gorbachev will ultimately squash him, but he'll sure have his hands full until he does, and the damage to his rep should be long-lasting. That's the project's real objective, Henry. For the near-term. For the long-term, there will be other targets of opportunity."

Steve set down his glass, rose abruptly to walk to the panoramic aft window of the salon; not a row of portholes, but a smoke-tinted strip that presented a wide-screen view of Annapolis Harbor and the hazy Chesapeake Bay beyond. A small cabin cruiser drummed along the marina's slips, a few knots too fast. Its wake set smaller moored boats arock, but Claiborne's fifty-three-footer barely acknowledged the surges.

"Does Washington know about this?"

Claiborne picked up his empty glass and toyed with it absently. "Let's say the right people in the right places have helped expedite selected FRETSAW paperwork—and have looked away when looking away was of vital importance."

"That's pretty vague, Burlington."

"That's the way it has to be. Look at the Iran-contra thing. Its workings were pretty vague, as you put it. That protected everyone." Claiborne nodded at Steve's snifter on the coffee table. "Refill?"

"I don't need it. You've already got me reeling. How far into this thing are you?"

"The point is, how far into it are *you* willing to go?"

No, the real point here was how far could he push Claiborne into divulging obviously confidential FRETSAW information.

"Look, Burlington, I'm a patriotic American who is just as tired as you are of the way this country lets itself be pushed around by a bunch of Slav peasants in the Kremlin. I'm willing to put some serious cash into action, but I want to keep something of a handle on it. You follow what I'm saying?"

Claiborne had been leaning forward, forearms resting on his thighs. Now he leaned back, still fiddling with his empty glass.

"Where are you from, Henry?"

"Chicago."

"You want to give me a little background?"

Steve was ready for this. He'd concocted it in the Honda, as he'd pushed the little car eastward on Route 50.

"Degree in civil engineering from the University of Illinois."

"In Springfield."

"In Champaign-Urbana, Burlington." Got you there. Nice little test, but I really did graduate from dear old U of I. "I got into site preparation work with a consulting engineer in the Chicago area, then worked for an Indiana real estate developer. Went off on my own ten years ago to buy up low-cost land parcels with overlooked potential, make a few improvements, then sell when progress boosted values. I hit it lucky not too far back with a twenty-three-acre parcel of weeds and scrub outside Seymour, Indiana. Fellow who owned it got tired of waiting for the city to stretch out that far. After I took it off his books, a shopping center developer from Montreal decided to put an enclosed mall in or near Seymour. Seems I had just the property he needed. Now I've got a fair amount of cash on my hands, and I'd like to put some of it where it could help guarantee the survival of free enterprise."

Hell of a speech, Steve thought. But so much smoke if Burlington Claiborne decided to check out that story. Steve was pushing for what he could pull out of the man here, this afternoon; then one Henry Mifflin from Chicago would putt away in his Honda to become a man who never was.

"FRETSAW appreciates higher levels of commitment," Claiborne said from his plush, seagoing sofa. "Like most non-profit organizations that depend on contributed support, we've got what you could call an inner circle of major donors."

"A President's Club? Or Golden Circle? That sort of thing?" He'd wondered when Claiborne would get around to this.

"Exactly. Ours is the FRETSAW Advisory Council."

"Do you get to give any advice?"

"Anytime you want to pick up the phone, you've got the executive director's ear. Right in Washington."

"How much?"

"You mean the entry level for Council membership? Ten thou, Henry. Then ten thou minimum per annum to stay aboard. Some of us kick in more than that."

"How often do you meet?"

"We don't meet. No demand on your time at all, and direct access to FRETSAW anytime you want it."

Steve ran his fingers along the polished edge of the stereo cabinet. So FRETSAW was a front—or so this waterborne playboy had told him. Plausible?

Claiborne seemed to read his mind. "I can see you're a man who's careful about where he's going to invest important bucks, Henry. I can't say I blame you if you're a little taken aback by all this. Tell you what I can do to help convince you. There's a shipment going out just about"—he studied his complex chronometer—"just about fifty-five hours from now. Port of New York. You want to meet me there day after tomorrow at nine P.M., East River Pier 33, you'll see exactly how effective FRETSAW can be."

That was a surprise. Up to now, Claiborne could have been spouting pure smoke too. But this offer to Steve to witness a shipment had to have some substance. Talk about being caught off-balance.

Claiborne sensed that. "What about it, Henry? Shall I get you cleared?"

"Cleared?"

"We're not exactly running a public spectacle up there. A certain degree of security is prudent."

This, Steve did not like. Two days gave Claiborne time to do a lot of checking.

"How much information would you need?"

"Information? Hell, all I'm going to do is call FRETSAW and tell them I've got a buddy with money who's a potential major donor. All they need is my say-so. Okay?"

A calculated risk. Like being here in the first place. "Okay," Steve agreed. "East River Pier 33, nine P.M., day after tomorrow."

God knew what he was getting into.

Claiborne avoided the open transmission of his mobile telephone. He called from a dockside booth.

"I think I've got him," he told Buttonwood exuberantly. "As you said, letting him witness the actual loading should be the clincher."

Buttonwood's next words threw him. "What was his name again?" asked the executive director.

"What? You're the one who told me he might be getting in touch with me. The man's name is Mifflin, Henry Mifflin." Buttonwood should have known that.

"Ah . . . an alias is not unusual for initial contacts, we have found. Fairly big man, mid-forties, dark hair cut short, cleft chin?"

"That's Mifflin. Look, if I sell this guy, what . . . well, I think he might be good for—"

"Are you asking what's in it for you, Burlington? Next time

you're in D.C., maybe I can set up lunch with one of the National Security Council people."

"How about the Secretary of Defense? I've always wanted—"

"I'll see what I can do, Burlington."

Claiborne hung up the pay phone with a heady sense of power.

9.

"Maybe Claiborne was a little too open, too easy to get information out of," Steve told Marcie that evening. They ate in the kitchen again. There was something reassuring about their meals together here; something intimate. Wrong word. He pushed it out of his mind.

"And maybe he accepted you at face value, Steve. I'm sure you were convincing."

He took a last bite of almond chicken catered by Beni Hana via the freezing compartment of Marcie's big almond refrigerator.

"Two possibilities. Either he was conning me just to cadge FRETSAW a substantial check, or he was on the level, and the Foundation is in the international interference business. I have a problem with that."

"But you said he told you, or at least intimated that key people in Washington know about it; that they even help."

"That's the problem."

"Why? We have a CIA that plotted to kill Castro, a National Security Council that sold missiles to Iran and shipped money to the contras in the face of a Congressional ban. All that was done by people in government. What's so shocking about the possibility that that same government is only looking the other way while a private organization is providing some sort of logistical support to a Soviet dissidents?"

"That's no shock at all, Marcie, and that's my problem. If that is FRETSAW's true purpose, and one of their Advisory Council members was so eager to lay it out for Henry Mifflin, why would they kill two of their people over it?"

Her smooth lips compressed. "Something doesn't make sense." She was crisply efficient tonight in black designer jeans and a white sweater whose sleeves she had pushed up above her elbows.

"So it seems. But I don't have much choice at this point, do I? Call it all off and go back to sanity in Fort Myers, or follow through?"

"Go to New York the day after tomorrow?"

"Correct. Either Claiborne's on the level, or there's an elaborate deception underway for my benefit."

"Or . . . Oh, Steve." She reached across the kitchen table to touch his hand. "It could be . . ."

"A trap to get me out of the picture altogether? I've thought of that. But why talk me into going two hundred miles up to New York when they could handle that right here?"

Horace Buttonwood slumped morosely behind his desk, elbow on the arm of his chair, the ball of his thumb supporting his hirsute chin, his forefinger crooked across his nose. He stared at his closed office door. Just beyond it, Alix would be bent over her desk terminal, calling up the mainframe's word processing program. He had spent most of the day dictating a promotional brochure and cover letter to go out in the July mass mailing. Now she was committing it to first draft hardcopy.

The dictation hadn't been easy; too much like working with a turncoat whose cover had been secretly blown. He had begun to delude himself that she enjoyed their frequent evening trysts, liked what he gave her: straight, face-to-face coupling, always comfortably in bed—no undignified erotics on her living room floor, or standing up in her shower stall. Nothing like that. None of those weird techniques he'd read about . . .

Then she had stolen the Advisory Council list. That was how she repaid his regard for her cushiony, warm, maddeningly lush body! By God, he could have made her do any number of wildly twisted things, but he never had so much as hinted at anything like that. And her response to that respect for her dignity had been treachery.

It was damned depressing. And that wasn't the only depressing factor that seemed to push him deeper into the seat of his executive swivel. This morning, Pope had been on his butt again.

"You contacted all the Advisory Council members," the sandstone block repeated, as if Buttonwood hadn't just said precisely that. Pope wore a suit the color of old ivory, almost a perfect match with his unblinking eyes. The pinpoint pupils skewered Buttonwood like twin lasers.

"All but the five who were out of town, but Gammon wouldn't be able to reach them either."

"And he did the obvious. Started with the most accessible, the nearest."

"With Burlington Claiborne, yes."

"What did you authorize Claiborne to tell him?"

"Exactly what we agreed upon after we went over the OmniSecure finding on Steven Gammon. He is a registered Republican, is active in the local Chamber of Commerce, and he's apparently conservative in his political outlook. OmniSecure sent a man to his office, posing as a salesman. The magazines in the waiting area were *National Geographic, First Monday*—that's the Republican National Committee's monthly publication. That sort of thing. He's no liberal. Engineering graduates and land development types usually aren't. Also, he put in two years in the army in the early sixties. Volunteered. Made it to master sergeant in a military intelligence unit. I've got every confidence that we will succeed in coopting Gammon. Might even get a donation out of him after the New York activity."

Buttonwood had judiciously left out the portion of the OmniSecure report that had offered a personality analysis of the man. Mr. Straight and Honorable. Also known by a couple of his clients, so said the Fort Myers *News-Press* file on Gammon, as a "pit bull" in the development field. Persistent. One deal, perfect on the surface, had collapsed on Gammon's recommendation after he'd spent almost an entire month tracking down the history of an obscure corner of the thousand-acre offering, and discovered the entire package had been fraudulently assembled. The pit bull of real estate development. That wasn't at all reassuring.

Following his optimistic, off-the-hook report on Gammon, Buttonwood glanced at Pope. The bald president of FRETSAW only nodded, then glumly dismissed him. Buttonwood had hoped for some kind of, hell, pat on the head. He had done what Pope had told him to do. And what had he gotten for it? A backhand wave out of Pope's office. Considering how FRETSAW had been set up, this was maddeningly perverse treatment, by God. Yet he put up with it.

Then, at the door, he paused. "To hell with all this verbal pirouetting! Why don't we just kill the son of a bitch?"

"Use your head," growled Pope. "How many coincidences can we absorb? The Maui affair was bad enough, but we had little choice there. James Gammon was perilously close when our people finally had a clear-cut opportunity."

"They could have detained him in Honolulu long enough to terminate the Van Hayden problem."

Pope had nodded, a single dip of his spade-like chin. "They could have. Interesting that occurs to you now. I have a fervent hope, Horace, that one day I can leave micromanagement to you in toto. But . . ." Again had come the backhand wave of dismissal.

Now Buttonwood brooded. Why did he take that kind of crap from Pope? Because it serves my ends, he rationalized.

That made him feel better, but there was a larger concern. Was FRETSAW poised on the edge of its planned final stage, or was it starting to come apart? He was the micromanager, but damned if he could determine which. He had given Kolker explicit instructions to relay to OmniSecure's subcontract people in New York. If they followed through, the Steven Gammon problem could be converted to an asset at best; should fade away at worst. If they blew it up there, though, he hated to think of the damage potential.

He needed a diversion. Desperately. He picked up his phone, buzzed Alix.

"We're working late tonight," he told her.

"Yes, Mr. Buttonwood." Her voice was flat, lifeless. That was how she was in bed, too. He didn't mind that. He wasn't after love; he didn't want love. He had to be free of encumbrances, free to pull up stakes in a hurry. She was a service. Comfortable physical therapy. Except that now he knew she was a FRETSAW security leak. There wasn't anything comfortable about that.

Georgie Prescott was confused. He had just assured Kolker that Gammon had never left the Crossmoor Arms at any time today. And Kolker had laughed at him.

"The woman," Georgie said hurriedly, "left around noon."

" 'Around,' Georgie?" Kolker said that with a smile. He seemed to be in disturbingly high spirits, and Prescott knew there had to be a verbal club coming his way before he got out of this stark office.

Prescott pulled out his notebook. " 'Gammon woman departed alone in Honda at twelve-seventeen.' That's what I put down, Kolker. She didn't come back until after dark. Gammon never left."

Milo Kolker, his butt hooked on his desk corner, swung a leg playfully. "Gammon," he said with obvious relish, "was in Annapolis from approximately one-forty-five P.M. until after three. I assume he stopped on his way back to grab something to eat, and to stall around until it got dark so you couldn't make out who was driving the Honda when it came back."

"But he didn't leave. I didn't see him leave."

"Two different things, Georgie. You didn't see him crouched down in that car. Let me ask you this. What time did the taxi show up?"

"Taxi?" Damn, there *had* been a Capitol Cab around 1:00. Prescott didn't have as good a line of sight from where he now parked the OmniSecure motor pool Chevette, but the taxi hadn't gotten by him. "I wondered why it pulled around behind the building."

"Instead of stopping at the front entrance where you could have seen her get out, right? Jesus, Georgie, this Gammon's making a real ape out of you. Maybe you're trying too hard. After your shift today, take the next two days off. Get yourself fixed up, sleep late, do something to sharpen your edge, you hear me?"

"What about Gammon? Who's going to be on him?"

"I'll put Hutchins on the day shift tomorrow. Canella tomorrow night. Day after that, we won't need anybody."

"What do you mean, we won't need anybody?"

"The client says he knows exactly where the subject will be, day after tomorrow. No need for surveillance."

"The client knows?"

"That's what the man said." Kolker slipped off the desk. "Get your butt out of here. I've got other projects."

Prescott didn't move out of the hard visitor's chair. "How would the client know what Gammon's going to do the day after tomorrow?"

"Come on, Georgie. It's a setup."

Steve spent most of the day tracking down the balance of the Advisory Council members, or trying to—a real AT&T credit card workout. Of the twenty-one listed individuals remaining, five were out of town and unreachable, according to their secretaries, wives, or house-sitters.

He failed to contact seven of the remaining sixteen for other reasons. One of them was still unavailable after three tries through the middle of the day: Arthur MacIlvane. The discovery of his name on the list had sent a weird little chill through Steve. Van Hayden's lawyer and friend *had* lied out there in Phoenix. MacIlvane was a member of the Council, right along with his semiretired, now totally dead partner. When Steve had talked with him, MacIlvane hadn't acknowledged that he'd ever heard of FRETSAW. On the other hand, come to think of it, he hadn't seemed surprised when Steve had mentioned it.

All that didn't mean much now. According to his receptionist, MacIlvane was "not in yet," "was in conference," then had "gone for the day." Three tries, three zeros.

Two of the names on the list didn't answer at all. The other four had proficient secretaries to provide excuses: "in conference," à la MacIlvane; "in a meeting"; "I'm not sure where he is in the building." That one did have a touch of originality. Each of those four did offer callbacks, but Steve decided against giving out Marcie's number. He felt as if he were picking his way through quicksand, and he didn't want to involve her any more than was essential. He had dropped the name Mifflin, and was now using Johnson, just in case any of these people decided to check with FRETSAW.

The nine-name balance of the list offered varying responses. One of the two women on it, a Mrs. R. Dwight Randall of Dallas, was almost wildly enthusiastic about her affiliation.

"I do indeed support the Foundation, sir! To the tune of five high figures yearly." That checked out with the tabulation of her impressive giving history: $220,000 over a three-year giving period.

"My late husband was absolutely livid about the way Washington lets every country in the world walk right over us. I shared his views then, and I certainly do now. I can think of no better way to invest a generous portion of the income he left me than to help the Foundation achieve its aims." Her voice projected the steel of irrefutable self-righteousness.

"I'm not certain I want to put serious money into what appears to be nothing more than newspaper ads, Mrs. Randall. I'm looking for . . . a bit more direct involvement, you might say." That approach had worked wonders with Burlington Claiborne.

"Nor would I, Mr. Johnson. You said you have talked with Mr. Buttonwood?"

"A prudent man checks with more than one source, Mrs. Randall."

"Suffice it to say, then," she offered after a pause, "suffice it to say that I would not invest one penny in anything of this sort, were it taking no more action than the placement of advertising in newspapers and magazines. You do understand me, sir?"

And so went the conversational essentials with the other eight he was able to reach. A Milton Balder in Fresno, "retired from forty years in West Coast highway construction, Mr. Johnson, and now I'm happy to do what I can to help keep this country great." Similar sentiments flowed quite glibly out of two other retired business types—one a St. Louis ex-stockbroker, the other more recently out of the lucrative world of low-death-rate Seattle life insurance. Both were enthusiastic in recommending FRETSAW as action central (McGroom, the Seattle insurance retiree, actually said that) for converting money into covert effectiveness.

The remaining five—four of them Eastern Establishment business executives, plus a Cleveland woman publishing exec who answered her own vice-presidential phone—all offered minor variations of that major theme.

FRETSAW, all nine respondents had obliquely allowed, was in a business a hell of a lot more significant than funneling money to Kinnon & Fields Advertising for its conversion into newsprint. Taken all together and interpreted, the nine Advisory Council members he had succeeded in reaching had corroborated what Burlington Claiborne had told him. There was no way Steve would miss going to New York tomorrow.

He'd had it with the telephone for a while. He wandered to the kitchen for a beer. It was then that he heard Marcie in the bedroom. Still in her housecoat in mid-afternoon, she sat on the double bed, surrounded by shirts, socks, trousers, coats, ties. The floor was littered with Jim's clothing.

"Marcie?"

"Oh, God, Steve," she almost whispered, "I thought I could get through this without . . . I thought I was doing so well. I'm . . . not. I loved him, and I miss him." Her voice hardened. "God*damn* his assignment to FRETSAW!"

"Let me ask you something. Do you think he knew about what seems to be FRETSAW's real purpose? 'Foreign affairs'?"

"Oh, Steve, he had to. Or he never could have raised the kind of money that's listed on that Advisory Council printout. Major donors were his speciality . . ."

"Then something doesn't jibe. Van Hayden would hardly have urged Jim to rush to Maui to tell him something he and the Advisory Council members already knew."

Steve took an Eastern flight from Washington National to Kennedy, and a so-called limo from there through commuter-clogged Queens to Manhattan's East Side Airlines Terminal. He had time to kill and knew New York well enough to realize he could do that a lot more comfortably in a midtown hotel dining room than down on the Lower East Side where he wasn't due until 9:00 P.M.

Lizabeth had liked the Essex House for its staid elegance and panoramic view of Central Park from the ninth floor suite she always insisted he reserve. After the split, he had determined never to stay there again. But he did like that part of the city. The Plaza, two blocks east, became his headquarters for the several business trips he'd subsequently made to Manhattan. He appreciated its controlled bustle and the quality of its facilities. Not so much the famed Palm Court as the undersung Oak Room with its English pub decor.

He bought a *New York Times* in the Plaza's marbled lobby, and walked down the corridor to the Oak Room. At this early hour, he was offered his choice of tables and and took one along the paneled wall.

He ordered brandy, the house salad, and the London broil, rare.

"The brandy later, sir." The elderly waiter with his worldly-wise expression offered that not as a question, but as a statement of protocol.

"No, I'll start with the brandy."

"Very good, sir." But the waiter couldn't disguise his discomfort at what he seemed to feel was a breach of tradition.

Steve realized he had unconsciously taken a seat facing the entrance. This FRETSAW thing was affecting everything he did, almost as if he were in large measure controlled by it. Certainly here in New York, he was, through FRETSAW's proxy invitation. Would Burlington Claiborne have offered to let him witness the loading of a "shipment," had not FRETSAW approved?

In advance? *Shall I get you cleared?* Claiborne had asked. But surely he would not have made such an offer, had it not already been cleared—or even set up—by FRETSAW. Though Steve had used the name Mifflin with Claiborne, and had made his phone calls to the rest of the Advisory Council roster with the Johnson cover, was it possible FRETSAW had somehow discovered that he had been provided the Advisory Council list?

Steve swirled the brandy, just arrived.

Question: if the Foundation's real business was supplying what Claiborne had termed support to foreign antigovernment factions, and official Washington turned a blind eye, why hadn't Horace Buttonwood come right out and told him that?

* * *

The taxi driver, a middle-aged black man who could barely squeeze behind the wheel of his Plymouth Reliant cab, wanted badly to get out of these gloomy waterfront blocks. But he still showed concern for his passenger.

"You sure this is the place, chief?" He looked at the looming shed that jutted five hundred yards into the black water of the East River. The oily surface reflected the lights of the Manhattan Bridge, a long block to the right. From the sluggish river water also bounced the isolated glare of floodlights far out on the pier. A small freighter was being loaded out there.

The taxi had pulled up below the soaring bridge, beneath the elevated FDR Drive. Both carried streams of cars with drivers and passengers, Steve imagined, who were glad they were up there, on well-lighted throughways, not down here on this unsavory waterfront, staring at the forbidding, soot-black shore end of the pier shed.

A naked bulb flared over a doorway cut into the big loading portal. The little door became a dim rectangle as someone opened it from the inside. A man's figure was silhouetted in its wan light.

"Wait here," Steve told his driver.

"Uh uh, chief. Not me. I said I'd bring you here, but I ain't sitting around in the dark on this particular street."

Out in the river, an invisible boat's whistle yowled once. Then again. The doleful sound echoed off the blacked-out row of buildings inland, behind the elevated highway's columns. Then it was swallowed in the surflike wash of traffic overhead. Down here, the waterfront was silent.

"Henry? Henry Mifflin?"

He recognized Burlington Claiborne's confident voice, crossed the broad ramp between curb and pier, and took Claiborne's outstretched hand. The taxi's taillights vanished as the driver swung away from the waterfront at the next available cross street.

"You're right on time," said the yachtsman, his pale blue blazer and navy slacks wildly out of place on this grubby freight pier. "It's the *Marrakech Sands*, Morocco flag out of Port Lyautey."

They walked past several parked vehicles just inside the entrance, then through the cavernous, minimally lighted warehouse of a pier, empty most of its length, but echoing the activity that was under way at the huge structure's far end.

"I hope you realize how privileged we both are to be able to actually see a FRETSAW loading operation," Claiborne said pleasantly. "Being told what your support is accomplishing is one thing. Seeing it in action is quite a different experience."

"You've seen this before?"

"Me? Hell, no. That's why I was so . . . well, thrilled when FRETSAW arranged for us to be here. Damn, Henry, this is *exciting!*"

If Claiborne was a FRETSAW shill, he was one damned good actor, Steve decided. The man's face was flushed, and he appeared to be having the time of his life. A darkened pier on the New York waterfront, a freighter registered in Morocco, a secluded loading operation. Almost too melodramatic, but Burlington Claiborne of the million-dollar lifestyle was eating it up.

They reached the center of activity. A mountain of crates, stenciled AGRICULTURAL IMPLEMENTS, had been stacked on pallets in a big L in the center of the floor. Three electrically powered front-end loaders plied between the stacks and the open ramp that flanked the freighter's rusted hull, fork-lifting several crates per trip through the shed's gaping dockside portal.

Out there in the floodlit night, the crates were placed on cargo nets, flat on the open dock area, then hoisted aboard, four at a time, with the freighter's moaning deck winches. The place was rank with diesel fumes from the winch engines, ozone from the loaders' whining electric motors, and the piercing odor of creosoted wood.

Steve tapped his knuckles against one of the crates. "Agricultural implements?"

"They're all marked that way, but I'm assured that's not the whole story." He glanced around. "Frank?"

One of the several men assisting the loading operation, apparently the foreman, said something to the others and ambled over to Claiborne and Steve.

"We're ready now, Frank."

"Right. Over here, where it's a little more, like, secluded." He was built close to the ground with impressively powerful biceps bulging his denim shirt. "Them deckhands don't have to know what they're carrying."

He led them to one of the crates in the rear row, hidden by the main cargo stack, and levered a nail-puller's tapered end under the top panel. The nails gave with a squeal. The cover rose enough for the foreman to get his fingers beneath its edge. He heaved the panel up.

Steve and Claiborne craned forward. The light back here was lousy, but they could see what was in there.

"You sure you have the right crate?" Claiborne demanded.

"I got the right box." The longshoreman's voice was hoarse from shouting orders, Steve assumed, and from the river's cloying dampness.

"What in hell do those look like to you?" Claiborne asked Steve, his face darkening.

"They look like what's stenciled on the crate."

"Fucking rakes!" Claiborne whirled on the foreman. The man grinned, held up a pacifying hand, then reached between the neatly spaced rake handles to raise what turned out to be a shallow wooden tray.

"Now this is more like it!" Claiborne said. He reached into the crate and pulled out one of the plastic-wrapped parcels. Though it was covered with some kind of preservative gunk inside the clear plastic, Steve could see what it was. No doubt now about what FRETSAW was up to.

"Iver Johnson Model PP30, the Super Enforcer," Claiborne announced, adding with evident self-satisfaction, "I have a smattering of gun knowledge."

"Not exactly a pretty thing." The weapon, a foot and a half long, was mostly fat wooden stock with a stub of a barrel: a bulky, oversized pistol.

"Semiautomatic, with a thirty-round magazine. A lot of damage potential here, a whole lot of damage potential." On impulse, Claiborne hefted the weapon.

"Jesus, watch it!" the foreman warned. Claiborne quickly jerked the package back down, replaced it in the crate. "There's nothing quite as convincing as a handful of ugly machine pistol."

Steve looked at him, and in that same glance, he spotted a man high on the upper deck of the *Marrakech Sands*, a badly sunburned little deckhand in a knit watch cap who suddenly appeared to be making it obvious that he wasn't at all interested in what they were doing down here. But from his elevated vantage point, could he have seen the package Claiborne had so enthusiastically hoisted from behind their cover?

"The guy up there on the ship," Steve said. "I think he could have seen . . ."

"What guy?" Claiborne asked.

Now that part of the upper deck was deserted.

"Okay, then." Claiborne fitted the gun back in the tightly packed interior of the crate. The foreman replaced the tray of rakes and pounded the nails back in place with the curved end of the nail-puller.

"That's it?" Steve asked.

"No, that's not quite it. We'll want to see those guns go aboard."

They walked to the short side of the L of remaining crates and watched the incessant back-and-forth shuttle. The cargo stack was rapidly diminishing.

"How does FRETSAW know that guy Frank can be trusted?" Steve asked abruptly. It had struck him that despite the security measures Claiborne had taken, here was a potential weak point.

"Bribes," the nattily dressed yachtsman assured him. "Money does the talking, not these people."

None of the front-end loaders came close to the gun crate for twenty minutes. Then one of them, its yellow paint battered and scraped like the others, and with half the R missing from its vertical HI-LIFTER logo lettering on its fork track, rolled around the end of the shrinking cargo stack. Its driver, a lanky younger man with greasy blond hair straggling beneath what looked like an old golf cap, maneuvered the big steel prongs into the pallet slots. The crate lifted easily, despite what had to be several hundred pounds of PP30s crammed beneath its false top of garden rakes. The front-end loader turned away from Steve and Claiborne, started to swing around the far end of the remaining crates, then stopped.

A large panel truck had materialized from the far side murk of the pier. Showing only its parking lights, it cut across in front of the loader carrying the crate of guns and halted. The loader driver pulled around the truck's far side, and above the rumble of the truck's idling engine, Steve heard angry shouting. Then the loader emerged past the front of the panel truck, rolled out the big door and gentled the crate onto one of the sprawled loading nets.

Frank and another longshoreman opened the rear doors of the truck, pulled out a bulky parcel wrapped in burlap, then carried it to the ship and up a narrow gangplank into the hold.

"Wonder what that was all about?" Claiborne said as they watched the cargo net's corners lift around the gun crate, then hoist it clear of the floodlit dock.

"Little present for the captain's wife," the man called Frank told them when Claiborne asked a few minutes later. "Redwood planter, they told me. Something she's been bugging him for."

That, Steve decided, was a bizarre capper for a bizarre evening.

"We've seen what we came to see, Henry," Claiborne said. "Can I give you a ride back to your hotel?"

"I'm flying out tonight." He didn't feel at all secure about leaving Marcie alone. "But I'll take you up on a lift to anyplace I can catch a limo or cab to Kennedy."

On the flight back to Washington National, he pondered the whole strange sequence of the evening's events. He had been painstakingly shown what FRETSAW's funding truly backed, or so Claiborne had assured him. He had seen the guns, dozens of them in that one case alone. He had seen them go aboard the Moroccan freighter.

Now he knew as much—more, possibly—as anyone on the Advisory Council, except, probably, his fellow witness, Mr. Burlington Claiborne. And, Steve reflected, I haven't given FRETSAW a nickel.

Why had they extended this dubious distinction to him?

The *Marrakech Sands* sailed at the turn of the tide, just before 5:30 A.M. But not before the little "sunburned" man wearing the knit cap left the ship, ostensibly to check what he claimed was a frayed cable on one of the cargo nets. He did check the cable, rubbed his flat nose, then signaled that it was still serviceable. As the net rose under the winch's pull, he ambled to the pier's big loading door, then melted into the blackness of the long shed.

He knew there was a telephone a hundred feet toward shore. He dropped in the unfamiliar American coins and dialed the number he had memorized. The number, though he didn't know it, was that of a man registered with the USSR United Nations delegation staff as a minor protocol functionary.

"Feodor Constanzi?" The *Marrakech Sands* crewman didn't know whether that was the man's real name, or a code phrase, or both.

"The very same, my good friend." That *was* the proper code response.

"*Marrakech Sands,*" the sailor said in heavily Turkic-accented English, "out of New York for Odessa." That was all he had to say to whoever was at the other end of the line. Now shipping records would be checked, and the captain of the *Marrakech*

Sands would have an ugly surprise waiting at the terminus of the last leg of the voyage to the Black Sea.

The man in the watch cap was not sunburned. He had a permanent windburn, his flat Uzbek cheeks blasted ruddy as a ripe apple by the Kyzylkum Desert winds near his native Tashkent. Not every field operative of the KGB was a big-nosed, raw-boned Russian.

The rusted hull of the *Marrakech Sands* would throb and vibrate across three thousand miles of Atlantic swells, benign in this final month before the onset of the official hurricane season.

She would put in at Port Lyautey, her home port, for reprovisioning and refueling, but no additional cargo would be taken aboard, and only the redwood planter would be off-loaded to accompany the captain on his way to a two-day shore leave with his surprised wife.

The freighter would set sail again fifty-seven hours after she had arrived, make her way through the Strait of Gibralter into the Mediterranean, pass north of Crete, then through the islands of the Cyclades into the Aegean Sea.

In a hazy dawn, she would begin her push through the Dardanelles, forty-two miles of perilously narrow passage on her way northeast into the lakelike Sea of Marmara, thence into the port of Istanbul.

Here her captain would negotiate clearance through the Bosporus, that narrow, turbulent twenty-mile strait into the Black Sea. The final leg of her lengthy journey would take the *Marrakech Sands* northward along the western reach of that landlocked waterway, with the rugged coasts of Bulgaria, then Rumania barely visible as rough blue rims along the western horizon.

Finally, her scaly black paint considerably more sun-faded than it had been when she set sail more that two weeks ago from New York, the *Marrakech Sands* would round the southernmost breakwater and enter the Ukrainian seaport of Odessa.

One tug would thump the little freighter into position along an evil-smelling cargo pier.

Then her puzzled captain would find himself and his crew impounded aboard his own ship, while three burly men in ill-fitting dark suits opened every crate in the ship's hold.

What they would find, after three hours of upending, dismantling, and making a substantial mess of the once neatly stacked crates, would be just what the cargo manifest said they would find: agricultural implements.

They would leave with expressions grimmer than those they had worn when they boarded. The weatherworn Moroccan captain, hands thrust in his surplus U.S. Navy pea coat's pockets, would wear a confused expression as he watched them leave. This would be the second odd happening on this otherwise routine voyage. The first had been the delivery of a redwood planter as a gift for his wife. He hadn't ordered it; the planter had simply appeared.

Standing in the stern, the first mate, the wind-burned Uzbekistani in the watch cap, would find himself mystified—and more than a little apprehensive. He had seen the crate of guns come aboard, had he not? Only the captain's package had been off-loaded in Port Lyautey. Nothing at all in Istanbul. Those were the only stops the *Marrakech Sands* had made before its arrival here in Odessa.

What had happened to the guns?

10.

"Phone, Steve." Marcie's voice came softly through the spare-room door. "Are you awake?"

"Barely." He hadn't heard the phone ring. The return flight from New York had been delayed twenty minutes at JFK, then he'd had to wait fifteen minutes at Washington National for a cab—not surprising at close to 2:00 in the morning.

He had fallen into bed, and now at—he squinted at his watch on the tiny night table—10:08, he felt as if he hadn't slept at all. Felt grubby. No doubt looked grubby.

"Who is it?"

"Steve, it's Horace Buttonwood."

Buttonwood?

He stumbled from the daybed to the desk, picked up the handset with clumsy fingers.

"Mr. Gammon? Horace Buttonwood. I wonder if you might see your way clear to visit the Foundation this morning?"

Damned if he would be rushed into whatever Buttonwood had in mind. "This afternoon would be better."

"All right. Say around two?"

He pondered that unexpected invitation while he showered,

shaved, and dressed. He insisted on getting his own breakfast. "You're not my innkeeper, Marcie. You've got your own work to do." He added a Swiss cheese sandwich to the orange juice, bacon, and coffee, and called it brunch; read Marcie's *Washington Post,* couldn't concentrate on anything but Buttonwood's call, took the rented Skyhawk out too soon, and had to kill time wandering side streets near Dupont Circle.

Alix Cortland already waited for him at the entrance desk.

"Nice to see you again, Mr. Gammon. Mr. Buttonwood is ready for you."

Halfway up the stairs, her voice decibels lower, she said, "I don't know what this is about, Steve."

"Makes two of us."

He followed her along the hallway past the mingled voices in the phone bank rooms, and into her office. She tapped on Buttonwood's door, swung it open to let Steve pass.

"Ah, Gammon. Good of you to come on short notice. I appreciate that." Rounding his antique desk, green eyes shining in a squinty smile above the dark beard, Buttonwood bore down with his hand outstretched.

But his grip was clammy cold.

"Sit down, Mr. Gammon." He spread open fingers toward the midnight-blue sofa. "Miss Cortland, bring us two coffees. Cream and sugar, Mr. Gammon?"

The man brimmed over with affability. "I trust your stay in Washington is proving to be a pleasant one?"

Eyewash, Buttonwood. What's really happening here?

Alix returned with a silver tray of eggshell-thin Limoges cups and saucers, a matching coffee pot, creamer, and sugar bowl. Buttonwood waved her out and poured. Like a social call to your friendly pastor's study, Steve marveled. If Buttonwood wanted him off-balance, he was succeeding nicely. Off-balance; not off-guard.

"Cream and sugar, you said? There you are, sir."

FRETSAW's executive director sat back in his executive swivel and stirred his coffee with a sterling spoon. Then, in the same offhand, pleasant tone, he said, "Now that you have learned what we are up to, Mr. Mifflin-Johnson, what do you think?"

Christ! They'd been on to him all the way.

"Oh, yes. You make a fair detective, Mr. Gammon, but a less-than-successful undercover operative."

Steve took a scalding swallow of coffee. As the sting receded, he discovered he'd never tasted better. Buttonwood was in total control, and Steve didn't find that at all comforting. He had been played like a marionette. With strings pulled even by Alix Cortland? Had this whole thing been a setup from the beginning? Had he been taken by Becky Rossmyer as well, with her offer to pave the way for him to get to Alix? And Alix's obtaining of the Advisory Council list—another setup? And Burlington Claiborne's eagerness to show him the New York operation? Had all of it been a precisely planned and scheduled scenario to get him back to this office, properly conditioned . . . for what?

"I see you are a tad taken aback, Mr. Gammon."

"What I'm wondering is why you didn't just come out with it when I first showed up here. A simple statement that 'we run guns to dissident factions' would have saved us all a lot of trouble and expense."

"A logical deduction, but we didn't know you then as we do now. We didn't know you had what might be considered, ah, parallel interests."

"In sending crates of Iver Johnson PP30s to the Ukraine? That's a hell of an assumption, Buttonwood."

"In generally supporting efforts to destabilize unfriendly governments," Buttonwood countered smoothly. "I doubt you'll deny that."

"As much support as any average American, I suppose, but well short of active participation."

"Passive, then?"

"Passive?"

"By doing nothing about what you have seen."

Interesting. Steve was silent. Let Buttonwood fill the vacuum.

The executive director of FRETSAW stroked his beard, unconsciously fingering the half-obscured strawberry mark. "In the long run, you understand, your attempt at interference would amount to no more than sound and fury signifying nothing. You can't seriously believe a government that has aided and abetted private arms supply efforts to Central American dissidents is going to prosecute very actively a private attempt to destabilize the Ukraine. Let it go, Gammon. Your brother's unfortunate death was an accident. There's no way to avenge a single-car accident. Return to Fort Myers, get on with your life. Passive support, you understand? And one day, you will pick up the newspaper and see that Gorbachev is up to his nose in internal complications that can only benefit this nation. Go home, Gammon. It makes sense."

Steve rose, put his elegant cup and saucer back on the tray on Buttonwood's desk.

"Gammon?"

"You make a persuasive case, Buttonwood. I'll give you that much."

"You and I are going out, Marcie. Put on the best you've got. We're getting out of this apartment. What's your favorite restaurant?"

"You mean it?"

"Damn right." God, how he needed a break from FRETSAW, from what now appeared to be the slick duplicity of Becky Rossmyer, Alix Cortland, and Burlington Claiborne. From the vivid, recurring tableau of a white Nissan, crumpled nose-down in a Maui rain forest.

"How about Hogate's?" she suggested. "I've always loved it there."

"Hogate's it is," and he called for reservations.

At 6:00 she came out of her bedroom in swirling butter yellow with a bright green sash, an absolute knockout with her russet hair.

"The Honda again?"

"No," he said. "The Skyhawk. I don't give a damn if every security man FRETSAW has hired latches on to us. We're going out for dinner. Besides, I think the case is closed. I know what they're up to, and they know that I know. Now they're hoping I'll keep my mouth shut because they don't want the publicity."

In the elevator, a new thought struck him. "Or aren't they worried about potential publicity? Who was it—Mencken? He said nobody ever went broke underestimating the taste of the American public. Substitute reasoning for taste. Ollie North admits he destroyed evidence and lied, and the public loves him. PTL goes broke paying horse-choking salaries to people whose responsibilities seemed a little gauzy to me, and the public sends more money. So if word comes out that FRET-SAW is running guns to dissidents, who knows what such publicity might do for their fund-raising activities? Maybe the take would double. Maybe Buttonwood's real message was, 'Go ahead, Gammon, make our fiscal year.' "

"My God, Steve, that's one strange line of reasoning."

"That's because I seem to be dealing with a strange group of people." He pulled out of the service road onto Connecticut, not caring a damn if FRETSAW had someone on him now. Traffic southward was considerable this early evening. That didn't bother him either. What was a matter of concern that kept resurfacing in the back of his mind was FRETSAW's inconsistency.

"First they're all over me with surveillance," he thought aloud as they crossed the bridge over Rock Creek, "then when I get my hands on the Advisory Council list and talk to Claiborne face-to-face, they clear me to witness the loading of guns bound for Odessa. Hell of a turnabout."

A buttery haze filtered through the city. The setting sun, finally visible after days of lingering clouds, flashed low through cross-street breaks in the building line. He had the car's windows closed to shut out street noise. Vented air sighed in, faintly sweetened by Marcie's little-girl scent. Spring wildflowers, just a trace.

"I don't think it's hard to follow their reasoning, Steve. First they hoped you'd drop the whole thing, accept their claim that they were just as mystified as you were about Jim's disappearance. Then you went to Hawaii and found his body. Now they called it an accident, and wanted you to accept that and go home. But you kept pushing, and next you were into their Advisory Council roster with a personal call on the man in Annapolis."

They sank swiftly beneath ground level into Connecticut's tunnel under Dupont Circle. When the Buick ascended the ramp on the other side, Farragut's statue, four blocks ahead, was touched with the gold of the setting sun.

"And Buttonwood shows me what goes on in the backroom," Steve said. "A 180-degree turnaround. That's what throws me. Why did they open up?"

"Because you made them open up. Now they're banking on you as a true-blue American to leave them alone, to go home and let FRETSAW do its patriotic work."

"You believe that?"

"I believe they do. Or that's their fervent hope. Besides, what if you were to blow the whistle? You said Buttonwood told you that would be sound and fury signifying nothing. Who's really going to care? Charismatic Ollie North conditioned the country. Public opinion came down on the side of law-bending patriotism. Isn't that what this is?"

They skirted Lafayette Square. A block south, the grandeur of the White House looked oddly faded in the dusk's failing light. He turned hard right down Fifteenth, then left onto Pennsylvania Avenue's impressive expanse.

"If they trust me not to blow the whistle, why didn't Buttonwood explain the whole thing to me at the beginning? He said it was because they had to get to know me. I have a hard time buying that. It's as if they made me dig out the truth so it would be convincing."

They rushed through the Ninth Street tunnel, its lights flashing past like strobes. "If Buttonwood had laid it all out at the beginning, I wouldn't have believed him. Maybe that *is* the answer. They had to make me convince myself."

They emerged into the lesser bustle of waterfront Washington below the federal section. Steve guided the Skyhawk into Hogate's brightly lighted parking facility.

"But why would they have cared?"

"What, Steve?"

"If Buttonwood had told me right off what FRETSAW's real purpose was, why would they have cared if I didn't believe him?"

They entered the restaurant's rough wood, riverside orientation and were taken to a corner table. The District's waterfront, Steve reflected, appeared far more benign than had the gloomy dockage of the East River.

They ordered mariner's platters. Anything else in this eatery seemed a sacrilege. First to arrive, though, concurrently with their drinks, was a basket of Hogate's trademark, hot rum buns.

"Unless," he said abruptly, "unless that isn't what they are really doing."

Her frown was softened by the table's candlelight. "What are you saying, Steve?"

"Their advertising campaigns are a cover for the weapons supply activity—or that's what I'm supposed to believe now. But doesn't it strike you that the whole New York thing was too pat? It was as if they knew I'd go to Annapolis—that wasn't hard to figure. That's where the nearest Advisory Council member happened to be. Then Claiborne led me to New York. Part of the plan. And up there, they made sure I saw the guns go aboard."

"But doesn't that prove the point?"

He nodded glumly. "That's the problem. I saw the guns in that crate. I stood there with Claiborne, and that crate was picked up and put straight into a cargo net. No, wait a minute.

A truck showed up. The front-end loader pulled around it, then went to the cargo net."

He visualized the whole sequence in detail. The panel truck's sudden appearance, necessitating the loader's detour around its far side. The loader's reappearance, its driver's straggly blond hair bouncing beneath his golf cap in the floodlight glare. The crisp black lettering on the fork-lift's upright track: HI-LIFTER.

"By God!"

Marcie's Scotch sour stopped an inch from her lips. "Steve, what is it?"

"The lettering! When the fork-lift picked up the crate, I noticed part of the R in HI-LIFTER was missing. But after it had gone around the truck, then come back in sight, there was nothing wrong with the R. The lettering was perfect!"

"That doesn't make sense."

"Yes, it does, Marcie. They made a switch. That truck pulled across from the far side of the pier behind us. It must have been there all the time, waiting. When the leader picked up the gun crate, the truck driver rolled into a preplanned position. He was a shield."

"For what?"

"For another loader that had to have come across beside him, across the pier shed—on the truck's far side, where I couldn't see it."

"And that loader had another crate on its fork?"

"Right. The loader with the gun crate pulls up behind him, the drivers trade seats, and the guy I'd seen pick up the gun crate reappears. Only now he's driving a different machine. Looks exactly the same, except for one little slip."

"Now the broken R is whole."

"So now the truck backs up across the pier, and the driver of the broken R loader reverses it to stay in the truck's cover. Simple enough. The switch of loader drivers behind the truck couldn't have taken five seconds, and I was supposed to be diverted anyway by watching a couple of other men off-load something from the truck."

Marcie put down her drink untasted. "But why, Steve? Why all that to convince you that they're running guns?"

"Because, my dear Watson, I'll bet you six figures that running guns is not what they are doing at all."

Hank Loper appeared so suddenly and silently that Alix jumped. "Damn, Hank, you startled me!"

He handed her the daily sealed envelope from the third floor. "Has he gone?" Loper's old man's face wore a scrunched look of concern.

"Mr. Buttonwood is at a luncheon meeting, Hank. And I'm eating in, thank you."

"I'm not here to bug you about a lunch date, Alix." He darted a glance back down the hallway. "You know that Showalter and I belong to the same aviation history group?"

"No, I didn't." What was this odd little man up to?

"Saw him last night during the break over at the Air and Space Museum's workshop in Suitland. That's where we meet."

"Hank, I've got work piled up—"

"Hear me out, Alix. I was kidding around, told him that I . . ." Loper's sallow cheeks unaccountably colored. The man was blushing! "I, uh, mentioned you, and he said, 'Stay away from her, Hank. Problems.' "

"He said what?" So far, the conversation was inane, but she was beginning to feel little prickles of uneasiness along her arms.

"That was my reaction, too. Then he told me about the . . ." Loper leaned closer and lowered his voice to a near-whisper. "About the Advisory Council printout."

"The Advisory Council printout?" She made an effort to keep her face blank, but she could feel perspiration begin to bead her upper lip.

"Showalter runs the mainframe room."

"I know that, Hank."

"What you don't know is that every request, every keyboard call-up in the building is monitored by a taped recording device down there. It prints out what data was requested, who called for it, and when. The previous day's tape is delivered to Buttonwood every morning. They know, Alix."

"They know what?"

Loper leaned even closer, and his voice dropped to a hoarse whisper. "They know you printed out an unauthorized copy of the Advisory Council listing."

The prickly apprehension coalesced into an ice ball just below her heart.

"You realize what's missing in all this?" Steve had asked Marcie when they'd returned from Hogate's last night.

"The answer to the great, big why? Why were Jim and Van Hayden killed?"

"That's got to be the key, but I'm talking about the process of getting to it. What keeps turning up missing along the way is anything at all on the backgrounds of either Buttonwood or Pope. It's as if they sprang to life there at FRETSAW. Nothing in the D.C. papers. Nothing in *Who's Who.* Not a lead anywhere. All I know about either of them outside that building is that Buttonwood has a hold on Alix Cortland and takes it out in trade."

Marcie had smiled. "Well, there you are."

"There I am?"

"She told you that about him. What else might she be able to produce?"

An interesting suggestion. He mulled it with his coffee this morning, a dreary morning after yesterday's sun. Washington was again overcast in pearl-gray, and already beginning to work on its infamous summertime humidity.

Could he trust Alix? Yesterday's conversation with Buttonwood had left him with the impression that all three of them—Buttonwood, Alix, even Becky Rossmyer—had been part of the intricate manipulation that had taken him to the New

York pier to witness the carefully orchestrated "loading" of the gun crate. Surely Frank, the foreman up there, and at least four of the dockworkers, had been bribed to participate in the deception.

And Claiborne? It was possible he had been manipulated as intricately as had Steve. But hadn't Claiborne told Steve where to stand to watch the crate go aboard? Their observation from any other location at the end of the pier could have made the switch of loaders impossible. Or was it only coincidence that Claiborne had led him to that particular observation point? If he had wandered elsewhere, Frank could have talked them back where he wanted them.

A toss-up on Claiborne.

Use Alix Cortland again, Marcie had suggested last night. If Alix had been part of the complex New York charade, then she was loyal to Buttonwood, no matter how convincing a story she'd given Steve about their personal relationship. And if she was a FRETSAW loyalist, what would be the consequences were he to ask her to pump Buttonwood for leads on his background?

They would know he was still probing FRETSAW.

But they could interpret that a couple ways. He could be checking into the organization with an eye toward active support. Not very likely, Steve decided. They were far from stupid. They would realize he was still intent on uncovering exactly why his brother and Walter Van Hayden had met sudden death on Maui.

The confirmation of that scenario would likely be the reappearance of the FRETSAW—he assumed it was put there by FRETSAW—car in the vicinity of the Crossmoor Arms: his tail.

On the other hand, if Alix was what she'd told him she was, a woman trapped by a blackmailer, then there was the possibility that she could make the breakthrough on Buttonwood that Steve had been unable to make.

Worth a try, and worth the risk. He heard Marcie pull a

frying pan out of the kitchen's pan drawer as he picked up the phone on the spare-room desk. He and Marcie would kick this around again, but the outcome was going to depend on Alix Cortland.

Her position had become so complex that Alix went carefully over it again as she made a final check of herself in her bathroom mirror. She fingered a stray blonde tendril back in place and adjusted the drape of her ankle-length, soft coral lounger. Normally—if there was anything at all normal about this arrangement—she wouldn't care all this much about her grooming. Horace Buttonwood cared only about basics, not finesse. But tonight was going to be different.

Talk about crosscurrents! Buttonwood knew that she had illicitly acquired the Advisory Council list printout, but he didn't know she was aware of his knowledge. Steve Gammon had called her yesterday with a remarkable request: that she use her unique relationship with Buttonwood—hell, that she use *herself*—to get some scrap of information, anything, that would give Steve a lever to pry open a window into the man's background.

When she had hung up, she realized how little any of them at FRETSAW knew of Buttonwood's personal history, save, logically, Richardson Pope himself. Nor did anyone with whom she was on conversational terms know anything about Pope. Now that Steve's call had brought it to fine focus, she was struck by the fact that the Foundation's president and its executive director had seemingly dropped into place fully formed, with no evident curriculum vitae having gone before. They had been the Foundation's initiators, and its first two staff members. Thus all who had come on board thereafter, which included all other FRETSAW employees, were denied the insight of an office grapevine's gossip nuggets on an incoming president or executive director.

Fascinating.

She leaned closer to the mirror, and with the tip of a little finger, blotted away a tiny excess of coral lipstick at the corner of her mouth. Then she strode into the bedroom, trying to show confidence she didn't feel.

Getting Buttonwood to arrange his personal schedule for this precipitous tryst had been a matter of transmitting female signals to him through much of the day. A glimpse of high thigh during dictation. Several lingering glances. A brush of breast across his shoulder as she set down his coffee. An enhancement of sandalwood in mid-afternoon. Child's play.

Now FRETSAW's executive director sprawled on the cushions of her white wicker settee near the bedroom's double windows, legs crossed. One arm was curved along the settee's back, the other offered her a half-filled, squat glass. He'd brought a bottle of Leroux Peach Basket Schnapps this time, his idea of flair. A stiff drink apiece, which she customarily welcomed for its numbing effect, then into her double bed.

Propped there in his shirt sleeves among the lime-green cushions, he looked like what a pathetic john must look like to a call girl, she thought. He had neatly hung his coat and tie across the back of the straight chair by her little white Ethan Allen desk in the room's corner.

First, the pro forma drink. Then off would come the buttoned-down Arrow shirt, the white Haines T-shirt, the gleaming black shoes and calf-length black socks, the gray banker's trousers. Then he would abruptly scramble into bed with his boxer shorts on. He shucked those only when he was safely concealed beneath the sheets. A quirk, like his always taking her in the missionary position. Not that she cared.

Alix crossed the room in barefoot strides, took the offered glass with its two inches of Schnapps. Her tentative swallow had a nonaggressive peach smoothness that left a warm afterglow just beneath her breasts. She was dismayed by her unexpectedly faltering resolve. The man's eyes appeared somehow different tonight. Hard, above that faint smile that demarked beard from mustache. A false smile?

She had to deal with the problem of the list.

"Before we . . . go further, Horace, I must tell you something." She sank to the edge of the bed and fixed her eyes on the glass she held in her lap, a properly contrite tableau, she hoped. "I meant to tell you earlier, but it simply slipped my mind."

Buttonwood's eyebrows inched upward in mild interest.

"A couple of days ago, Steven Gammon asked me for a copy of the Advisory Council list." Head still downcast, she raised her eyes to watch his reaction. His ginger-ale-bottle-green gaze caught hers, but revealed nothing. Nor did he say a damned word. She looked down into her glass.

"He told me it had been authorized by Mr. Pope. But I thought you should know."

Buttonwood took up his own glass from the little marble-topped table between settee and bed. She flicked another glance toward him. His eyebrows slowly sank.

"He lied to you," he said.

"Oh, my God! And I gave him the list."

Now Buttonwood was assessing the bed, not her. Had the crisis passed this easily? She had gambled that, faced with the choice of firing her because of her flagrant breach of office security, or keeping intact his access to her, he would opt for the access.

"As a matter of fact," he said dryly, "your unauthorized action appears to have worked in FRETSAW's favor. But you must check with me before releasing that kind—*any* kind—of information, you understand?" His voice hardened on the last two words, but the problem had been resolved just as Steve had predicted it would be when he'd pointed out the inescapable fact that she would have to confess to the unauthorized list printout.

Now that was out of the way, appearing in retrospect to have been the less demanding of her two efforts tonight.

Buttonwood drained his glass, set it on the table with a decisive clank, and clambered out of the settee.

"Horace," she said gently, "don't hurry."

He stood there, uncertain of how to react. She'd never before made a single bedroom suggestion.

Her move again. She took two more swallows of the Peach Basket Schnapps, felt its warmth flood her stomach, and she stood to set her glass on the table beside his. Maybe she would desperately want more of that stuff before this night was over, but she wouldn't be able to handle this through an alcoholic haze.

"It's got to be the phases of the moon, or the hazy weather, or something, but, Horace . . ." She sighed in abject helplessness. "I want to undress you."

Would he buy that?

"I'm not sure I—" But she was already at work on his shirt buttons.

"This is so strange," she murmured. Hell of an understatement. "I mean, when we started these . . . meetings, I felt so—you know what I mean. But now, I think I've begun to, well, look forward . . . even to hope that you— Oh, it's crazy, isn't it, Horace?" She peeled off the shirt, tossed it aside, and pulled the undershirt over his head. Then while he stood there afluster, but, she hoped, enjoying a heady burst of ego, she poured him a stiff one. "Here, this will help. I'm sorry, maybe I'm going too fast."

"No, no. It's fine. I like it fine." His face had flushed a delicate rose above the precisely trimmed beard. The thumbprint birthmark on his right cheek had turned flaming scarlet. After countless episodes of simply hopping aboard under the sheets, Horace Buttonwood was embarrassed. He took a grateful drag of the Schnapps.

She stripped him slowly to his blue-and-white-striped boxer shorts, and he stood tense as a soldier, immobile with anxiety, yet obviously intrigued with what she might do next.

"Now," she ordered, her voice low in his ear, "you just watch."

She unzipped the lounger ever so slowly, let it drift open, then shrugged it off her shoulders. The soft fabric pooled around her ankles. She wore nothing underneath. All this he had seen before, but always from beneath the security of the bedclothes. This time she moved languorously toward him until her breasts brushed his chest.

Then she reached down and dropped away his last shred of refuge. Never before had he stood before her naked, his control of what was happening so visibly askew.

He drained his glass, and she set it down. That should be enough. She didn't want him soused out of this. She straightened, interlaced her fingers with his, raised their arms together high above their heads to press the whole length of her body against his. Then she kissed him deeply.

"Oh, Jesus!" he whispered.

Delicately, she tongued his ear. "So to bed?"

She slipped in behind him, but when he made his clumsy effort to pull her beneath him, she waggled a forefinger before his glazing eyes. His pupils were big as marbles, as if he were on something. He *was* on something: pure erotic excitement, maybe for the first time in his life. She knew she had him.

"Relax, Horace. My turn." She trailed her fingertips along the rough beard, beneath the furry jaw line, down his bristly chest, past his navel. Her lips followed her fingers.

"Oh, my God!" he muttered.

"Don't Buckeyes do this?" she said, her voice muffled now.

"Buckeyes? I'm not from . . . *Oh, God, Alix!*"

"I thought you were from Ohio." She bent back over him.

"New York. Ahh . . ."

"City?"

"No, no. Gridley. Little town upstate, near . . . Elmira." He was having a lot of trouble concentrating. How much could she ask before he would realize he was being interrogated?

She slid her naked length upward to lie along his perspiring body, to whisper, "It's never been like this before." No lie, that. She felt his hand searching, kissed his ear. "After Gridley, what?"

His fingers stopped their crawl. "What do you mean, 'after Gridley, what?' "

Oh, Lord. Was he not as far gone as she'd thought?

"What?" she asked in what she hoped sounded like drowsy confusion, deftly reaching.

"I asked . . . I asked . . . Oh, my sweet *God!*" She had abruptly tripped his start switch. She fervently hoped she had punched his erase button as well.

11.

The boxy, turboprop-driven Shorts 330 commuter left Steve at the Chemung County Airport northeast of Elmira at 1:27 P.M. There, he rented a Ford Tempo from a company he'd never heard of, but which was happy enough to accept his American Express plastic. Following the New York State map he'd bought in the small terminal, he drove north on Route 35 some ten miles until the county road intersected State Route 414.

This was pretty country, with distant rolling mountains smoky blue, and the nearer hills a lush, late-spring emerald. The air smelled fresh and oxygen-charged. He shut off the A/C he'd turned on through habit, and opened the driver's window to let the clean air blast in.

Gridley, five miles short of Watkins Glen and the southern tip of Lake Seneca, was smaller than he'd hoped, but larger than he had expected. Route 414 was its main street, arrow-straight through its cluttered commercial valley after winding down the north side of a respectable hill just south of town. He passed an A&P, a lumberyard, hardware store, assorted retail shops. The flanking side streets pushed back a block on either side, then ascended steeply into sparse hillside residential areas east and west. He passed Gridley Consolidated High, a substantial and classic three-story brick structure set well back on a broad lawn.

Where in hell was the *Gridley Call,* the weekly newspaper the D.C. library info desk had told him was published here? He didn't spot it until he had driven the entire six-block length of downtown. It was just past the Citgo station, a hulking, one-story, gray granite thing, solid as a powder magazine. He swung the little Tempo into one of the two visitor spaces out front, went up the three, wide slab entrance steps, and found himself in a narrow space between the entrance and a waist-high counter. Behind it was a big, brightly lighted room of mostly empty desks.

Two harried-looking women bent over manual typewriters. One, middle-aged with sparse, blue-hued hair, and wearing a baggy tan cardigan with the sleeves pushed back, glanced up.

"Help you?"

"I hope so. Do you have a morgue?"

"A morgue? Oh, a library." Her voice was high and wispy. "Nobody calls them morgues anymore. Sure, on microfilm. We wanted electric typewriters, but they put the money into microfilm."

On her feet, she was a little bit of a woman. She pushed up a hinged section of the countertop to let him through.

"In the back. You have a particular date in mind? Saves a lot of time if you know what you're looking for."

"I have a name. Buttonwood, Horace Buttonwood. He's about fifty now, I guess. That would put him here anytime from fifty years ago to I-don't-know-when."

"That narrows it down." She opened a door in the rear of the big work area and eyed him curiously as he entered a smaller room with a microfilm readout machine on a big reference table flanked by racks of film cartridges.

"Only fifty years' worth? We publish weekly, so that means you only have to look through 2,600 editions. Unless . . ."

"Unless what?"

"We didn't convert to microfilm until four years ago. Before that, we saved one copy of every paper, and we kept a file of subject cards." She pulled a long, green metal file box from a drawer of the reference table. "This file. Then came the big austerity drive, and we went to microfilm, but without the index filing. Cost money to make the switch, but it got rid of the librarian's salary."

She set the file box on the table. "A lot of papers don't even let the general public have access anymore. We still do, but you have to know what you're looking for, or you're going to spend a whole lot of time rolling film strips through that viewer."

"So if my guy, Buttonwood, did anything notable before the microfilm years, he should be in that file box."

"That's right. Filed alphabetically by subject. Here, let me give it a try. Buttonwood, you said?" She pulled out the long tray, and her fingers began to rifle through the three-by-five cards.

"Butterfield Farms . . . Buttler, Aaron K . . . . Button Collectors Club . . . Buttram, Peter W. I'm sorry, no Buttonwood."

Damn it! The 6:30 A.M. rush to Washington National, USAir to Philadelphia, Allegheny's flying box to Elmira, twenty miles into the Finger Lakes boondocks. For nothing. Alix had told him Buttonwood was from Gridley, New York, but she hadn't found out how long he'd lived here. Maybe his family had left when he was still a child. Maybe he'd been a nonentity, never making it into the local paper.

"Is there anything else?"

"Oh, no. Thanks for your help."

Back in the car, he drummed his fingers on the steering wheel. Where now?

Maybe he changed his name.

If he had, this was it. Dead end.

Or was it? He visualized Buttonwood, smug and self-confident behind his expensive antique desk, jumping up to greet his visitor, unctiously shaking hands. Pouring coffee. Stroking his beard with thumb and forefinger. Bright green eyes, the strawberry mark . . .

One slim possibility might still exist here in Gridley. The library or the school? He hadn't seen a library, but he knew where the school was.

Gridley Consolidated, unlike the schools in Southwest Florida, was still in session on this late May afternoon. He sidestepped a gaggle of fast-moving students in the wide and echoing main corrider, found the administration offices, and made his request to a youngish-looking secretary who wore her brown hair in an old woman's bun. She, too, wore a cardigan, bright orange, but no informally pushed-up sleeves here.

"The yearbooks for the middle '50s?" She compressed thin lips, mulling over this out-of-the-blue request from a stranger. Apparently she could recall no regulation barring access. "We have those books in the school library. Next door on the right, down the hall. Oh, sir, you cannot take those books out," she called after him, her regulatory instincts satisfied.

The school librarian, heavy-legged, white-haired, and obviously nearing retirement, was equally protective. "These books must not be taken out. They must stay right here in this room, you understand." The era of pervasive security had permeated even isolated Gridley.

He selected the 1954 through 1957 volumes of the *Gridley Griddle*, half-inch-thick books of glossy coated paper with embossed Leatherette covers in alternating blues and reds, obviously the school colors. He turned to the section on graduating seniors in the 1954 volume and began to leaf slowly.

Not there.

He took the other three volumes to a nearby reference table and sat in a hard, armless chair. Not in the 1955 volume, either. Another blank? He opened the 1956 edition. If this long shot didn't produce, he was going to be hard put to—

His eyes stopped on the middle photo in the left-hand column of three head shots on page 7. He would never have recognized that sallow face, the purposeful eyes, penetrating even then, because the beard had changed so much of the facial contour and had hidden what the yearbook picture revealed as a weak chin. But there was no mistaking the birthmark, the strawberry thumbprint high on the right cheek, a gray smudge in the black and white graduation photo, but the very same imperfection.

Aaron Kenneth Buttler: Horace Buttonwood. *Track team, Gridley Senior Players. Idol: Preston Tucker. Favorites: a short beer, the long green. Ambition: to make it BIG.*

A kid with drive and presumably a flair for acting, and who liked money.

Who was Preston Tucker?

Tucker . . . Tucker. Hadn't he been something of a post-World-War-II Delorean, without the cocaine charge? Promised an automobile that would revolutionize road travel as the world knew it, turned out a few, sold franchises, then faded away. Nice idol for a high school kid whose ambition, two decades before the ME Generation, was "to make it BIG."

With his first solid lead into Buttonwood's past, Steve drove back to the bunkerlike offices of the *Gridley Call.* The blue-topped staffer—"I'm Maggie," she allowed this time—pulled out the three microfilm cartridges that were indexed on the *Buttler, Aaron K.* file card, showed him how to insert the film strips in the viewer, then left him alone in the stuffy little library room.

The machine had a manual advance lever, generating his first-ever thumb cramp before the first Aaron Buttler story slid into focus.

GRIDLEY YOUTH ARRESTED IN TIRE SWITCH.

A local 19-year-old, Aaron K. Buttler, was arrested by Sheriff Neville Nesbitt late Thursday on the complaint of Edward Westover, 1919 Hillside Street.

Westover had ordered two top-grade tires from Yardley's Cities Service repair garage, where Buttler worked part-time. After the tires were delivered and installed on Westover's 1954 Lincoln, they were found to be "seconds" of a brand inferior to the brand ordered.

Initially, Buttler claimed to know nothing about the mix-up, but Charles Yardley had witnessed his young assistant's departure with the proper tires. Further questioning revealed that Buttler had switched the top grade tires for the inferior replacements and a cash difference at Rattner's Garage near Watkins Glen. Buttler allegedly had pocketed the cash, stated by Samuel Rattner to be the sum of $27.62. Rattner further stated that he believed the tires to have been owned by Buttler, and that the exchange was a legitimate one. He was not charged.

Buttler, son of Horace and Irma Buttler, 837 Euclid Road, has been charged with theft and the exchange of stolen property. He will appear before Circuit Court Judge Jacob Moffat August 31.

The story was datelined August 7, 1956. Steve thumbed the film strip forward rapidly. A follow-up story should have appeared in the issue after next.

Here it was: BUTLER RELEASED ON PROBATION. Moffat, apparently not a hanging judge, had taken into account the fact that the tire scam had been Buttler's first offense and had let him off with a reprimand and a year's probation.

The next listing on the Buttler file card was on microfilm cartridge 1958-13, thirteen weeks into that year. March. Buttler, now a junior at Triple Cities College in Endicott, New York, had been disciplined for leading a student protest over alleged civil rights infringements against minority students. During the protest, the administration offices were ransacked, and approximately $400 in undeposited student cafeteria funds disappeared.

Buttler-Buttonwood, today's self-confessed gun-runner, a civil rights champion? Or had the $400 been the inspiration of his political awareness?

The fourth story on Aaron K. Buttler appeared in a February 1960 edition of the *Gridley Call.* At twenty-three, he was detained by Schuyler County authorities for allegedly converting to his own use $1,500 in cash, which a Montour Falls widow named Enid Fuller had entrusted to him for investment. Buttler, operating as a "financial consultant," claimed he had invested the funds for her, but that the local construction company in which he had made the investment had gone bankrupt and departed the state with all its records.

Judge Moffat, in view of Buttler's prior appearance before him, and in consideration of the lack of documentary evidence, offered Buttler the choice of facing a jail sentence on the minor charge of harrassment of the widow, or leaving Schuyler County promptly and permanently. Buttler stated that he would be "out of this miserable part of the Empire State" within twenty-four hours.

The final mention of Aaron Buttler was as the sole survivor of Horace and Irma Buttler, who died, apparently incapacitated by inebriation, in the accidental destruction of their home at 837 Euclid Road on New Year's Eve, 1961. The fire was determined to have been caused by careless smoking in bed. At that time, their son was believed to have been living in the Midwest, but he was not located. There were no other relatives.

And that was that on one Aaron Kenneth Buttler, boy scam artist, according to these three-decades-old documents. Surely, his boyhood goings-on were far cries from ordering murder in Maui. Yet they were quite an insight into Buttonwood's developing character, Steve realized, as he drove the Tempo back down 35 to the Chemung County Airport. And that early background reinforced a suspicion Steve had been nurturing since he'd tumbled to the fact that he had been elaborately duped on that gloomy Manhattan pier.

The next logical move would be to call or appear at Triple Cities College in Endicott to see what the school records on Aaron K. might reveal. He didn't have to make the trip to arrive at one entry sure to be in those records. With Aaron-Horace fleecing Widow Fuller in February of 1960, he was not in college where he should have been completing his senior year. So Horace Buttonwood was a college dropout—or dismissee. Which could mean that the Triple Cities alumni office would not have been as interested in keeping in touch with him through the years as it would have been had he graduated. Failed or canned students weren't notoriously supportive of the institutions that evicted them.

Steve slowed for the swing into the airport road. He could press on with this laborious probe into Buttonwood's past in the hope that it would lead into his current activities—which Steve already had discovered were not precisely what Buttonwood claimed them to be. Or, and it was one big *or,* he could take direct—and inescapably high-risk—action.

Would it be worth placing himself, and possibly Marcie, in jeopardy?

Then a mental image blotted out the approaching terminal building and hangars. Crumpled white metal beneath a tangle of vines. The Nissan, its front end compressed back to the shark's-toothed rim of the gaping windshield opening. Again he heard Sergeant Holo's chillingly soft voice: "The driver has no head."

Steve checked in, waited impatiently for the Philadelphia-bound Allegheny commuter to land, then taxi into place a hundred feet out on the ramp. He walked to the plane with two rumpled businessmen and a sharply dressed woman exec. Steve climbed aboard last, and in that moment, he made his decision.

"I don't know how thin I can stretch this, Steve." Alix Cortland's telephone voice was strained. "Buttonwood seemed to accept my confession about the Advisory Council list, but I know damned well I'm still here and not in jail only because he can't seem to do without my—"

"I know why you're still there, Alix, and it's quite likely that you may have more at stake than losing your job and facing possible prosecution for theft."

"You don't think he'd . . . go *that* far!"

"There are already two people dead, Alix."

"I think I'm going to have to disappear. Just vanish, move out of Washington to someplace they'll never find me." She sounded as if this weren't the first time she had considered that alternative.

"Maybe that's not a bad idea, but I need to get into the FRETSAW building one more time. After everyone has left for the day. I suspect I can't do that without your help."

He tapped the edge of the spare room's desk with his forefinger, waiting for her reaction. Beyond the window, Connecticut Avenue was shrouded in mist, sickly, yolk-colored under the streetlights.

Then she said, "You have part of Buttonwood's background now. You know they faked the gun-running. You think you know what they're really up to. Why don't you go to the police?"

"Because I don't have a nickel's worth of proof, Alix. That's where you come in."

"Again."

"Yes, again. I'm sorry for you that it's shaped up this way, but you can think of it as a chance to even the score with friend Horace."

She said, very quietly, "I was the one who stole the $1,200."

"And he's the one who has been taking it out in corporal ownership ever since. He probably set you up. And even if he didn't, I'd say you paid off that debt a long time back, Alix, but Buttonwood is obviously going to use you as long as it does something for him. Then what? A gentlemanly tip of the hat and a farewell bonus? Don't count on it. He's got you on a one-way street."

Silence again at the other end. He was getting through. And using her, it occurred to him, almost as blatantly as was Buttonwood.

"Hell, Steve," she sighed, "I should never have left Wilmington."

"The security, Alix. I have to know about the building's security setup."

He heard her draw a long, ragged breath. "There's a perimeter system, hard-wired, I think they call it. On every door and window. All three floors."

"Key-operated, or a number combination?"

"Combination. The panel is just inside the front entrance."

"Who knows the combination?"

"Buttonwood. Mr. Pope, I assume. Simmons, the receptionist. And, of course, the guard."

"The guard?"

"The security guard from OmniSecure. He comes on duty at five, closing time, and relieves Margaret Simmons. Then, I assume, when he sees that everyone has checked out, he arms the alarm system."

"How does he know the building is empty?"

"The sign-out sheet on the reception desk, I suppose. We sign in at nine, out and in again for lunch or for other out-of-the-building purposes, then sign out at five, the close of business for the day."

"The guard is still on duty when the building opens the next morning at nine? That's sixteen hours."

"No, it's a different guard when we open, Steve. I imagine they run two eight-hour shifts."

"Probably with the change at 1:00 A.M. We'll have to be aware of that. What do you take for sleepless nights?"

"What?"

After he told her what he wanted her to do, he heard another long, shaky breath. Then she said, "Oh, my God."

Behind the battered oak desk in his Spartan OmniSecure office, Milo Kolker enjoyed a newly acquired feeling of control as he hung up the phone. He liked to be on top of things, but through the past few days, he'd had the disturbing sensation of having blown something somewhere.

The FRETSAW people had ordered him to pull the Gammon surveillance. No explanation. It was as if something had gone wrong, they weren't telling him what, but they were going to have his ass for it. He'd quickly developed a couple of scenarios along that line, and managed to work up a serious mental lather when Buttonwood called this morning.

"Kolker, I want you to send a man up to Gridley, New York. Find out if anyone has been poking into the background of one Aaron K. Buttler. That's Buttler with two Ts."

"Gridley, New York." Kolker's tone was flat, businesslike, but he was elated that FRETSAW was putting him back in action. His gnawing apprehension melted into anticipation.

"It's between Elmira and Watkins Glen. I don't need backgrounding on Buttler, you understand. I just need to know if anyone has been probing into Buttler within the past few days, and, if so, I want to know who it was."

Curious assignment, Kolker thought, but perfect for Georgie Prescott. Since he'd pulled Georgie off Gammon, Kolker had tried to keep him busy with a couple of fill-in divorce surveillance shifts to relieve the unit on the Chenowith vs. Chenowith case over in Arlington. Kolker knew that wouldn't keep Georgie interested too long. The kid was real volatile, and inactivity sent him right to the edge of control, a real pain in the administrative can. But who else at OmniSecure, besides himself, was any good at wet-work?

Prescott liked flying, liked it better when he was airborne with the purpose of keeping a hard eye on another passenger. But at least this easy D.C. to Philadelphia to Elmira shuttle beat sitting on Valencia Drive down in Arlington from midnight to 8:00 A.M. to see if a wee-hours visitor might stay long enough at number 816 to bang Victoria Isabelle Chenoweth.

He rented a Chrysler LeBaron. Might as well enjoy himself. FRETSAW was picking up the tab, and the rental company at Chemung had one LeBaron among its gaggle of compacts. The drive north was a nice, relaxing ride through hilly country, with the AM dial picking up acid rock out of Syracuse.

Gridley started out as a drag, though. He was a field man, not a damned researcher. He didn't know where to begin.

Where in hell did you start when you were trying to get a line on somebody in a small town? He drove the LeBaron the length of Gridley, which sure didn't take long, then he turned around at the north end of town between the Citgo station and the hulking newspaper building, and guided the car back through the sparse local traffic.

He wished he'd listened more carefully to Milo Kolker this morning. They didn't want anything on this guy Buttler. Just wanted to know if anybody had been checking up on him, and if so, who? Lacking a name, what had he or she looked like?

Where in hell would he find that out? Goddamned Kolker had sent a man to do a boy's job.

There had to be a bar in an isolated little burg like this, a gossip center. That would be a starting point, anyway. And he could use a beer.

He found it just off the main drag on Euclid Road. The Gridley House. Pretty damned pretentious name for a hole-in-the-wall, asphalt-shingle-faced beer joint. It was grotto-dark when he walked in out of the afternoon glare, and it reeked of boozing past. He ordered a Miller Light and nursed it long enough for his eyes to adjust; long enough for a leisurely nod at a pair of old tipplers further down the battered bar.

Then he said, "Anybody been in here looking for Aaron K. Buttler?"

The bartender, probably the owner of the place and obviously the owner of an extra hundred pounds of body suet, stared at him through squinty little eyes nearly hidden in cheek fat.

"Jeez Chris'," he said, his belly beginning to jounce in silent, derisive laughter behind his huge-waisted chinos. "Ronnie Buttler ain't been back here since that business with the woman over to Montour Falls, I think it was. Back in '59 or '60, wasn't it, Denny?"

One of the stubbly oldsters gave him a beery, "Sommers 'round then."

"Used to live on this same road, mile up the side hill," the bartender volunteered. "His folks burned up with their house one New Year's thirty years back. He was gone then."

"That isn't what I asked," Prescott persisted in a voice gone steely. He hated being laughed at.

"What'd you ask?"

"If anybody's been here inquiring about Buttler. That's what I asked."

" 'Inquiring'?" The fat man was playing it for the old guys' chuckles. "Nobody 'inquiring' here, pal." The two barflies offered him the expected bad-teeth grins, then smirked at each other. High comedy in Gridley.

"So if somebody wanted to find out about Buttler, where would you suggest he look?"

"Hell, pal, the *Call* had files. I s'pose he'd look there."

"The *Call?*"

"The town's newspaper, Chris' sake." The bartender angled a pudgy thumb over his shoulder. "North end of town, just past Citgo."

Prescott felt like the dummy with the sloped forehead in the joke, battered that way from frustrated blows of his palm when he was told that two and two made four. The local newspaper files. Of course. He paid and left.

In the dungeonlike Gridley Call Building, he lucked out with the skinny, blue-haired broad who wore her sweater sleeves pushed back.

"Why, you're the second person this week who's asked about Aaron Buttler. I haven't even refiled the microfilms yet." She pulled up a hinged section of countertop. "They're in the back."

"I'm not interested in Buttler," Prescott said. "I want to know who was asking about him. Man or woman?"

"Oh, it was a man."

Who had made an obvious impression. Prescott felt a surge of satisfaction, if not excitement. A half hour ago, this had looked like mission impossible.

"Did you get his name?"

"I'm sorry, no."

"How old was he?"

"Maybe forty."

"How tall?"

"Six feet. A little taller."

"Hair?"

"Dark. Hardly any gray, as I remember. Why do you want to know all this?"

Prescott was ready for that one. "I was supposed to meet a friend of mine here. He's researching local history. Looks like I have the date mixed up. Anything else you remember?"

"I'm sorry, no. Oh, wait. He had a chin with a dimple. You know, like Cary Grant."

I'll be damned, Prescott thought, with a wash of elation. The skinny little bitch with blue hair had just described Steven Gammon.

12.

The afternoon—the whole day—was interminable. Yet Alix dreaded the approach of closing time. She was a wreck, found herself using the typewriter's automatic correction button much too often, had to visit the ladies' room down the hall every hour, it seemed. Her armpits were damp, and a bothersome film of perspiration kept forming on her upper lip. Surely Horace Buttonwood would detect these signs of agitation. Surely he would confront her any minute with an accusatory, "Exactly what is bothering you?"

But throughout the day, preoccupied with work, he barely acknowledged her uneasy presence. She struggled through his correspondence, took the letters in for his signature, and he didn't even look up.

Back at her desk, she reviewed for the dozenth time what Steve had told her on the phone. God, what a risky thing this was going to be! She had the timing down pat; at least in her mind. She had the vial in her purse. She had the motivation, the chance to end Buttonwood's control over her, the opportunity to terminate the sweaty sessions of his making her serve as no more than a depository for his loutish urges. She had the motivation, all right. But did she have the guts?

She had worn gray today, gray skirt, gray jacket over a cream blouse, in the hope that the suit's drabness would lend her a neutral sort of protection. Simmons's attention might be focused by a bright yellow sweater or orange scarf, but dull gray, Alix hoped, should be less than riveting.

By 4:55, her fingers were no longer capable of accurate typing. They tingled. Then they seemed numb. She rubbed her hands together.

It wasn't her hands that made her feel so obviously distraught. It was her heart, thundering so loudly in her ears that half the second floor must be able to hear it.

"Good night, Alix." Buttonwood spoke so close to her ear that she was visibly startled. Thank God he hadn't chosen this night as one of his. She had done her best to transmit negatives through the long day. No smiles, no close encounters. She had even made a point of wearing no scent.

He had pushed the little button on the face of his office door latch and pulled the door shut. It locked automatically. He had the only key she knew about. Then Buttonwood strode down the hall to the stairs, carrying his briefcase like a beaten-down public servant at the end of a grueling day; a dull, unimaginative man, she thought, with an out-of-character beard.

She covered her typewriter, took her purse from the desk drawer, and joined the cluster of people exiting the phone bank rooms. Downstairs at the front entrance, she waited her turn to sign out, managed to control the ballpoint enough to write a fairly neat signature, then she fumbled in her purse.

"Oh, damn! I've forgotten my scarf," she said to Margaret Simmons, who was watchdogging the sign-out from behind her reception desk. "I'll be right back." She had worn one this morning to have on hand to forget.

She trotted back up the wide staircase. At its top, she checked her watch. Five-oh-three. The guard should be arriving, typically a couple of minutes late, working in the front entrance through the departing employees, nodding at Simmons as she gathered up her belongings in preparation to leave.

In the empty second floor hallway, Alix paused to peer back down into the main floor corridor. Simmons was signing herself out now, then the blue-uniformed guard was alone down there. He set his bright red thermos and brown bag of sandwiches, his newspaper, small portable radio, and his bulky, round time clock on the desk. There was a man who came prepared. Then he walked to the alarm system panel set in the hallway side of the vestibule wall.

It was set too high for her to see from the top of the stairs. Her legs prickled at the thought, but she crept down three steps to get a clear line of sight. If he turned now, she would be highly visible up here, to say the least. And Steve's whole, intricate plan would instantly crumble.

But the guard was intent on keying the combination to arm the system. She couldn't make out the numbers from this distance, but she knew the panel's keyboard layout. Three rows of three numbers each, from one to nine. He tapped upper left, lower right, then center. One-nine-five. A green pinpoint of light in the top of the little panel was joined by a red pinpoint. The system was armed.

She pushed back up the steps out of the guard's line of sight, and retreated silently to the second floor ladies' room. Simmons, Alix knew, was a scheduling stickler: in on the dot of 9:00, out just as close to 5:00 as she could make it. Would she have remembered to tell the guard that Alix Cortland was still in the building? Or had she done what Alix and Steve were counting on? Departed without comment, dismissing Alix's return upstairs as insignificant, or even forgetting it altogether in her rush to leave. Now the guard, finding no blanks in the sign-out column, should assume the building to be empty.

Until she was certain of the guard's action, though, Alix decided on the ladies' restroom as a prudent refuge.

For a full five minutes, she heard nothing at all. She edged open the restroom door.

Then she quickly eased it shut. Footsteps. Coming up the stairs. A man's heavy tread. God forbid that it was somebody coming back to work late!

Her stomach shrank into a tight ball and jammed up under her ribs. Her breath came in raggedy gasps.

The purposeful tread, now muffled by the second floor hallway's carpeting, thumped closer. Then the steps stopped at the restroom door.

She bit her knuckle.

The heavy footfalls moved on. She heard her office door open.

"Alix Cortland?" That was the guard's raspy voice, irritated with the necessity to make this search. Damn Simmons! She hadn't overlooked a thing.

Alix heard her office door close. The guard retraced his steps along the hall. Then he paused again at the ladies' room door.

He rapped on the frosted glass. She could see his outline hazily silhouetted by the hallway's dim safety lighting.

"Anybody in there? He stepped closer. She caught her breath. Was he coming in?

She forced herself to rush as noiselessly as she could to the nearest stall, held the swinging door open to stop it from banging against the catch, and stepped up precariously to straddle the open seat.

She heard the restroom door swing open. "You in here, Alix Cortland?" His voice reverberated off the tiled floor and walls. The room's fluorescents flickered on.

There were three stalls in the row. Please God that he would just crouch down to look for feet.

In its unoccupied position, the stall door stood two inches ajar. She was horribly vulnerable. If he found her in here, obviously trying to hide, God knew what FRETSAW would do when he held her and reported in.

Her legs began to cramp. Her left foot slipped a half inch on the curved seat . . . an inch. She tried to shift her weight.

Only another few seconds of this, and she would be forced to—

The lights flicked out. The door opened, then closed behind the departing guard. She hoped that now he would assume she had left the building with Margaret Simmons having failed to notice her in the departing crowd.

How long would it be, she wondered, before the guard made his first official check around the building to key the time clock he carried to the several check-in stations? She had to be in a position where she could see him begin his security tour. Then she had to be certain that he was well away from the entrance hall when she made her next frightening move.

Alix took off her low-heeled shoes and left them on the top of the toilet tank. She inched open the restroom door, listened intently, heard the guard's radio playing softly downstairs.

She crept to the head of the staircase and crouched to gain a view of the reception desk. He had tilted Margaret Simmons's chair back against the wall, and had his feet up on the desk. Simmons would have killed him for either of those infractions, but at least he'd put a section of the newspaper he was reading on the polished desktop to pad his heels. Near the upraised feet were his brown-bagged sandwiches and the red plastic thermos.

He lounged sideways to her, facing across the hall. She realized that if he had good peripheral vision, he might be able to catch a sudden motion out of the corner of his eye. Sobering thought. Yet she had to stay here where she could watch or at least hear him. She was glad she had worn the colorless dark gray suit. It should blend fairly well with the subdued safety lighting up here.

She moved slowly behind the banister's ornate newel post, then leaned back against it, out of sight of the reception desk. She wrapped her arms around her knees in an unconsciously little-girl fashion. How long would she have to sit dead-silent up here? She was already worn down from the strain of the seemingly endless day. She was thirsty, hungry—and damn her nervous bladder. She felt as if she had to go to the bathroom again.

Put that out of your mind, girl. You're stuck right here, no matter how you feel. You're stuck here until that guard moves out of the hall.

This was so awfully risky! How could she have let Steve Gammon talk her into it? Was it worth all this to get out from under Buttonwood? Oh, that was well put, Alix. Never again to have to sprawl inertly and disgustedly compliant beneath his damp, mushy weight; his flaccid belly pressing hers, his insistent little hardness obscenely stabbing, then ineptly entering, then quickly spasming to leave her with . . . nothingness. Maybe that was the worst part. It didn't do anything for her at all, except make her want a long, hot shower. Like rape? Like nonviolent, victim-compliant rape. Almost every week.

That was why she was up here, damn him!

She pushed upward against the newel post. She had been sitting here a long time, and her rear end was numb.

Talk about a used woman. Steve Gammon was doing it, too. Not as degradingly as Horace Buttonwood. Not with her body. Seven was more insidious about it. He was using her position, her access, and the trap she was in.

No, that wasn't fair. She liked Steve. He was using her, but with her compliance. When she had agreed to do this, though, she'd had no inkling how scared she would be.

Alix craned around the polished hardwood post to look again at the guard down there in his slate-blue uniform with its gold and white OmniSecure shoulder patches. He was a big, heavily muscled man, in his forties, she judged. His visored cap was tilted over his eyes, but the lower part of his face looked sort of like Lorne Greene in his prime. Determined and set-jawed, and not about to believe anything she told him if he caught her in here tonight.

He reached out suddenly to click off his radio. Then he dropped the chair down on all four legs so abruptly and noisily that she jerked her head back behind the concealing banister support.

When she edged back around it far enough to see him, he had slung his fat disc of a time clock over his shoulder by its carrying strap, and he strode along the hall to the rear of the first floor.

It took the guard four minutes to complete his first floor check. When he reached the foot of the staircase, she padded silently to the ladies' room. She doubted that he would check in here again, but she took refuge in the stall once more to be safe. Safe?

She heard the guard clock into the station at the head of the stairs. Then his hazy shadow moved across the restroom's frosted glass as he walked to the station outside her own office cubicle. He clocked in there, then rounded the corner to check the storage areas at the end of the short front hall.

Alix slipped out of the restroom, darted to the stairs, and rushed down on silent, stockinged feet. She prayed that the guard's rounds would take him straight to the third floor without returning—or even glancing—down the main staircase. At the most, she judged she had four minutes.

She unsnapped the flap of her pocketbook, took out the prescription vial and set it on the desk. The thermos bottle's bulky top unscrewed easily. The thermos held coffee, probably the equivalent of three cups.

The damned plastic vial had one of those infuriating childproof caps. She bit her lower lip in frustration before she thought to line up the two little arrows. Even then, she broke a nail pulling off the obstinate cap.

Two of the pink tablets were enough to knock her for a loop. The thermos top, which was designed to double as a cup, looked as if it would hold a moderate cupful. It struck her that this was hellishly risky. If she overdosed him— Too late to worry about that now.

Before leaving for work this morning, she had used the bowl of a tablespoon to crush twelve of the tablets into powder on a sheet of paper. Then she had tapped the powder back into the prescription vial. Three tablets per cup . . . three cups' worth in here. She shook three-quarters of the pinkish powder into the thermos. Its top went back on a lot harder than it had come off. She couldn't get the cheap threading to mate smoothly.

Three minutes gone. The damned top finally yielded. She screwed it in place, shook the thermos to mix the contents, and set it back beside the brown bag. Then she hurriedly swept the vial and a sprinkle of spilled powder into her purse.

She heard the guard's footsteps near the top of the stairs. She was blocked from returning to the relative security of the second floor! She ran down the main corridor to the rear of the building, and ducked into the narrow carpeted hall that led to Pope's secluded office.

The guard's deliberate tread thudded down the staircase. She edged around the angle of the two hallways far enough to watch the man resume his seat, tilt the chair back against the wall and plunk his feet up on the desk. Then he reached for the phone, punched in a number and spoke only a few words, which she couldn't hear. He hung up and flicked on his radio.

She waited. Down the hall, beyond Pope's office, the building creaked. The guard didn't stir. The silence pressed in on her, so dense she could feel it, like unseen pressure on her damp face, against the back of her neck, down her legs to her stockinged feet, which were icy cold on the Oriental runner to Pope's office.

The tingle began deep in her nose and built swiftly into an overwhelming need to sneeze. How disastrous *that* would be! She clamped the bridge of her nose with thumb and forefinger to cut off the rising sneeze with an unavoidable gasp.

Had he heard that?

The guard's feet hit the floor with a thud audible all along the main floor.

Oh, God! Frigid sweat broke between her breasts.

He reached for the thermos.

Alix shuddered with relief, then watched him unscrew the top with deliberate twists. He inverted it and filled it with the doctored coffee. Then he leaned back against the wall, brought his feet up, and sipped contentedly.

How long would it take? Would one cup be enough? Would more than one overdose him? Oh, hell, would it work at all? If it didn't, his next round would be disastrous for her because there was no place to hide in this dead-end cross corridor.

Damn you, Steven Gammon, for putting me in this incredibly vulnerable position; for this shaky plan with so many holes in it that could end in calamity any second.

The guard had downed half the cup without visible effect. Maybe she had way overestimated her prescription's narcotic effect. Maybe his body weight was so much more than hers that the stuff wouldn't have any effect at all.

He tilted back the red plastic cup, drained it, poured another. And he sat there, feet up, chair tilted back, cup in one hand, the fingers of the other tapping in rhythm to WTOP's soft music. On and on and—

His chin dropped. He caught himself with an upward jerk of his head. The tapping fingers lost the beat, fluttered off the chair arm. He jerked upright again, shook his head, then quickly drained the second cup.

The music tinkled on. He tried to screw the thermos top back in place, but his uncoordinated fingers couldn't do it. He gave up, sank back in the chair. His chin inched toward his chest. His arms dropped straight down.

She felt the throat-tightening onset of panic. Was he . . . was he . . . Then she heard his soft snore.

Alix padded swiftly up the hall. She felt a ripple of anxiety as she neared the sprawled guard, but she forced herself to stop in front of him. He was out, all right; with his mouth slackly open. A string of saliva glistened down his chin onto his uniform collar.

She switched off the radio music and moved silently past the desk to reach up to the alarm system's control panel. She pushed the three square buttons in careful sequence. One-nine-five. The tiny red indicator gleam winked out. The system was disarmed.

She opened the solid oak door into the vestibule. Through the wrought iron and glass outer door, she saw to her surprise that the deserted street was bathed in the surrealistic greenish glow of a smoggy sunset. She felt that she had been trapped in the FRETSAW building for an eternity, but it was not yet 7:00. And she felt frighteningly exposed out here in the glass-fronted vestibule, visible from the street behind the outer door's ornate grillwork, should anyone out there look closely.

He could have planned this for later in the evening, when the street would be shrouded in darkness. But he'd pointed out the increased risk of her being discovered in the building—and the reduced search time available, with the second security shift presumably coming on at 1:00 A.M.

So here she stood, in fading daylight, shivering in the entrance of a building whose security she had just immobilized.

Then Steve strode into view on the sidewalk, trotted up the steps as casually as a salesman making an easy call, and slipped inside.

"Where were you! I feel like a target out here."

"Parked a hundred feet up the street. You haven't been out here for more than thirty seconds, Alix." He took her arm and urged her out of view of the street, closing the vestibule's exterior door behind them.

"I don't want to go back in there, Steve."

"At this point, I think you're safer in there with me than in your apartment by yourself, Alix." He glanced down at her shoeless feet. "Besides, you're not exactly equipped to travel."

"Steve . . ."

"Come on, I need you." He opened the interior door and strode to the reception desk to peer at the unconscious guard, took the man's dangling wrist, felt his pulse and nodded. "Nice job."

"Should I arm the system again?" She seemed to have gotten hold of herself.

"No. We might have to make a quick exit out the rear door or a window." Steve checked his watch. "I figure that with luck we have six hours before his relief comes on. Six hours to find out what FRETSAW is really in business for."

Horace Buttonwood had a case of gut-rippling jitters. He prowled around his drab apartment in Lanham's suburban sprawl, just inside the Capital Beltway east of Washington. The Sears living room and bedroom suites were not his. He had rented the place furnished, here in Morning Glory Heights. No complications. Free to travel. Except now he had acquired an encumbrance that was far more entangling than an apartmentful of furniture, or organization memberships, close friends, civic commitments, or a wife—all of which he had assiduously avoided through his building of FRETSAW into a productive organization.

That encumbrance was Richardson Pope.

Damn it! The inspiration for FRETSAW had been his, not Pope's. Unfortunately, the seed money—$50,000 of seed money—had been Pope's. When Buttonwood had met the man, Buttonwood's total assets were less than $2,000.

He had newly arrived in New York from the West Coast, where he had barely escaped the investigative outcome of the Los Angeles Police Department's Bunco Squad. Buttonwood had sold nearly $4,700 worth of advertising in the Official Program of the East Los Angeles Integrated Charities Gala before one of the advertisers, whom Horace pressed for advance payment, did some checking.

There was no gala; in fact, there was no ELAIC registered anywhere except on the stationery in the briefcase of one Gridley Watkins, as Horace Buttonwood then called himself.

He was forced to leave a number of lucrative accounts uncollected when the West Coast business climate soured, but he took with him a newfound appreciation of the power of charitable appeals. Well before the musty-smelling transcontinental Greyhound hissed to its final stop in Manhattan's crowded terminal, he had a plan.

No more low-profile widow-walloping or phantom programs or picayune Sunbelt scams. He was going, well, public. Right out front. Big time.

All he needed was the money.

The meeting had been ironically memorable, not necessarily because of its location, though they met in the mellow splendor of the Waldorf's lobby. Buttonwood had found the lobbies of prestigious hotels to be impressive sites for key get-togethers, and their use was free.

He had plucked Pope's name out of *The New York Times*; more specifically, out of a Sunday feature on the rash of health spa closures that was embarrassing the industry.

Richardson Pope had relentlessly promoted the franchising of a chain of health spas in three South American capitals, had exacted stiff franchise fees and heavy percentages of the membership dues. The health clubs had collapsed one after the other, following the fade of his promotional impetus. A gaggle of lawsuits roiled in Pope's wake, but the legal complexities of pursuing claims into another continent left half a dozen disillusioned *señors* and two chagrined *señoras* holding a collectively large and empty *saco.* Pope was stateside by then, scot-free. And, Buttonwood deduced from the extensively researched article, with money to invest.

It took four phone calls, beginning with one to the *Times* feature writer, to locate Pope, who was then known by his true name, Andrew Albertson, a native son of faraway British Columbia. Buttonwood finally reached the man in Baltimore, where Albertson was in the initial stages, he said, of setting himself up as a financial consultant. No licensing or background check required.

Buttonwood told Albertson enough to get him on the Metroliner to New York for their meet at the Waldorf. There he sized up his man before outlining his plan in toto. There were some drawbacks. First, Albertson's appearance was a shock. At a towering six-feet-four, the man was a virtual Telly Savalas; not because of the height, but because of the shiny, tanned skull. Not a hair in sight.

Next, there was the aura. Albertson was formally dressed in bland tans as if he had just come from a Florida bank's boardroom, and an emanation of powerful presence came right along with him like an invisible electric current.

"Mr. Buttonwood?" The voice using his newly acquired name—fresh project, fresh start—was a volcanic rumble.

"Mr. Albertson?" Buttonwood found he had unconsciously risen on his toes. Still, he was craning steeply upward. "Won't you sit down?" Please, for God's sake.

Seated, they were on eye level with each other. Albertson's height was all in his immensely long legs. Buttonwood offered to buy him a drink. Declined. Albertson was a man who wanted to get on with it, hear him out, then accept or discard the opportunity on the spot.

Buttonwood got on with it.

Albertson accepted. But with conditions. "After all, Mr. Buttonwood, I will be providing the total initial investment."

Albertson would accede to Buttonwood's insistence on control of day-to-day operations; to his being executive director. Then the dapper Canadian threw in, as if an afterthought, "I would like the title of president."

Buttonwood started to question that, but Albertson raised a silencing hand. "Trappings, that's all."

And Buttonwood believed him.

Not until they both had moved to Washington, and Andrew Albertson had become Richardson Pope as the midday Amtrak crossed the Delaware River—a prudent move that Aaron-Horace Buttler-Buttonwood fully understood—did Buttonwood get an inkling of what was happening to FRETSAW's executive echelon.

Pope's office was ground floor and larger. Pope never visited Buttonwood; he summoned him. Pope selected, seduced, and dominated the damn fool board of moneyed putty that believed so vehemently in "enlisting the support of right-thinking Americans everywhere."

The Advisory Council had been Buttonwood's idea, but it was as internally toothless as was the small Board of Directors. So the real power had become Richardson Pope, lurking in his secluded office in skinheaded eminence, fronting at occasional unavoidable public functions, relishing his presidency. And Buttonwood found himself "on call," and frequently on the carpet, dominated by the very man he had recruited for the project he, himself, had created.

When FRETSAW had been mortally threatened by the far-too-perceptive Walter Van Hayden, the solution had been initiated by Pope, but Buttonwood had been delegated to transmit the order to OmniSecure. And when Jim Gammon had appeared on the Hawaiian scene, it fell to Buttonwood again to forward Pope's decision on Gammon.

The preservation of FRETSAW, Buttonwood reflected glumly, had propelled him from his former status as a penny-ante grifter to murderer by proxy. "The stakes," had rumbled Richardson Pope, "make any risk worth that risk. Bear in mind that it is relatively short-term."

Only when he was ordering Alix Cortland into bed did Buttonwood enjoy any feeling of control. But even that illusion of power had been shaken to its shallow roots three nights ago when she had left him disoriented and gasping. One of those gasps, he had realized later, had been a reference to Gridley.

How could he have said that? How could he have let her get him to the mind-blown point where he would say it? How could he ever have believed that superficial crap she had given him about why she had illicitly acquired the Advisory Council list? One thing was painfully clear now: she had been working with Steven Gammon all along.

Jesus, he hated to lose her. Secretaries were a dime a dozen, but not sleek, blonde animals with gorgeous thighs to which he had engineered permanent pass privileges. He would sorely miss that, but there was no way he could keep her at FRET-SAW now. Or keep her at all.

He was almost ready to close the biggest deal of his life, but a blonde bed bunny and a chillingly persistent amateur investigator were threatening to trip him up. He'd managed to force his Gridley slip to the back of his mind until he had returned to his apartment that night, still glowing. When the glow faded, nagging worry set in. He had called OmniSecure the following afternoon.

Twenty-two hours later, Kolker had a report for him. A man answering Steve Gammon's description had been in Gridley, upstate New York, inquiring about "your man, Aaron Buttler."

Excellent work, he told Kolker, and it unsettled the hell out of him. Now he prowled his substandard digs, chewing at a ragged end of his mustache. His brain was a whirl of crosscurrents. He wondered what Gammon had been able to learn about him in Gridley. He wondered why he had let Richardson Pope-Albertson virtually take over FRETSAW, *his* baby. And he wondered just what forces were at work out there, chipping away at everything he had built out of what had been, just a little more than three years ago, no more than a midnight inspiration on a transcontinental bus.

13.

"If there is anything revealing in this building," Steve said, "I'll give you odds it's in one, maybe all, of three places."

They rushed down the ground floor hallway. Steve's shoes thudded on the parquet, but Alix's stockinged feet made almost no sound. He stopped at the foot of the broad staircase.

"Three places?" Alix prompted.

"Pope's and Buttonwood's offices, or the computer mainframe storage."

"The computer room? But neither Pope nor Buttonwood has a terminal. I input all of Buttonwood's stuff, and Pope is one of those execs who makes a point of not needing a secretary, then uses everyone else's."

"That seems to narrow it down to the two offices. You have a key to either one?"

She shook her head.

"Not even to Buttonwood's?"

"No, he always opens it himself."

"Let's take a look at Pope's."

They hurried to the cross corridor at the rear of the building, past the small rear door. Its upper panel was clear glass, but their risk of being seen in here was minimal, Steve thought. The door gave into a service alley, surely deserted by now in this area of converted office buildings.

At the door to Pope's sacrosanct office, Steve fingered the brass lock housing and checked the jamb.

"So much for the credit card trick. You couldn't slide even a piece of paper past this tight fit. And the lock could be a dead bolt."

"Buttonwood's isn't. He just pulls the door shut, and it locks itself."

"Spring lock. Let's take a look."

They returned to the stairs. The guard hadn't moved. The building was dead-silent except for Steve's own footfalls, Alix's light padding, and the guard's rhythmic snore.

"You've done a hell of a job," he told her at the top of the stairs. "It will be a damned shame if we can't get any further than this."

At that instant, the phone down on the reception desk tore into the silence, as loud as a fire alarm. Steve felt his blood freeze right down to his feet. Alix gasped, and her fingers dug into his arm.

The phone clamored again. They stared at the sprawled guard, not three feet from the shrilling bell.

He didn't even twitch.

The phone fell silent after its sixth, seemingly endless, ring.

"Let's move," Steve urged. He heard her long, shaky exhale.

The door to Buttonwood's office was as tightly constructed as had been Pope's. Though this office was secured by a spring lock, there was obviously no space to insinuate a plastic card between door and jamb.

"Now you know why I'm a development consultant, not a detective," Steve muttered. "This is some great scheme of mine. You've immobilized the guard and disarmed the security system. We're inside, with enough time to dismantle the place. But none of that does us a damned bit of good because we can't— Wait a minute. What about the guard? Wouldn't fire regulations require him to have access to every room in the building? How dense can I be?"

In the second floor's low-wattage security lighting, her face was dead-white. He had put her under a hell of a tension load, and it hadn't let up yet. "Steve, I'd just as soon not—"

"I'll do it. You wait here."

He hurried down the steps, unconsciously lightening his footfalls as he neared the inert guard. The keys hung on a ring from a belt loop on the man's right hip beneath his dangling arm. Steve moved around the desk, carefully pulled the arm aside and pressed in the spring closure of the key ring. He lifted the keys free and let the limp arm swing back. The heavy snoring never stopped, but Steve's palms were wet. He wiped them down the sides of his sports jacket.

"Got 'em," he said when he had rushed back up the steps, two at a time.

"Steve, if we've caught in here . . ."

"Steady, now. You've done beautifully, and I think we're in the final stretch."

". . . breaking and entering—"

"Just entering. We'll leave without a trace. Chances are the guard will never know what hit him. He might even come out of it before his relief comes on, and what's he going to say? 'I've been asleep on the job?' Don't get the retrofrights on me, now."

He wished he felt as confident as he tried to sound.

The seventh key slid into the lock on Horace Buttonwood's office door, turned, and they were in. Steve reached for the light switch.

"Wait," Alix cautioned. She walked across the office and pulled shut the draperies on the two corner windows. Then she switched on the brass desk lamp. It threw much of the office into shadow, but it was ample for them to work by.

"You take the desk," Steve suggested. "I'll handle the rest of the room."

"But what am I looking for?"

"Anything that seems to be other than standard Foundation business. You should be able to spot something like that better than I could."

He felt a little melodramatic as he checked behind Buttonwood's undecipherable paintings for a hidden wall safe. If he did find one, how were they going to get in it? But he found nothing.

He bent low, craned upward to peer beneath the big couch, then under the desk and the two visitor's chairs. He helped Alix examine the undersides of the desk drawers, took the lamp from the desktop to aim its light into the empty drawer spaces before they put the desk back together again, feeling increasingly ridiculous. But a search was a search.

They found nothing.

"How about his papers?"

She shrugged. "Routine correspondence, the usual phone books, appointment calendar, memo file, Foundation checkbook."

"Wouldn't the treasurer have the checkbook?"

"Buttonwood also acts as treasurer."

"Let me see that."

The checkbook was half full of Foundation-imprinted beige business-style checks. He ran through the stubs. Deposits were entered twice weekly, averaging some $15,000 per entry. Higher in some previous months.

"Those must have been the returns from mail campaigns started in those months," Alix said. "Hank Loper told me we get the maximum per-day response for the two weeks following the week of the mailing."

Steve made a quick calculation. Fifteen to $20,000 per deposit, twice a week, would aggregate something approaching $2 million a year. Just what *The Foundation Directory* had reported to be FRETSAW's annual income.

He riffled through the check stubs again. "What's this biweekly remittance to Bartell Services?"

"It's a payroll management company," she said. "Bartell handles our payroll deductions and issues the paychecks."

The rest of the stubs recorded monthly checks to the Chesapeake & Potomac Telephone Company, Potomac Electric, insurance premium payments. The stubs were a compendium of routine office operating expenses—plus notably large remittances to the advertising firm of Kinnon & Fields. In fact, that was where the bulk of FRETSAW's money ended up, but that was exactly where Horace Buttonwood had told him it was going: into newspaper and magazine ads.

He returned the checkbook to the desk's center drawer and grimaced to Alix. "If there's anything incriminating in there, I've missed it. What haven't we checked out?"

"We haven't torn up the wall-to-wall carpeting or ripped off the wallpaper. I can't think of anywhere else to look. Especially since we don't know what we're looking for."

He sat on the edge of the desk, frowning. Then he stood abruptly. "The bookcase. We haven't checked the bookcase."

He pulled out several volumes on the bottom shelf to make room to grope behind the books still in place. Not very thorough. He began handing her four or five volumes at a time, and he was suddenly struck with the awkwardness—hell, the potential catastrophe—of this whole thing. He had coerced her into drugging the guard, and God knew whether the man was just sleeping it off or verging on coma. Now they were trampling Buttonwood's privacy. Maybe that wasn't so reprehensible, in view of what had led to this. But they weren't finding a damned thing.

Then Alix said, "This one rattles."

"It what?"

"Rattles. Her left arm clutching a half dozen books to her chest, she shook a hardbound copy of *How to Generate Major Grants* by somebody named Wallace Willis with her free hand.

He stepped back from the wall-mounted bookcase. "Let me see that."

A hot wave of elation broke through him. "It's hollow!

Look, a space has been cut out of the pages." Steve pulled out a blue passport embossed with a gold seal, and leafed through it. "Buttonwood's photo, but the thing is made out to Butler A. Gridley."

"How could he get a passport like this? Don't you have to show ID?"

"Know the right people and pay them the right amount, I imagine. Oh ho, what's this? A passbook, Bank of the Islands, Grand Cayman."

"Grand Cayman? Where's that?"

"In the Caribbean, south of Cuba. I've heard it's one of those no-questions-asked refuges for the financially adventurous." He flipped open the maroon Leatherette passbook cover. And whistled.

"My God! Now we know what FRETSAW's really been doing with its money."

Her arms tight around the books she still held against her chest, she stared at him.

"It's a gigantic scam, Alix. They're *stealing* it."

Georgie Prescott had begun to resent the hell out of the FRETSAW work. The first trip to Hawaii had been fine. Better than fine. He'd handled the Van Hayden termination slickly, left not even a bruise or toenail gouge on the old man, made sure he did indeed drown, his lungs clogged with swimming pool water. Like a pro, Prescott. With Kolker watching the performance.

The second Hawaiian trip, though, dogging James Gammon's big brother, had been an exhausting drag. Then pilot fishing the man around D.C. had been worse, particularly that thing Gammon had pulled in the parking garage. Made a dog turd out of me, Prescott recalled grimly, just when Kolker thought I was getting hot.

Got him sent out to grow mold on the Chenowith split work, and that had been a dud. Through the eight hours he'd sat on the residential side street in the cramped little OmniSecure

Chevette, nobody had shown up to split Victoria Chenowith. Nobody even passed the place, except the paperboy. An hour after dawn. Bor-ring.

The one-dayer to Gridley, though, did work out okay. He was a little surprised on his return that he hadn't been put back on the Crossmoor Arms watch. But Kolker had told him there seemed to be some confusion over that. FRETSAW hadn't ordered reinstatement of the watch, but here Prescott was now, back in his own hot Camaro, heading for FRETSAW headquarters.

He didn't mind that Kolker's phone call had interrupted something. Well, not all that much. He'd picked her up in a New York Avenue singles bar; liked her name, Leteece, though she'd probably made it up. He'd thought she'd shown promise, but when he had gotten her onto his unmade bed and given her a strategic little tweak, she had frosted over.

"I'm *not* into *that!*" Icecubesville, even when he'd tried something more or less standard.

Then had come Kolker's unwittingly timely phone call. "Our night guard at FRETSAW, fellow by the name of Harrison, didn't make the required hourly check-in call at seven," Kolker said. "We also got a monitor log entry of the FRETSAW arming light out at six-twenty-two, and it still shows the system disarmed."

"You try to call the guard?"

"No answer."

"It's seven-ten now, Kolker. You said the arming light went off at six-twenty-two." Prescott enjoyed this one. "How come you waited till now?"

"I don't have to answer to you, Georgie, but there was a frig-up in the monitoring room here when the shift changed. Anyway, it's not an alarm signal. It's only a not-armed indication. Could be a dozen things, including an electrical screw-up. But you get your ass down there pronto, you hear me? And carry your piece. If it's something critical, I don't want a body count, you understand? Search and detain, Georgie."

Whatever was going on at FRETSAW, it could be more diverting than Miss Inert Filler, still naked among the sheets, and staring at him with a mix of expectancy and apprehension. When he hung up and turned his full attention back to her, he saw gooseflesh sweep along the taut thighs. Too late, babe.

"Get yourself dressed and get out," he told her, curiously finding more satisfaction in that than he figured he would have found in her. He washed his face hurriedly and obliterated the last of her musky scent with a heavy dash of marjoram-laden Herbissimo.

He was barreling across East Capital Street's Whitney Young Bridge by 7:21, mentally thanking lanky Leteece for one thing, anyway. Her misleading eagerness had gotten him back to his apartment early enough to catch Kolker's call. His luck was turning. Hell, yes! He could feel it. Definitely turning.

He took the Camaro slowly past the darkened FRETSAW building. Couldn't see a thing. Except, by God, a blue Buick Skyhawk at mid-block.

He parked a half block distant, and walked back to the building entrance, his now nervous right hand involuntarily patting the bulge his Smith & Wesson 459 made in his navy blue blazer. Kolker carried a clumsy .45 Colt, the unbalanced military version that could blow a man backward no matter where you hit him—if you hit him. Beyond fifty feet, that thing of Kolker's could miss a barn.

Prescott's 9mm S&W had better balance, greater accuracy, and it carried a twelve-shot clip. He had fired it in OmniSecure's basement range, but he was the organization's accident specialist. He'd never fired a shot "in anger," so to speak. He was itching to experience that, to see what it felt like to plant one right in the middle of a chest. "Search and detain," Kolker had ordered. But there was always self-defense; OmniSecure wouldn't expect him to just stand there and be taken out.

Prescott mounted FRETSAW's entrance steps noiselessly. He peered through the glass and iron front door to see only another door on the other side of the dusk-darkened vestibule. The inner door was solid wood. He wished he'd been in this place before, but Kolker had been the only OmniSecure rep to come here, except for the uniformed guard shifts.

He walked back down the steps, trying to look like someone who'd arrived for normal business, then found the place locked. On the short entrance walk, he darted his eyes the length of the block. Nobody on either sidewalk of this tucked-away street of outdated townhouses converted to low-rent offices. He could hear the wash of traffic over in Dupont Circle, but this block was deserted. Silent. Eerie in the evening's deepening greenish haze.

A narrow, overgrown concrete walkway angled off the entrance walk and bent around the right side of the building. No doubt it led to a service entrance in the rear, a relic of the building's original design as a residence. Prescott checked the street again, then he followed the walk's narrow, cracked slabs around the corner of the building. He pushed through the grasping branches of some damned shrub that should have been pruned back years ago. Lousy yard maintenance. He ducked beneath the low-hanging limb of a yellowed and struggling pine, and emerged in a tiny rear yard abutting a service alley that split the block behind twin rows of what once must have been pretty fancy townhouses. Could have walked up to the cross street, then down the alley, Prescott realized, instead of clawing through all that underbrush that had left dismaying scratches in the soft leather of his Italian loafers.

The building had a narrow rear door with a single pane of glass in its upper half. Truly lousy security by itself, but they had the guard and the alarm system. He mounted the stone stoop and peered inside.

A long hallway ran from here straight through the building to the front entrance. Side hall off to his right. Big staircase a third of the way up the main hall. Yellowish security lighting, except down by the front entrance where a brighter light—what the hell! On the top of a desk down there, he spotted a pair of sprawled legs. In OmniSecure blue. The rest of the guy was hidden by the staircase. But the splayed black shoes told him that Harrison was dead to the world. Or dead.

Prescott moved to the left of the glass pane, squinted for better focus. Yeah, there was the alarm system panel, set in the front wall near the inside entrance door.

No little red light. The system was not armed. He tried the door. Locked. Then he pulled out the S&W and wrapped his handkerchief around its butt.

"Stealing it?"

Steve handed Alix the passbook. "No name. It's numbered, like a Swiss bank account, but I've read that even fewer questions are asked in the Caymans."

She sank to the sofa. "But they had your brother killed, Steve. Two people killed. Does this justify murder?"

"Look at it, Alix."

She opened the passbook with fingers that noticeably trembled. He didn't blame her. Her voice sounded strangled. "My God, Steve, this shows a balance of nearly five *million* dollars!"

"Enough to kill for."

"How did he do it? How could he possibly take this much out of FRETSAW without anybody noticing?"

"He's the treasurer. He and Pope are the only officers. There's no way an organization's executive director could clip off this kind of cash without the president in on it. I'll bet you half of the Washington Monument we find an escape kit just like this one down in Pope's office. Why here, though? Why didn't Buttonwood keep this at home, or in a safe-deposit box?"

She was fascinated by the deposit book. "The mechanics of stealing this much money. How could he possibly . . ." She pushed up from the sofa. "How risky is a call out?"

"A call out? Probably no risk at all."

She was already scrabbling through Buttonwood's D.C. White Pages. Then she punched in a number on his desk phone. "I just hope he's home. I'm sure he's not big on night life—Hank? It's Alix . . . Yes, yes, I'm okay. This may sound odd, but can you tell me about how much money came in through the mail operation during the past week? . . . No, not day by day. Just the approximate total . . . I know it's confidential, Hank, but something serious has come up . . . No, I can't tell you now. I need that figure, Hank. Please!"

She waited, the phone held to her ear with both hands.

Then she said, "Sixty-five *thousand?*" She raised her eyebrows at Steve. He took the checkbook out of the desk drawer again and flipped it open.

"Thanks, Hank. A lot." She hung up and leaned across the desk to peer at the deposit records Steve was already studying.

"Uh huh," he said. "Here's at least part of how it's done, Alix. Your friend says he gave Buttonwood $65,000 through the past five working days. Obviously he didn't deliver it through you."

"Yes he did, but in sealed envelopes marked 'Confidential.' I never see how much is in them."

"So Buttonwood deposits only half of what comes in. I'll bet you the rest of the Washington Monument that he splits the skim with Pope, and off go half the checks to their numbered accounts in the Caymans, probably laundered through some kind of dummy account so the stolen checks show what looks like a legitimate cancellation stamp. Throw in a hefty bite out of major gifts from the Advisory Council members, and it's not hard to see how Buttonwood goosed this personal nest egg of his up near five million. We find the counterpart to this in Pope's office, and we've got both of them. They've used the mails to defraud. I'm sure the area's U.S. Attorney will be intrigued by that for starters. Then along the line, I hope he will be able to prove murder one."

He replaced the checkbook and slipped the passport and deposit book in his jacket pocket. "Come on, lady, we're going to give Pope's office bookcase a housecleaning."

He snapped out the desk lamp and made sure the office

door locked behind them. They walked lightly along the second floor corridor to the head of the stairs.

Then Alex grabbed his arm again. Her stunned whisper was right in his ear. He could feel the little puffs of her hot breath. *"Did you hear that?"*

He had frozen in midstride, his right foot one step down. The crystalline shatter at the rear of the lower hallway had been no louder than the sound a dropped wine glass would have made, but it might as well have been a cannon blast.

He backed away from the stairs, pulling her with him. "Somebody's breaking in through the rear door."

Her fingers clawed at his upper arm. "I don't think I can take much more, Steve. I just don't."

"Hold on, Alix," he whispered fiercely. "We're almost home."

In the main floor hallway, they heard the rear door open, quietly close, then cautious footfalls moved along the polished parquet.

A shadowed figure passed the bottom of the staircase and approached the reception desk. Youngish man, Steve noted from the darkness at the top of the stairs; sculptured, blow-dried black hair, dark sports slacks, navy blue blazer. Looked like expensive shoes. The man's right arm was extended, and the hallway's security light glinted on a pistol.

He reached out to shake the unconscious guard's shoulder. No response. He shook him again. "Harrison!" His low voice was barely audible up here on the second floor landing. He felt the guard's dangling wrist, shook him again. But the guard snored on.

Then the man with the gun turned to peer back along the hall. Then up the staircase. They pulled back barely in time.

"He's sure to come up here," Steve whispered. "Back to the office!"

They rushed silently down the second floor's carpeted hallway. Alix had to steady the key with both hands. Then they were in the concealing darkness of Buttonwood's office. Secure or trapped?

They waited just inside the door in silence, a long, long silence. Then Steve heard a muffled footfall on the carpeting in Alix's cubicle on the other side of the door. Under the light pressure of his fingers, he felt the knob turn. The door rattled slightly.

Then, he assumed, the man with the gun moved on to check the rest of the building.

"Steve—"

He silenced her strained whisper with a finger against her lips. He pressed his ear to the varnished oak. For a long time, he heard only his own pulse throb. Then there came a distant rattle as the man apparently tried another locked door.

"Where is he now?" She stood so close that he felt her body heat.

"Third floor."

More dead-silent minutes passed, then Steve heard light footsteps descend the staircase to the first floor. He turned the knob slowly and inched the door open. Alix's cubicle held a lingering tang of lime and spice.

From downstairs came the faint sound of the rear door opening, then closing.

At the head of the stairs, Steve touched her shoulder. "Wait here." Then he crept down the steps and stood at the bottom to listen again. All he could hear now was the guard's burbling snore. He turned to motion to Alix, but she was gone.

God, had the guy faked his departure, than rushed back upstairs, waited in one of the phone bank rooms for them to reappear, then grabbed her?

Had there been time for that? They had come down the second floor hall just after they'd heard the back door close.

Steve started back up the staircase. Then he stopped. If there had been two of them—

While he stood there cursing his indecisiveness, she reappeared, holding a pair of shoes in her hand. She hurried down to him.

"I left these in the ladies' room. You sure he's gone?"

He wasn't sure of anything now. "I'm sure of nothing except that searching Pope's office at this point could be sticking our heads straight into a noose. I don't know who that guy was, but he knew the guard's name. My guess is that he's with OmniSecure, and he's gone for help." He steadied her while she slipped her shoes on.

"Why wouldn't he have used the phone, Steve?"

"Maybe he did. All the more reason for us to get out of here. But I've got to put the keys back. No sense in our leaving a blueprint."

At the reception desk, Steve snapped the key ring back in place on the guard's belt loop. The man breathed more heavily now, and he twitched in his sleep. Going further under, or about to come out of it?

The green light on the alarm panel still glowed, despite the broken pane in the rear door. The circuit was still intact. Alix armed the system, and they slipped into the vestibule. The electrical contacts, Steve noted, were on the outer door. The only alarm system he was familiar with was his own, in his house near Fort Myers. It had a thirty-second delay after it was set, long enough to permit a normal exit before the system became active. Was that standard? Surely they didn't have much time to pause in here.

He peered through the front entrance wrought iron work. The street was still deserted.

"Let's get out of this place."

The lock on the ornate entrance door clicked into place behind them. They stood on the sidewalk, both of them breathing deeply of the moist night air and, Steve realized, feeling the exhilaration of a clean escape.

"My car's parked down that way."

They walked rapidly southward on the uneven, tree-darkened sidewalk, softly crushing fallen oak catkins underfoot.

"Steve, what do we do now?"

He patted his breast pocket. "Turn this over to the U.S. Attorney first thing tomorrow, and let him take it from there."

"But you'll have to tell the U.S. attorney about tonight, won't you?"

"An edited version, leaving you out of it. I went in before closing time, hid somewhere."

"Steve, they're not going to swallow that."

"They'll have to, if I stick to it. How heavy will they come down on a man checking into his brother's murder? I'll take my chances."

The rented Buick was parked in midblock, in front of a converted townhouse set back from the street by a ragged, chest-high privet hedge. Steve reached in his pocket for his keys.

Then he caught the faintest scent of spicy lime, and the hairs on the back of his neck prickled. He knew what it meant, but much too late.

"Gammon, hold it right there!"

The voice came from behind the hedge. Steve heard Alix let out a frightened squeal. He whirled. But he already knew who was there.

"You ought to get rid of that blue Skyhawk, Gammon. It's an ID the size of a billboard."

The owner of the youthful voice with its overtone of disdain had to be the same guy who had spotted his rented Buick out here, prowled FRETSAW looking for him, then had made a sufficiently noisy exit for them to hear—and waited confidently behind the privet for him to return to the car.

A simple enough trap, and Steve had fallen straight into it. Worse, he'd brought Alix with him.

Georgie Prescott was enjoying gut-bubbling elation. Damned if he wasn't one slick security op. He'd come across Gammon's car right off, so he knew who he was looking for when he got into the FRETSAW building. Gammon must have gotten Harrison to open up, then slugged him with something comparable to a two-by-four, though Prescott hadn't found a mark on him. That was odd, but the situation was obvious.

After he'd checked the building and found no one other than the unconscious guard, something else was obvious. He didn't know the layout of the place, and he realized Gammon could futz him around in there all night. That was when Prescott hit of the idea of making an exit with just the right amount to noise, then staking out Gammon's car. Surefire, unless it wasn't Gammon's car, or unless the guy had left by taxi or something.

But to Prescott's delight, the Buick was Gammon's, and the man performed precisely as Prescott had predicted. The surprise was the appearance of the woman. Real piece of tenderloin, too, with that blonde hair, nice chest there under her gray jacket. And hips that he'd bet could kill.

Now he had them in the Buick, Gammon behind the wheel, the blonde next to him, Prescott behind her in the back seat. He could almost smell her terror, and that gave him a warm feeling between the legs.

Real neat, Prescott. Then he realized he had a problem. He needed to get to a telephone. OmniSecure, in the same austerity mode that had dictated its fleet of underpowered Chevettes, had turned down his requisition for a cellular phone for his Camaro. And there sure wasn't a phone here in Gammon's rented Skyhawk. Jesus, he was always being snagged by logistical details.

There were phones in the FRETSAW building, one of them right on the guard's desk. He'd look kinda stupid, though, now that he'd gotten them in the car here, telling Gammon to drive half a block, then ordering them out to force them around back to see if the alarm was set—

So *that* was why the broad was here: to disarm the system and let Gammon in.

Yeah, Prescott reflected, I would look stupid, and there would be too much risk in going back there. Too many opportunities for Gammon, maybe even the blonde, to make a panicky run for it, mess this up. He'd handled it neatly so far. He would keep it neat.

He jabbed the gun muzzle into the nape of the blonde's neck. "Who are you?"

She said nothing.

"Reach your purse back here, then. Slow and easy."

He opened the purse with his free hand.

"Start this thing, Gammon. I'll tell you where to turn." The blonde's name was Alix Cortland, her Woodward & Lothrop charge card told him. He was right: her medical insurance card said FRETSAW. And the little prescription vial told him what had happened to Harrison. That, he shoved in his pocket.

He told Gammon, through terse instructions at intersections, to go to Eye Street. More precisely, to the service alley behind OmniSecure's Eye Street headquarters. At one point, when Gammon appeared to balk at crossing Fourteenth, Prescott put steel in his voice and told Gammon, "You try anything out of line, and I wouldn't mind hurting this lady." In truth, he'd love to hurt the lady, in the right way. He began to think about that.

But it wasn't possible at the moment. When Gammon pulled the Skyhawk beneath the single naked bulb over OmniSecure's rear entrance in the service alley, Prescott ordered them out, then up the four concrete steps to the gray-painted steel rear door. He pressed the adjacent button.

"ID?" a metallic voice asked from the little speaker box above their heads.

"Prescott, four-three-four."

The electronic lock buzzed, and he pulled the door open with his left hand, motioning Gammon and the woman inside. They climbed a flight of concrete steps single-file, Gammon in the lead, the blonde between so that the provocative flare of her butt was level with Prescott's eyes.

He took them to OmniSecure's interrogation room, or so it was called; really more of a windowless conference room, its oddly pink walls naked except for a narrow door in the middle of the wall opposite the hall door. The room was furnished with an eight-foot-long K-Mart-class table with a top in late-century Formica woodgrain. The room also had six gray steel folding chairs, and a Coke machine in one corner. The lock on the entrance door was operable only from the hallway side.

Prescott tossed Alix Cortland's purse on the table, left the two of them in there, and threw the dead bolt from the hall side. Then he strode down the corridor to Milo Kolker's office. OmniSecure's stark hallways were gloomy enough in the daytime. They were downright dismal at night; like he imagined KGB interrogation facilities might be in Lubyanka Prison.

He snapped on Kolker's office fluorescents, made a point of sitting in Kolker's chair behind Kolker's desk, lit up a Sherman's Amigo, and dialed Kolker's home number.

When the man gave him a sleepy "Yeah?" Prescott wondered about Kolker's bedtime habits. It wasn't yet 9:00.

"I have them, Kolker." Prescott had a hard time suppressing a gleeful giggle. "I searched, and I detained. Gammon and a woman. Her ID says she's Alix Cortland, a FRETSAW employee."

"Any trouble, Georgie?" Not "congratulations" or "great work." Just "any trouble?"

"No. But Harrison's back there flat out. I think they gave him something. You want me to have the dispatcher here send somebody over?"

"You're not at FRETSAW?"

"I'm at OmniSecure. I got them buttoned up in the interrogation room."

"Oh, fine, Georgie. Just what we need for a low-profile project. You find out what they were after?"

Prescott realized that, in point of fact, he hadn't found out much of anything. "I thought you'd want to handle that part, Kolker." Not a bad recovery.

"You keep them right there, Georgie. I'll call the dispatcher, and I'll apprise the client, then I'll be on my way there. Leave them alone until I get there, you hear?"

That was it? The pay was good, but praise was sure hard to come by in this grim outfit.

Behind the narrow door on the far side of the barren conference room was a bathroom, equally austere with a toilet, beat-up porcelain sink, and a pink plastic wastebasket for used paper towels. No window.

"They have no right to do this, you know," Alix said from one of the hard chairs.

"I'd say it's moot. I had no right to be in the FRETSAW building."

"But this is *kidnapping,* Steve. When we get out of here, I'm going straight to—"

He held up his hand. Something had just occurred to him. He gestured around the room, then cupped his ear.

"I don't give a damn if the room is bugged," she said bitterly. "They have no right."

"Possession is nine points." He felt oddly subdued in this pink cell. Not eager to argue. Even relaxed a few notches, after the tension of prowling FRETSAW.

She fell silent, then she took her purse from the conference table and went into the bathroom. He shifted on the unyielding chair. The kid who had caught them hadn't come across as much of a slick operator. Steve still had Buttonwood's passport and deposit book in his pocket. These people had him, but he had those.

If they body-searched him, they surely would find them. Would it be possible to conceal the two documents in here, then later notify the police that he had slipped the incriminating passport and deposit book under the carpeting? If there were carpeting on this naked tan linoleum. Taped beneath the table? No tape. Up under the Coke machine? Why hadn't he had the sense to slip the two documents out of his pocket behind the front seat cushion of the Buick during the drive here?

Then he realized that all they had to do to get him to tell

them anything they wanted to know would be to threaten to harm Alix. Would they dare? This was obviously the dirty action arm of FRETSAW, and they had dared to kill, hadn't they? He'd gotten her into this. That was bad enough. He wasn't going to jeopardize her further.

In the end, he did nothing with the two documents. He left them where they were, in his sports jacket pocket.

When Alix came out of the bathroom, he inserted quarters in the Coke machine. They nursed the soft drinks in silence. The overhead fluorescent fixture buzzed softly. The Coke machine's refrigeration unit cut in periodically with a click, then a ragged hum. The corridor outside was dead-silent.

"What do you think they're doing?" she asked in an uncharacteristically subdued voice.

He leaned back in his chair. "It's pretty obvious, Alix. They're letting us sweat."

14.

A column of ice speared straight down Horace Buttonwood's spine. It shattered into frigid shards that permeated his gut, then coalesced into a cold, hard lump just beneath his heart. He needed a few more seconds to try to jerk himself back together.

"Give me that again, Kolker."

"Like I told you, Mr. Buttonwood, this guy Gammon was loose in your building for maybe an hour, along with one of your people, an Alix Cortland. They immobilized our first-shift night man, and secured the alarm system. When our monitoring room reported the system disarmed after your closing time, I sent one of our people out there. He detained Gammon and Cortland leaving the building."

"Where are they now?" Buttonwood managed to keep his voice near normal.

"At OmniSecure. I figured you'd want them held."

"Did they take anything?"

Kolker's silence disturbed him.

"Kolker? Didn't your man search them?"

Kolker cleared his throat. "He found what they'd given the guard to flatten him."

"I'm talking about a body search. A strip search."

Kolker cleared his throat again.

Had they found the documents on Gammon or Alix and were holding out on him, Buttonwood wondered? The anonymously numbered Cayman bank passbook wasn't negotiable without his Butler A. Gridley signature—but the copyable signature was in the passport, wasn't it?

More likely, the documents were safe in his office, and Kolker was only suffering from the embarrassment of just realizing his man's stupid oversight in not having thoroughly searched his two detainees.

"I'll take care of it," Kolker said lamely.

So they didn't have the documents.

"No, leave them for me. First, I want to check the building."

"I'll meet you there, Mr. Buttonwood. I already sent two people over to take care of the guard, but I want to check out the situation personally."

And salvage some face, Kolker?

"It will take me about twenty-five minutes to get across town. Just try to stabilize things, Kolker." Whatever that meant. Buttonwood didn't quite have himself together yet.

He gunned his metallic-green Audi south on the Beltway to Exit 19. When he was inbound on the John Hanson Highway, Buttonwood tried to sort the thing out. That goddamned pit bull of a Gammon had lived up to his reputation for persistence, all right. He would never make the CIA or FBI professionally jealous, but the man had managed to find his brother's body, connect that with Van Hayden's death, worm his way into Alix's confidence, secure the Advisory Council list, then interview a number of the people on it, evidently see through the New York dock charade Pope had so intricately arranged, and now he had gotten himself through FRETSAW security and into the building after hours. Jesus. What had the man done in there? This was the biggest score of Buttonwood's life, and Gammon's tenacity threatened to unravel it.

Or did it? Buttonwood hadn't planned to fold FRETSAW

this early, and Pope might give him a hard time, but flexibility was the soul of survival.

At 9:12 P.M., Buttonwood braked the Audi to a rocking stop behind a big gun-metal-gray Mercury station wagon in front of FRETSAW. On the sidewalk beside the Merc, he recognized Milo Kolker; wide, compact, overdramatically dressed in some sort of dark jumpsuit. What did he think they were going to do? Storm the place?

Kolker nodded a greeting, grim-faced. "The guard was drugged, all right. My people took him to a doctor we have on call. That'll maintain confidentiality. Incidentally, my man had to break the glass on the rear door when he responded to the alert."

"Alert?"

"OmniSecure alarm systems are double monitored. An amber light shows in our monitoring room when the system is armed; a red light if the alarm is tripped. Also, our guards check in by phone once each hour. When FRETSAW's amber went out during normal activation, and the guard here didn't call in, I declared an alert, sent a man over. He saw the guard was out of it, so he broke in through the back. I had our people nail temporary plywood over the broken pane." Kolker looked down at the sidewalk, then back up. "Our man got in too easily, Mr. Buttonwood. That back entry ought to be secured with a solid steel door."

Buttonwood listened with towering impatience. The important point was not how OmniSecure discovered how Gammon got into FRETSAW, but what Gammon did after he was in there.

"You finished?"

"Yeah, Mr. Buttonwood. I—"

Buttonwood was already past him, up the steps and pushing through the outer door. Kolker rushed to follow.

"Check out this floor, Kolker."

"Already did."

"Check it again. Then the third floor. I'll take the second." He didn't want Kolker hanging over his shoulder in his office.

The blocky OmniSecure man strode toward the rear of the building in a combat-ready crouch. Buttonwood took the main staircase two steps at a time, scrabbling in his pocket for his office key. He felt a small lessening of tension when he found the office door locked. But that didn't prove anything, did it? It was a spring lock, not a dead bolt. With cold fingers, he inserted his key, shoved the door open, closed it behind him, clicked on the recessed overhead fluorescents, and rushed straight to the bookcase.

He yanked out Willis's fund-raising text. Shook it. Flipped the cover open. *Son of a bitch!* Gammon and the woman had found them.

Now what?

He paced the office. Now *what?* He forced himself to sit behind his big desk, and found that he was pulling at his beard, literally tugging it. *Think.*

Since Kolker had made no mention of the passport or deposit book, either OmniSecure was retaining them for no good purpose, or Gammon and Alix had hidden them. Or still had them. He doubted the first possibility—because of what Kolker had said, and because OmniSecure was in this too deeply to try that kind of double cross. The location of the documents lay with Gammon in either case. Shouldn't be too difficult to find that out. With OmniSecure's persuasive help, if need be. Kolker had already killed for FRETSAW, so he wouldn't be overly squeamish about applying basic motivation to one Steven Gammon.

Assume, Buttonwood told himself, that I will reclaim the documents. Would Gammon have managed to notify anyone that he had them? Federal offices had been closed by the time Gammon entered FRETSAW. But D.C. police never closed. The FBI surely had night numbers. Yet no police or feds had shown up here. Nobody had appeared here but the OmniSecure people.

Before he'd been apprehended by OmniSecure, had Gammon perhaps phoned his sister-in-law? A possibility there. Anyone else Gammon might know in Washington, someone in a position of authority?

That was an unanswerable question, and its potential answer was devastating. FRETSAW, Buttonwood realized at that instant, was finished.

He had hoped to milk this efficient cash cow for at least another six months. Yet $4.8 million was quite a haul. By far the biggest of his life. And it wasn't worth risking, just to reach his $5 million dream goal.

Pope had a like amount in his own Cayman account. They had consistently split the skim 50-50. So Buttonwood's Greyhound bus-borne inspiration had netted almost $10 million. Not the greatest score of all time, but it ranked up there among big-dollar cons.

Should he alert Pope, or let him twist in the aftermath wind? Richardson Pope had been a pain in the backside since he'd advanced the start-up money, now fully repaid. Pope had worked relentlessly to take over the entire operation, yet Buttonwood felt compelled to alert the man. Since they had separate numbered accounts, money was not a consideration. What Buttonwood did not relish was the thought of six feet four of hairless fury relentlessly tracking him down after Pope got out of federal custody some years hence. That was not a comforting thought at all.

Buttonwood picked up his phone and tapped in Pope's number. Waited, fingers of his free hand twisting in the beard. If Pope wasn't in his Chevy Chase apartment on this most crucial of all evenings—

"Yes?"

"It's Horace." He rapidly sketched the events of this unsettling and pivotal night, his voice strained by a rapidly drying throat. Sweat ran along his nose, or was that tears of apprehension? When he finished the distressing litany, his ear was filled with silence. Then he heard Richardson Pope draw a long breath.

"No question about it. We have to quietly and promptly fold our tent." The bald giant sounded surprisingly calm and unvindictive. Then he said, "You were an ass, Buttonwood, to keep those items in your office."

They'd had this discussion before. A safe-deposit box was out of the question, of course, because its access would have been limited to banking hours. Buttonwood had held his unshakable conviction that the office, secured during nonbusiness hours by the building's burglar alarm system and an armed guard, was a hell of a lot safer repository than an apartment. Maybe Chevy Chase was less prone to residential break-ins than Lanham, but logic had told him FRETSAW was more secure than either. Tonight Gammon had blown that theory into so much crapola, and had made Buttonwood look as naive as the moneyed simpletons FRETSAW had persuaded to pour hard cash into "getting the word out to America." That had been one of his more effective direct mail slogans, resulting in a seven-figure take.

He wasn't going to argue fine points now. "Pope, there's no way around this, I'm afraid. If Gammon managed to use a phone before he was apprehended by our people—"

"I'm gone, Buttonwood. First plane to Miami, then a shuttle to the Caymans."

FRETSAW had just collapsed. Pope was heading for the nearest exit. But if Gammon *had* managed to contact the police, FBI . . . hell, even the postal authorities before he and Alix had been stopped, it was entirely possible that local airports—National, Dulles and Baltimore-Washington International—would be shortly, perhaps already were, under surveillance. Buttonwood didn't want to chance that.

"Good luck, Pope." That sounded inadequate, even hypocritical, given their near-adversarial relationship over the past months. But he didn't know what else to say. This hurried parting had been inevitable from the start, he realized, but now it seemed so anticlimactic. There should have been a champagne toast to the intricate scheme that had netted them close to ten mill. Shared grins. Some kind of celebration. But the cut-off click of Pope's phone was all there was.

Buttonwood found Kolker in the second floor hall. The rent-a-security-chief jabbed his thumb upward at the third floor. "Nothing disturbed up there that I could spot."

"Forget it. You've got them at OmniSecure. That's where we're going. I'll follow you." If Gammon hadn't yet disclosed what he'd done with the documents, Buttonwood didn't want to give Kolker the opportunity to get it out of him without Buttonwood's being there.

Somewhere between FRETSAW and OmniSecure's drab Eye Street building, the idea came to him. But first he had to have that damned passport. Then he could leave with only the clothes on his back. And he sure as hell needed the deposit book, or he would be in fat trouble as soon as the couple hundred dollars in his wallet ran out.

Think of this as just another fire to be put out, he told himself. The Van Hayden thing had been bad, and he'd handled that. How could he have foreseen in his remotest fantasies that in the intricate laundering process, Advisory Council member Walter Van Hayden, Esq., retired, would have a holdover client who had a disastrously placed friend?

Buttonwood and Pope had established separate accounts in money-market trusts. Buttonwood's was in Boston. His money-market trust accepted Buttonwood's multicheck deposits in his "Horace Buttonwood, Executive Director, FRETSAW" account. It distributed withdrawal checks to him made out the same way. He then exchanged those withdrawal checks, always in amounts under the $10,000 IRS reportable transaction break-point, for cashier's checks made out to Butler Gridley. Four Washington area banks were used in rotation for that step, and he appropriately adjusted FRETSAW's books to cover.

Off went the cashier's checks to the Bank of the Islands, Grand Cayman, where a 1976 Bank Secrecy Law made it a criminal offense for a bank to release any information whatever to anyone concerning a customer's account.

The system was far from foolproof. Buttonwood and Pope, who used a similar mechanism, were well aware of that. But it was convoluted enough to gain them time in an investigation beyond FRETSAW's protective set of ostensibly legitimate books, which were made readily available to anyone who asked to see them.

As he followed Kolker's Mercury wagon to Eye Street, Buttonwood vividly recalled the near-calamity that converted Van Hayden from an asset into a liability. He had been a particularly lucrative mark, and Buttonwood had handed Jim Gammon the assignment to sell Van Hayden on a planned giving arrangement whereby the attorney would turn his assets over to FRETSAW, then receive the income tax-free for the balance of his lifetime. That setup, common enough in the high-income world, would have offered FRETSAW some fascinating possibilities. A timely Van Hayden demise, for example. But all that went by the boards when Buttonwood received the agitated phone call from the man.

"Horace, a peculiar sort of situation has come up," Van Hayden had said, in that clipped, deadly-calm voice the rich use in announcing distress. "A former client of mine, whom I've been working on for a FRETSAW contribution, has a friend on the board of the Washington Potomac Trust—"

It was at this point that Buttonwood's pulse began to gallop.

"—and this friend of his told him that FRETSAW has a very active account there."

"Washington Potomac Trust?" Buttonwood echoed. How much had Van Hayden stumbled on?

"This friend told my client that a recent audit turned up a record of several FRETSAW checks having been cashed, with the funds reassigned to a Butler Gridman or Grid-something. Nearly $88,000 worth."

Ice points of frigid sweat erupted in Buttonwood's armpits.

"I assume," the deadly flat voice forged on, "that those were perfectly legitimate transactions, Horace, but your personal assurance—"

"They were to pay certain invoices, Walter, if you follow what I'm saying. Obviously, I didn't want it entered in the books here."

Van Hayden had been an avid donor whom Buttonwood had correctly judged to be more interested in direct action than in passive advertising campaigns. He had been discreetly apprised of FRETSAW's nonexistent arms supply operation, whereupon his contributions had increased to the Advisory Council level.

Would he swallow Buttonwood's implication that the Grid-something checks were clandestine payments for hard goods?

He'd seemed to at the time, but Van Hayden proved as deceptive as Buttonwood. The next time Buttonwood tried to recycle one of the money-market withdrawal checks through Washington Potomac Trust, he was told to "wait just one moment." One hell of a traumatic moment. He couldn't just walk out. They had FRETSAW's name, address, phone number. He stood on jellied legs until his contact reappeared and told him the cashier's check would have to be issued in FRETSAW's name.

"Fine," Buttonwood had replied, but that wasn't what he thought. He never went back to that bank, and he instinctively knew Van Hayden's client's friend was probing.

So Van Hayden had stumbled on part of it, and FRETSAW had kept tabs on Van Hayden through frequent and subtle contacts with Arthur MacIlvane in Phoenix. MacIlvane had unwittingly fingered Van Hayden's sudden departure for Hawaii. Jim Gammon's simultaneous disappearance from Washington had been simple enough to trace. All it had taken was a phone call by FRETSAW to American Express. Coach fare to Honolulu had been approved that same morning. OmniSecure subcontracted a day's surveillance on Oahu until Kolker and Prescott could get there.

The Hawaii terminations had pulled the muscle out of the Washington Potomac Trust's embryonic investigation.

Now, here was another fire—this one potentially cataclysmic. As Buttonwood pulled in behind Kolker's Merc in the alley behind OmniSecure's glum headquarters, he felt the same nauseating stomach clamp that had assailed him when Van Hayden had made that fateful call short weeks ago.

He got out into air so moisture-laden that it drifted through the wan light from the single bulb over OmniSecure's rear door in visible swirls. He followed Kolker up the gritty backstairs, along the grim, carpetless second floor hallway to a door, beside which perched a youthful-looking man in a dark sports coat, his chair tilted back against the wall.

"Georgie Prescott, Mr. Buttonwood. He apprehended your trespassers."

Buttonwood nodded. "Good work, Prescott." He'd heard Kolker speak of this man, but had never met him. Prescott looked surprisingly youthful and—what? Feral? Was that what made Buttonwood glad Prescott had not thought to search Gammon and Alix; that Prescott apparently hadn't discovered the documents?

"I'll see them alone," Buttonwood told Kolker.

The security chief nodded at Prescott, and Prescott reached over his shoulder to twist the toggle on the door's external lock. Interesting arrangement.

The two of them looked up as he entered. They seemed properly shaken, though he could sense that Gammon's rising irritation would shortly blossom into anger that would benefit nobody.

"You realize this is kidnapping, Buttonwood. A federal crime." Gammon was reaching for the initiative.

"And you realize, I'm sure, that you are not in police custody, not charged with breaking and entering, not charged with theft. Not charged with anything. Why don't we keep it that way?"

He pulled out one of the cold metal chairs and sat stiffly at one end of the conference table. "My God, Alix, I'd expected better of you. You disappoint me. You really do disappoint me."

He resisted his strong impulse to leap out of the chair, grab Gammon by the lapels of his sports coat and shout at him.

"This is a deplorable situation." He struggled mightily to keep his voice level, under control. "But we can resolve it quite easily. I'm going to ask you this just once: where are the passport and the deposit book?"

Neither of them said anything. Alix studied her nails. Gammon fixed him with that smoldering glare.

"All right, if you want it this way. I don't have the time to conduct one of those charming, Hollywood-style cat-and-mouse interviews between captor and captive. I want to know what you have done with those two items, Gammon, and I want to know it now."

The stubborn bastard didn't move, didn't deflect his challenging stare as much as a degree. Buttonwood's anger surged.

"Kolker!"

The door from the hallway opened. "Sir?"

"I need information from these people, and I need it now."

"Right. Prescott, you heard that."

The young OmniSecure man strode into the room, his angular jaw set in a weird little smile.

"Strip search!" Prescott ordered. He turned to Alix and stood very close. "You first. Everything off, down to the skin."

"What the hell, Buttonwood!" Gammon exploded. "Leave her alone. Your problem is with me."

"Simply tell me where you put those documents, Gammon, and she will be left intact." Buttonwood was impressed with the way the young OmniSecure man had cut straight through the bullshit and hit Gammon where it had counted, without even touching him.

"Everything off, right now," Prescott repeated.

Alix stood slowly, her face white. "It's all right, Steve," she said softly. She slipped off her jacket.

Gammon jumped up from his chair so suddenly that it toppled over backward and folded flat with a metallic crash.

"The hell it's all right! What's next, Buttonwood? Gang rape by your boys here?" He thrust his hand in his jacket's inside pocket, jerked out the two Leatherette booklets and threw them on the table. "There are your goddamned documents!"

Buttonwood scooped them up and turned to Kolker. "I suspect this wouldn't have been at all necessary if your man at FRETSAW had half a brain." In fact, he realized, the guard's apparent incompetence was going to cost a couple hundred thousand through FRETSAW's premature demise.

"You've got what you wanted," Gammon rapped behind him. "Now we would like to get out of here."

Buttonwood swung around slowly. "You must be joking."

Out in the hall with Kolker and Prescott, he said, "Hold them in there until I tell you otherwise." His brain was clicking nicely now, the numbing shock of the missing passport and deposit book wiped away by their recovery. "Kolker, I need a phone and some privacy." Pope was welcome to the risk of airline terminals here and in Miami. On the drive here from FRETSAW, Buttonwood had been struck with the possibility of what should be a far less exposed and probably more pleasant exodus. And it offered a neat—and final—solution to the Gammon-Alix problem.

Kolker showed Buttonwood to his own office and closed the door to leave Buttonwood in privacy with the phone. Buttonwood, referring to the list of key numbers he habitually carried in his wallet, dialed the unusual combination. After an infuriating delay, Burlington Claiborne came on the line.

"Horace, Burlington." Mindful that Claiborne was using his mobile phone, and that put this call into open transmission, he said, "Please call me right back from a pay phone." And he gave Claiborne OmniSecure's number and Kolker's extension.

The desk phone rang in less than three minutes.

"I assume, Burlington, that you are still docked in Annapolis?"

"Yes. Yes, we're still here."

"You recall that you several times offered me a cruise on your impressive yacht?"

"The, uh, offer still holds, Horace." Claiborne sounded like a man regretting an invitation tendered in a moment of unguarded expansiveness, but too much of a gentleman to renege. Buttonwood was counting on that.

"When would you like to go?" Claiborne asked hesitantly.

"Tonight."

"Tonight. *Tonight?*" Silence.

Buttonwood said, "It's for the good of FRETSAW, Burlington."

"Just a cruise? How can that . . . How far? To where?

"South. Past Florida."

"Pete's sake, Horace, that's not the kind of jaunt you take by just shoving off and turning south. It takes preparation."

"Like what?"

"Like provisioning. How many people are we talking about?"

"Five." Himself, of course. Plus Alix and Gammon, and the two OmniSecure men to assure Buttonwood's rapidly evolving plan.

"Five of you and two of us." Claiborne's voice was far from enthusiastic.

"Who's the other?"

"Rustie. You met her. She's fully checked out on the operation of this big bathtub toy. She cooks, navigates, takes the helm. I need her."

For other services as well, no doubt. Now Buttonwood recalled the small, red-haired woman Claiborne traveled with.

"Okay, so it will total seven, Burlington." Claiborne seemed to need some incentive. "You will bill FRETSAW for the entire trip," Buttonwood threw in, "so don't worry about that end of it. How long will it take?"

"Where are you talking about going?"

"I told you, past Florida. How long that far?"

"In 340-nautical-mile legs, it should—"

"We can't do it nonstop?"

"Are you kidding?" Claiborne gave him a disparaging chuckle. "The cruising range at twenty knots can be stretched to 340 nautical miles before refueling. That's just under four hundred land miles. We can make it to . . . say, Wilmington, North Carolina, on the first leg. We would be coming in on the fumes, but I think we could stretch it that far. Then probably Jacksonville, Florida. Miami, then where?"

"I'll tell you when we get aboard." It could be imprudent to tell Claiborne more than he needed to know at the moment. "We'll be in Annapolis around midnight."

"Horace, damn it, I—"

"This is important to the organization, Burlington." Buttonwood could sense that wasn't going to be enough. "It's so important that I'll tell you what FRETSAW can do. I can swing a, let's say, $20,000 charter fee for the use of the boat."

"Horace, you're aware that money is not a problem."

Jesus, the man's bullheadedness was going to blow this nicely evolving bailout into rat shit!

"There is something you might consider," Claiborne tossed into Buttonwood's mute desperation. "I've been hoping that a position on the FRETSAW Board might, uh, one day open up."

"That," Buttonwood said in relief he hoped wasn't obvious, "I can arrange." Hell, he could offer Claiborne the whole damned now-collapsed operation. Anything. Claiborne's payoff for this wasn't going to involve cash or prestige.

15.

All six of them crowded into Kolker's Mercury station wagon in the alley. Steve was wedged in the rear seat between the blow-dried man who had caught them outside the FRETSAW building and the other, more muscular OmniSecure employee, who was obviously the younger man's superior. The young one was named Prescott. George Prescott. The other, Steve noted, insisted on calling him Georgie in an unmistakably derisive tone. Georgie's boss was Kolker, so Buttonwood called him.

Up front, Alix sat between Buttonwood and a bull-necked third OmniSecure minion Kolker had addressed as Mason. In the snatches of conversation Steve had heard as the six of them descended the echoing rear stairwell, Mason's job was to "bring back my car." Kolker had said that, so the wagon was his. Mason was along to drive it back here, which meant the rest of them were headed elsewhere. All five?

In what had seemed like an interminable wait in the barren room upstairs, Steve had tried desperately to devise an escape, first from the room, then from the building. His jangled imagination insisted on flashing ahead, to a deserted stretch of road. He and Alix marched at gunpoint into isolated woods.

The younger OmniSecure man ordering them to turn, face him. A man like him would want to see their faces as his pistol flashed blinding blue-white.

Not possible? Anything was possible when a con artist with a history like Buttonwood's found himself in a bind with close to $5 million at stake.

But the car was to return empty, except for Mason.

For several blocks, Steve was disoriented as Mason expertly wound the Mercury through the thin 11:00 P.M. traffic of this deteriorating section northeast of downtown Washington. Then they swung left, off a murky side street into brightly lighted New York Avenue. A few blocks further, they passed the entrance to the National Arboretum, barreled straight through the splash of lights at the interchange with the Baltimore-Washington Parkway, and they were now on the John Hanson Highway. Route 50 to Annapolis.

Annapolis. Of course. Burlington Claiborne's big, ocean-going diesel yacht was the perfect getaway vehicle. A fast cruise down the East Coast with two fewer passengers arriving in the Caymans.

Thin rain began to slick the pavement. Mason switched on the wipers. The driver, Alix, and Buttonwood were silhouetted against the occasional flares of oncoming headlights. The two OmniSecure men flanking Steve were only shadows in the darkness, but Steve could smell Kolker's faint aura of meaty sweat and Prescott's aftershave. Or maybe cologne. Lime-based spice. Still viable at this time of night? The guy must have splashed himself with it just before he'd gone to FRETSAW.

The only sounds were Prescott's wheezy breathing, the muted rumble of the Merc's big engine, the tires snicking along wet pavement, and the monotonous clop-clop of the wipers. Nobody said a word for miles.

Then they swung sharply right off Route 50 into a broad Annapolis approach highway. The misty pool of city lights ahead was deceptively reassuring. What could he do, wedged back here between Buttonwood's two security men? They didn't even have to shove their gun muzzles in his sides to immobilize him. They had only to sit here.

The fat-necked driver rolled the Merc into Church Circle's one-way counterclockwise pattern, turned out of it into Duke of Gloucester Street. The pavement arrowed downslope to the waterfront. Another turn, sharply left along Compromise, then they stopped at the end of the dock where Claiborne's fifty-three-footer was a sleek silhouette against the lights of the Naval Academy across a black arm of the harbor.

"Out," Kolker ordered. Steve followed Prescott out of the wagon to the wet asphalt. Kolker leaned back in to say something to Mason that Steve couldn't catch. The Merc's idling engine picked up smoothly, then the station wagon's tail lights dwindled up Compromise Street.

The five of them walked out on the rain-slickened boards of the dock in a compact group, Buttonwood in the lead, Kolker and Prescott behind. Not a chance here, either, Steve realized. The dock area was deserted in post-midnight limbo. No traffic on the adjacent street. No one visible on any of the gently swaying power cruisers and sailboats moored nearby. Rising wind drifted cold drizzle into his face.

Kolker kicked at a weathered piling. "I hate boats, Mr. Buttonwood," Steve heard him murmur. "There are easier ways to do this. Plenty of side roads and woods. I could—"

"No!" Buttonwood growled. "You and your people have helped put us here, damn it. No more opportunities to bungle. You know what micromanagement is? It's me, on site, so I know this is done right."

Then Burlington Claiborne's broad shoulders loomed above them on the forward deck. "Bring your people aboard, Horace." He lifted the hinged section of railing and stood aside as they stepped up from the dock to the deck and filed the few steps aft to enter the sumptuous salon.

Prescott offered a low whistle. At the elegant furnishings, or the redheaded sprawled on the L-shaped sofa with *The New York Times* crossword puzzle?

"Georgie . . ." Kolker warned.

Claiborne followed them in and secured the doorway. "Welcome aboard, gentlemen. And lady. This is Rustie, my galley slave." Was Claiborne's offhandedness a trifle forced?

She was a neat package of frizzily curled carrot-orange ringlets, blue pixie eyes, snub nose, pointed little chin, and the rest was a lot of skin that showed past her black tank top and gold shorts, all of it heavily dusted with tiny freckles, cinnamon sprinkles on a creamy dessert. She looked like a vapid confection, along for Claiborne's convenience, but she had nearly completed the crossword puzzle.

"Rustie, this is Horace Buttonwood, executive director of FRETSAW, and, well, greetings again, Mr. Mifflin. I'm sorry, Horace, you'll have to take it from here."

"Alix Cortland, my executive assistant," Buttonwood said smoothly. "My associates, Mr. Kolker and Mr. Prescott."

Alix managed to catch Steve's eye. She had noted it, too; the surrealistic aspect of all this. As if it were a pleasure cruise. And Buttonwood had let the Mifflin reference ride. The OmniSecure hired guns were his "associates," now.

"Rustie and I use the master stateroom aft below," the big yachtsman said, smoothing back his bronze mane. "The guest stateroom forward sleeps two in a queen-size. Below there are two stacked bunks in a small utility stateroom forward of the engine room. You'll have to sort yourselves out." He looked past them. "No luggage?"

Buttonwood ignored the question. "Mr. Mifflin, why don't you and Alix take that room below?"

"Ooh, friendly!" Rustie chirped from the sofa.

Buttonwood ignored that, too. "I will be in the forward stateroom. Kolker and Prescott will make do here in the salon and on the bridge. If I recall, Burlington, there are two sizable lounges up there."

If Claiborne was thrown by these dictated and peculiar arrangements, and the total lack of luggage for a trip of more than a few days, he showed no obvious sign of it. He did smooth his hair again, a recurring gesture Steve didn't recall from his first visit here.

Buttonwood offered Claiborne a wan smile. "I assume we are ready to shove off?"

"Fortunately I topped off the tanks this morning, and Rustie found a store open after you called this evening. Catering by 7-Eleven, I'm afraid, but when you give short notice, you have to expect short shrift."

A touch of irritation there?

Buttonwood turned to Steve and Alix. He nodded downward. Behind them, Prescott stepped closer.

"Time to go below," Buttonwood said. Again, Claiborne's expression was unreadable.

"The door between the galley and the inside steering station." Claiborne pointed to a narrow doorway set in the salon's forward bulkhead. "The bunkroom access is the portside hatch at the bottom of the ladder. That's the door on the left at the bottom of the steps."

"Prescott," Buttonwood ordered, "help them find it."

The salon's forward door opened into a narrow stairwell, at the foot of which was a short passageway with three doors. Prescott shut the salon door behind them, followed them down the four teak steps, then checked each of the doors at the bottom. Straight ahead was the guest stateroom Buttonwood had claimed for himself, a generous space in mahogany veneer and cream Formica, dominated by the sprawling bed. Above its headboard, a broad window, now with its gold drapes drawn, looked out on the small front deck.

Prescott closed the access to the stateroom and shoved open the door on the right. Behind it was the hallway access to the stateroom's small bath. Then he opened the portside door, stood back, and motioned Steve and Alix to descend the five narrow steps that jutted from the midships bulkhead of their little prison chamber.

The bunks were set in the far wall, one above the other. The room—more of a cubicle—had a skinny closet just aft of the bunks, a small built-in storage cabinet forward, and a starboard doorway adjacent to the steps. It opened into a minimal bathroom.

"Stay put," Prescott ordered. He slid open and inspected the mirrored medicine cabinet in the bath. Nothing in the way of potential weapons in there, Steve noted, unless he intended to gag Prescott to death with Crest or knock him flat with Brut fumes. The guest razor was a Gillette Atra. Damned hard to inflict more than a skin scrape with that.

A metal hatchway was set in the room's aft bulkhead. That one, Steve saw past Prescott's shoulder, led into the now-silent midships engine compartment.

Prescott shut the hatch and turned quickly. "This'll do fine. Have fun," he said as he climbed back up the access steps. "You'll have to be acrobats on one of those two-by-four bunks." The upper door slammed shut.

Alix sank to the lower bunk. "You know what they're going to do, don't you, Steve?"

"Do I?"

"It's obvious. On their way to the Caymans, they're going to . . . lose us."

He didn't answer. She had the picture, all right.

"So here we are," she said bitterly, "down in the windowless, upholstered bilge of this floating hotel suite, one outside access, which is straight into the salon where at least one of Buttonwood's thugs is sure to be. And there isn't a damned thing down here to use as a weapon. Nothing but toothbrushes, toothpaste, soap, mouthwash, and shaving stuff in the medicine cabinet. Only blankets in the closet. Not even a stray coat hanger. Nothing we can pry loose as a club. My God, Steve, these people mean to kill us, and we're forced to just sit here and wait for it to happen."

"They won't do it while we're tied up to an Annapolis dock, Alix."

In stunning response to that hollow reassurance, they heard an electric starter motor whine on the other side of the aft bulkhead. Then one after the other, the twin Marlin V-12s thundered into life. Feet scurried and lines dropped overhead. The brown indoor-outdoor carpeted decking beneath their feet vibrated as the *Take Over* swung slowly away from its mooring and drummed out of Annapolis Harbor into the mouth of the Severn River. Then the big boat heeled southeast into the black expanse of the Chesapeake Bay.

When he awoke in the guest stateroom forward, Buttonwood lingered a few moments in the comfortable airfoam bed, his mind racing. This was going extremely well, this hastily assembled escape cruise of his. He had posted Prescott in the salon and Kolker on the open bridge where Claiborne had elected to be the first to take the helm. There was an inside steering station in the front right corner of the salon, Buttonwood had noted. If they hit bad weather, Claiborne could handle the boat from there. Or Kolker, or even Prescott. Buttonwood had instructed them both to observe closely, ask questions, learn to operate the boat.

A few days from now, they would have to do just that, because Claiborne and his little frizzy-haired boat buddy were not scheduled to complete the return trip.

"Jesus, we can't navigate this thing back to Annapolis," Kolker had protested in their subdued conversation just before they had gotten under way. They were alone in the salon. Prescott had been despatched to the bridge to watch and learn. And to preclude any unconstructive moves Claiborne might attempt. Buttonwood was not totally sold on the man's FRETSAW loyalty. The redhead had retired to the master stateroom below to rest up for her coming watch several hours hence. She didn't look as if she could handle a canoe, but Claiborne assured them she'd know what she was doing at the helm of this big bastard. Gammon and Alix, Prescott had assured Buttonwood, were secure in the below-decks bunkroom because its only topside egress was into the salon.

"You won't have to bring the boat back here," Buttonwood

had assured Kolker. "We need Claiborne to get us there, but he's a potential liability after that. He can go over the side anytime after you leave Grand Cayman. And his girlfriend. Then all you and Prescott have to do is steer in close to the Florida coast at night and sink this ark."

"*Sink* it! What happens to us?"

"You've been on the bridge. You saw what's under that canvas cover behind the lounges up there."

"Looked like a boat."

"It's a little Pursuit with an outboard. You bang some holes in this thing's hull, launch the Pursuit, and go ashore in South Florida."

Buttonwood wasn't sure whether that plan would work. He didn't have to be. By the time Kolker and Prescott went through all that, struggled ashore on some deserted Florida Atlantic Coast beach, then flew back to Washington to find there was no FRETSAW, no payoff, he would be long gone from Grand Cayman, fairly choking on money. More money than he'd dreamed of, until he'd dreamed up FRETSAW.

"The redhead, too," Kolker said hollowly.

"Claiborne said they're a team, so she goes over the side with him." Buttonwood marveled at how glibly he was able to order . . . death. From stealing tires to this in a mere thirty years hadn't been all that difficult, had it?

"Gammon and the blonde," Kolker persisted. "When?"

"Quite promptly, Kolker. The less time Gammon has to think, the better."

"That amateur?"

"That amateur has come on with the determination of a mongoose, Kolker. And don't underestimate Alix." He had, and she'd gotten him to open the door to his past just a crack, which was enough for "that amateur," Gammon, to lever into near disaster.

"Okay," Kolker had agreed. "Whenever you give the word. Four terminations, Mr. Buttonwood. That calls for a substantial bonus."

"Mr. Pope will see to that, as soon as you return to Washington." Double cross all around, Buttonwood. Easy when you know how, but you'd better never show your face in the U.S. of A. ever again.

He rolled out of the wide bed and pulled on his trousers. He hated sleeping in his underwear, but the guest stateroom closet contained only foul-weather gear, no spare pajamas.

Dull light outlined the window over the bed. He drew back the curtains on a world of grays. Dove-gray sky, iron-gray water. Blue-gray, low-lying land distantly left and right. Port and starboard, Claiborne. They still plowed down the bay. Twenty or so knots to stretch fuel, the big yachtsman had told him. A little over that in miles per hour.

He checked his watch. Not much past 6:00 A.M. Less than five hours' sleep, and he didn't feel all that tired. Showed what tension could do for you.

Five hours at, say, twenty miles per. That put them one hundred miles down the Chesapeake. That was Virginia's eastern shore over there on the left . . . port. If it was like the eastern shore of Maryland, they could keep it. He'd been over there three times to nudge loose a sizable contribution from a well-heeled chicken raiser near Salisbury. The country was flat as piss on a pine board, and the people were hard-headed and tough to convince. He'd had to work for those eastern shore bucks.

Buttonwood found toothbrush and toothpaste in the small bath off the guest stateroom. He squirted an overload of paste on the small brush and realized he wasn't quite as together as he'd thought. Small wonder. He had engineered a cruise on a true ship of fools. "You can fool some of the people all of the time," he'd told Richardson Pope when they'd initiated FRET-SAW, "and those are the people we're after."

He rinsed his mouth and wiped his mustache clean. "Four fools, anyway," he muttered to his reflection. Surely Gammon and Alix knew this was no return trip for them.

He stepped into the narrow passage between the bathroom

bulkhead and the entrance to the bunkroom below. Prescott sat facing him at the top of the four steps that led up to the door into the salon. He looked frowsy, his cobra jawline darkened with stubble.

"You here all night?"

Prescott nodded. "Me here, Kolker up on the bridge."

"Bring them up to the salon, then get yourself some sleep."

"Where? Your stateroom?"

"No." Damned if he wanted to share bedsheets with Prescott. There was something twisted about the man. "Use one of the bunks below."

He pushed past the OmniSecure man and opened the upper doorway, instantly salivating at the rich smell of coffee that permeated the warm salon.

Claiborne was up here alone, relaxed at the round portside table, an overly handsome asshole in white ducks, yellow polo shirt, and a ridiculously jaunty white yachting cap. The man was playing captain of a ship he didn't realize had already been pirated.

"Coffee, Horace?" Claiborne held up the glass pot from the automatic coffeemaker in the galley. "It's Kona, best coffee there is, in my estimation."

Was the man as incredibly stupid as he appeared? Or was he one of the nation's most adept undiscovered actors?

"Why not the best?" Claiborne chortled as Buttonwood went to the chair across from his and spooned sugar into the fine china cup. The sugar was brownish, unrefined stuff. Fad sugar. "Why not the best to celebrate the recovery of expenses, the twenty-grand charter fee, and the trusteeship?"

"You want it all? I thought money wasn't much of a consideration."

"You offered it all," Claiborne reminded him.

The man wasn't acting. He was stupid.

Without knocking, Prescott shoved open the door that led down into the below-decks bunkroom. He half hoped he would catch them wrapped together in one of the bunks, but Gammon was dressed, pulling on his shoes. The woman came out of the little bathroom beneath the landing on which Prescott stood. She was dressed, too. They must have slept in their clothes.

"On deck." Prescott had the S&W out. For effect. He gestured with it. This was like a movie, holding his gun on two doomed prisoners—pretty damned obvious what was going to happen to them—on a boat headed for the Caribbean. Beat the hell out of pounding around Washington on Gammon's elusive tail, or even a trip to Hawaii. Too much lobby sitting that second time. And he'd hated the ass-chewing Kolker had laid on him for losing the guy on Maui.

Yeah, this was better, even if he had spent the night camped on the passageway steps. The payoff was going to be worth everything he was putting up with here. "This goddamned Buttonwood is ducking out, Georgie," Kolker had told him just after they'd come aboard. "That was a bank book he took off Gammon back at OmniSecure. You and me are going to dump Gammon and the blonde, like he's going to tell us. Probably the other two along with them. After that, we'll see. It's my guess Pope would be in a real good mood if we hauled Buttonwood's ass and his bank book back to FRETSAW. There's got to be a hell of a bonus in that, Georgie."

With Kolker planning to take over, this was shaping up just fine.

"You heard what I said," Prescott prodded. "Get your two butts up here."

Gammon and the woman climbed the short stairway out of the bunkroom and edged past him on the landing. He crowded her so that her buns brushed him as she passed. He followed them into the cramped hallway and prodded Gammon in the back with the muzzle of the S&W before he holstered it. A little reinforcement never hurt. The woman, even in her rumpled gray business suit, looked like she'd be a real bedful as she topped the four steps at the aft end of the passageway and entered the salon.

As soon as Prescott stuck his head into the salon behind Gammon and the woman, Buttonwood dismissed him with a wave of his hand. He walked back down the two flights of steps to the bunkroom. He was beat. He shucked off his jacket and fell into the lower bunk. The lingering scent of female told him the Cortland woman had used this one. He wondered what she'd be like, down here with him? This was going to be a long pull down the East Coast, he mused as the muted thunder of the engines began to dull his brain. Who knew what the possibilities might be?

"Coffee?" Claiborne asked them. "If you want something more substantial, you will have to fix it yourselves in the galley there." He nodded toward the small kitchen in the forward portside of the salon. "Normally, Rustie would do the honors, but Horace has insisted on quite a challenging schedule. So she's at the helm on the bridge, shortly to guide us between Cape Charles and Cape Henry into the Atlantic. Join us, join us."

"I'll do the honors," Alix offered. "Scrambled eggs and toast all around all right? You do have eggs?"

"Certainly," Claiborne said. "Seek in the refrigerator, and ye shall discover."

Steve took one of the two remaining bolted-down swivel chairs at the circular table. Buttonwood looked pale and rattled, but Steve could read nothing in Claiborne's face. The man had seemed an innocent dupe when they'd come aboard last night. Was there now a derisive edge to his conversation? Was he FRETSAW's man, or had he begun to realize what was really going on here?

"You slept well, I trust, Mr. Mifflin . . . Henry, isn't it?" Claiborne poured coffee then slid the cup on its saucer across the table to Steve.

"Under the circumstances."

Buttonwood shot him a look that appeared to be warning and apprehension in equal parts. If Claiborne weren't in on Buttonwood's hasty exodus plan, Steve wondered what his reaction would be, were Steve to blurt, *These bastards have taken over your boat, Claiborne. Alix and I, and no doubt you and your redhead, aren't coming back from this one!*

He took a swallow of Claiborne's coffee.

"Best there is," Claiborne told him enthusiastically. "Kona. Only coffee grown in the U.S.A."

Jesus, Claiborne. Captor or captive? Don't you wonder why Kolker is always on the bridge? Or have you approved his being up there to make sure your redhead doesn't run us into the coast guard station in Norfolk or doesn't pick up the mike of the ship-to-shore and blurt out a panicky Mayday?

He damned near said all that, damned near told Claiborne what was going on. Claiborne's reaction would tell the story. Then Alix clopped dishes on the table, and a platter of eggs and toast. And Steve, during that interruption, realized he had come close to making a major error. If Claiborne was not aware of the one-way aspect of this cruise, Steve's briefing him in front of Buttonwood would result in Claiborne's losing the run of the boat. And Claiborne's relative freedom could be useful, if he were not a full partner in the real purpose of this trip.

Buttonwood, Kolker, and Prescott were as obvious as a warning label. With Kolker assigned to watch her, Rustie could be tagged as a woman in a bind she didn't recognize. No threat. No help, either.

Claiborne was the imponderable. Captor or captive? Steve had to find a way to get through to the man without the others knowing about it.

Shortly after 8:00 A.M., the now ironically named *Take Over* drummed smoothly through the mouth of the Chesapeake Bay and into Atlantic swells. Claiborne's woman handled the boat well, Steve thought, but the heaving ocean set crockery and silverware rattling in the cupboards. Prescott's head poked through the passageway opening.

"What the hell is it? What's going on?"

"Your friend here," Claiborne said with a cheerful nod at Buttonwood, "prefers the open sea to the Inland Waterway." He stood, his sea legs compensating instinctively for the deck's roll. "I'm going to relieve Rustie, Horace. She has been up there for almost five hours."

He climbed the spiral steps in the forward starboard corner of the salon. When he opened the overhead hatch to the bridge, a rush of wind gusted cold spray down into the salon. The hatch slammed shut. A moment later, it opened again. Rustie's slender, now jean-clad legs appeared. Despite her designer pea jacket, she looked bone-cold. Kolker followed her down, looking, Steve noted, not only thoroughly chilled in his now-appropriate combat jumper, but also greenish. Buttonwood's hired muscle was seasick.

So now Claiborne was allowed to stay on the bridge unescorted. Run of the ship.

"It's getting awful up there," Rustie announced. She hugged herself, teeth chattering. "Oh, God, I need coffee. And sleep." She took a thick mug from the galley cupboard. "Burlington likes those dumb little cups and saucers. When I need coffee, I need *coffee.*"

"A storm?" Buttonwood asked. He reached for his cup, spilled part of its contents on his shirt and slapped at the spill, cursing softly.

"Storm?" Rustie looked surprised. "Just a cold, windy Memorial Day weekend on the Mid Atlantic, girls and boys." She held her mug high in a mock toast. "And so to bed." She took the coffee with her as she descended the stairwell midway on the salon's portside to the master stateroom below.

"You two finished?" Buttonwood demanded, still dabbing at his coffee stain with a napkin. "Take them back down to the bunkroom, Kolker, then grab yourself some sleep in my stateroom."

Steve followed Alix down into the passageway, looking properly cowed, he hoped, in Buttonwood's eyes. His stomach seethed, but not with queasiness brought on by the rolling sea. With anger. And with the realization that with every hour that passed, he and Alix were in greater jeopardy.

She was equally perceptive. When they were back down in the bunkroom and Kolker had closed the door to the passageway, she said, "Steve, we have access to the engine room. Why don't we do something to them? Disable them?"

"I thought of that a while back, Alix. But any superficial damage we could manage, they could probably repair just as fast. Back in Annapolis, if we'd had some tools—"

"We're getting down to limited choices, aren't we?"

"I'd say basically two. Do nothing and have it surely done to us nearly anytime now. Or do something first, and hope to hell it doesn't turn out the same way."

She sank to the lower bunk, and he crouched on the floor close to her. "We know where Buttonwood, Kolker, and Prescott stand. Rustie is along for the ride and doesn't seem to notice anything amiss. Claiborne is the imponderable. At first, I thought he was with them, but now I'm not so sure. We've got to get to him without the others knowing about it."

"How? Buttonwood keeps him separated from us, except when we're all in the salon together."

"Maybe I do know how. I've got a pen. We need paper. And a little luck."

"I've got a memo pad in my purse."

He liked that. She didn't ask how or what. She rooted in the purse and handed him the little pad.

FRETSAW nonexistent, he wrote. *Buttonwood has bankbook for $4 million + numbered Cayman account. Kolker, Prescott hired guns. Alix, I prisoners. You, girl, too. Call coast guard if you can.*

"Since this boat wasn't designed with all this in mind," Steve said, "we do have our handy access to the engine compartment."

He opened the oval hatch and stepped into the engine room between the big V-12 diesels. The cramped space smelled of rank oil, and the noise cut right through him. Their combined rumble was deafening. The boat yawed to port, throwing him toward the engine on his right. He thrust out his arm, caught his fall against the hot cylinder cover. His scorched palm stung as he searched for the engine's fuel line and its cutoff valve.

Then he found the copper line, traced it back to a valve with a thumbscrew. He folded the note tightly, wedged it beneath the valve assembly and slowly closed down the thumbscrew until the engine began to stutter and skip.

He returned quickly to the bunkroom to sit on the lower berth next to Alix. The starving engine's misfiring began to shake the deck under their feet.

"They can't put up with this very long. And I doubt that anybody up there knows much about these engines except Claiborne."

They put up with the rough running for fewer than three minutes. Then the door at the top of the bunkroom steps whipped open. Down came Claiborne. Right behind him came Prescott, gun holstered, but his hand was close to its butt. He accompanied Claiborne on Buttonwood's orders, Steve assumed, to inhibit communication.

Claiborne nodded at them noncommittally and pushed through the engine compartment hatch. Prescott stood in the open hatchway, his attention split between Claiborne's investigation of the balky engine and, Steve noted, the several inches of thigh Alix's skirt had exposed above her knees.

Then the engine's stutter smoothed. Claiborne stepped back into the bunkroom and secured the engine room access. His eyes passed over them without expression, and he preceded Prescott up the steps.

When the upper door closed, Steve reopened the hatch and ducked back into the engine compartment. The folded note was gone.

"Now what, Steve?"

"We're expected to wait for Georgie Prescott to come for us. For lunch, if we're lucky."

"Or for execution, if we're not."

"And I've got the impression that our luck's about to run out. Buttonwood's more shook up every time I see him." Steve looked up at the passageway door. "I said we are expected to wait passively, Alix, but that's not what we're going to do. Just hope that it's Prescott who comes for us. So far, Buttonwood has sent Prescott every time."

Then he told her what he wanted her to do.

She sat there, expressionless.

"I'm sorry, Alix. I realize you've been used again and again."

"Secondhand Rose."

"It's the best I can come up with on short notice. Prescott has twenty years on me, and he's got that damned gun."

She looked straight into his eyes. "Oh, hell, Steve, you know I'll do it. What pride do I have left? What do I have left at all."

He said, very softly, "You have courage, Alix. A lot of it."

"All right, Prescott," Buttonwood said just after 11:00 A.M. FRETSAW's executive director looked real sick now, and Prescott thought his voice sounded different. Like the voice of a man who had come to a decision he didn't want to face, but he was going through with it anyway. "Bring Gammon and the woman up here."

Prescott felt a hot rush in his groin. "Like now?"

"Gammon's got something in mind. I can feel it," Buttonwood said unsteadily. "I don't want to give him any more time. Potentially too dangerous."

Prescott was eager enough to get on with it, but Buttonwood's grayish pallor made him wonder if the man was thinking far enough ahead.

"They're going to know," he said.

"Who?"

"Big Stupe and his redhead."

"He's been bought, Prescott. If that isn't enough, we'll use the redhead to control them both."

Now that idea, Prescott could really go for. He quickly

reviewed the boat's status. Big, dumb Claiborne was topside on the bridge. His redhead was still sacked out in the master stateroom below. Kolker was in the forward stateroom, the one Buttonwood had claimed. Son of a bitch wouldn't let me use that one, Prescott thought, but he let the stumpy Marlboro Man crash there.

And he and Buttonwood were alone in the big salon. The time had come, and this was going to be a piece of cake. He could walk Gammon and the blonde through the forward starboard outside access door and put them over the side. Claiborne might not even see that from the bridge, and there was enough noise out there to cover the bark of the Smith & Wesson, if he had to use it. Which he wouldn't mind . . . Which he *wanted* to do, particularly to the blonde. If he couldn't do it to her one way, he'd do it another. With the gun.

Another warm flush bunched his crotch. He got up from the sofa, turning away from Buttonwood so it wouldn't show.

He opened the door to the passageway and went down the short stairs, both hands pressing the sides to counter the boat's roll. At the access door to the bunkroom below, he paused to pull the S&W from its shoulder holster. Then he opened the door and looked down into the compartment.

Gammon lay on his back on the lower bunk. Asleep? Prescott didn't see the woman down there, but the door to the small bathroom was shut. So she was in the can.

He walked down the narrow, jutting steps. The boat's constant roll made it a precarious, one-handed descent. The gun hand, he kept free.

Gammon looked up at him drowsily.

"You stay put," Prescott ordered. "She in there?"

Gammon didn't answer. He looked dazed, half sick. Out of it.

Prescott edged to the narrow bathroom door, eyes on Gammon. He rapped on the door with his free hand.

"Come on out of there!"

He waited. Nothing. He banged on the door again. "I said come out. You hear me?"

She'd probably locked herself in. He didn't need this. He tried the knob, and to his surprise, the door wasn't locked. He jerked it open.

Then he stared.

She stood facing him, left arm at her side, right hand holding a toothbrush to her mouth. Her face wore an expression he couldn't make out. He could make out everything else, though, in close-up, throat-thickening detail. Everything was right here, not even an arm's reach away. Tits with raspberry points. A golden bush with a little pink showing through. Not two feet away. *God!*

Georgie felt himself rising like an express elevator, straining against his slacks.

Then he felt something else. Something like a pile driver slammed into the small of his back. He was catapulted forward. He caught a tawny blur as she swung out of the way. He reached out with both arms.

Too late. His face smashed into the mirror over the metal basin. Pain shot across his face in a spidery burn. He'd been slashed by the razor edges of broken glass, but his problem was the gun. The impact of Gammon's full weight had jammed his hands against the edge of the bathroom counter. He could not raise the gun.

Fingers locked in his hair, slammed his head forward again. And again. The shock of the impact merged into a sickening spiral of pain, pulsating light and agonizing thuds that whirled him into helplessness.

The S&W slipped out of his fingers. His knees gave way. He tumbled to the floor. Hands grabbed his ankles, jerked him flat. Other hands yanked his arms over his head. Through swirling red, he made out naked legs straddling him, saw the golden juncture of those big, white thighs not three inches above his face. Jesus.

He was rolled over on his stomach. His wrists were pulled together behind his back. He was shocked at Gammon's and the woman's strength and his own weakness. It wasn't supposed to be like this. He was in control here, not Gammon, not the blonde.

Now they were tying his hands with what felt like a length of cloth. Gammon's tie? Prescott shook his head, tried to clear blood out of his eyes, saw a glistening crimson pool on the bathroom vinyl under his chin.

"You bas—" A hand reached around his neck, jerked his head up, stuffed a handkerchief in his mouth.

"Here, use my panty hose," he heard the woman say.

He felt his ankles clapped together. Panty hose, for Christsake! But the knotted nylon was strong as rope.

Now they shoved him over on his side and were tying the feet of the panty hose to his bound hands. Through a bloody haze, he caught glimpses of Gammon's big hands, her naked thighs. When she leaned over him, her chest was right in his face. He could smell delicate perspiration. He was seized by the damndest sensation he'd ever felt, erotic as hell, but shafted through with pain and white-hot anger. Pain plus blonde skin jumping all around him was bringing him damned close to—

Then they shoved his trussed legs back into the bathroom with the rest of him and shut the door. He lay facedown in his own blood, his feet bent up over his back and tied to his hands. A gray veil slid over his eyes, thickened. His ears began to ring. As he glided into unconsciousness, he wondered what Milo Kolker would have to say about *this!*

Steve checked Prescott's pistol. Eleven cartridges in the clip, one already in the chamber. He located the safety and thumbed it off.

"Stay here, Alix." She was yanking her skirt over her hips. "Keep an eye on our boy." He tried to hold his voice steady, but adrenaline pumped hard, filled him with desperate energy. By God, they had taken on that hard-eyed bastard and flattened him. Only two—or three—to go, depending on which side Claiborne put himself.

He started up the bunkroom steps, turned back. She was fastening her bra. "You did fine, Alix," he told her. Then he went on up to inch open the door into the passageway.

Horace Buttonwood sprawled at the aft end of the salon's big lounge, working hard to convince himself that the endless roll of the yacht was not making him seasick; that hollow queasiness roiled his stomach only because he was hungry. He tore his eyes from the ghostly turns of the unmanned wheel at the salon's auxiliary steering station. Hungry, that was all. It was nearly lunchtime.

Through the long, narrow windows down each side and across the aft end of the salon, he saw the heaving Atlantic. The slate-covered Virginia coastline was barely visible far off to the right when the boat rode upward, then was lost when the *Take Over* lunged sickeningly downward into troughs. They were maybe twenty miles out. Hard to judge.

Buttonwood mentally inventoried personnel yet again. Kolker was sacked out forward. Claiborne's woman was in the master stateroom beneath Buttonwood's feet. Prescott should be bringing up Gammon and Alix from the bunkroom about now. He'd been sent down there five, maybe ten minutes ago. And Claiborne was on the bridge. Alone.

Not good. What would be the man's reaction when he saw Gammon and the woman go over the side? He had been the jolly host up to now, but that couldn't last through what was about to happen. Buttonwood needed Claiborne where Claiborne could be watched and controlled. Where he couldn't suddenly decide to activate the bridge's radio.

There was an inside steering station down here; that's where he wanted Claiborne when Prescott took care of his particular responsibility.

Buttonwood pushed up from the lounge on wobbly legs. He felt rotten. He stumbled to the spiral stairs that led up to the bridge, pulled himself halfway up the six pie-shaped steps, and banged on the overhead hatch.

It jerked open. Salt wind gusted down into the salon. Claiborne leaned into the opening.

"Must be getting nasty up there, Burlington. How about using the inside steering station?"

"I'm fine, Horace."

"I want you down here." Spray peppered his upturned face.

"It's my boat, Horace."

"It's my charter, Burlington."

Claiborne shrugged. "Give me a minute to secure."

Buttonwood stumbled back down the steps. A moment later, Claiborne's tennis shoes and white ducks followed him down. The yachtsman paused to secure the overhead hatch, then he stepped down to the nearby steering station. He snapped switches and took the wheel in hand. His face was expressionless. Now what was the pelican-brained playboy thinking? Buttonwood didn't care. He'd gotten him down here where he wanted him.

Then the door to the passageway opened. Gammon emerged. Buttonwood looked behind him. Gammon seemed to be alone. Then the man's right hand snapped up. The son of a bitch had a pistol!

"Stay put, Buttonwood," Steve told him. The con artist had turned sickly gray above his beard. Steve stepped through the narrow door and closed it behind him. Only then did he realize that Claiborne, hidden by the open door, had taken the wheel at the inside steering station.

Steve moved into the salon, keeping the gun on Buttonwood for effect. He doubted that the man had it in him to make a sudden lunge. And he was reasonably sure Buttonwood was not armed, not with Kolker and Prescott here to handle that kind of work.

"Where's Kolker?" Steve demanded.

Buttonwood didn't answer.

"In the forward stateroom, I assume," Claiborne said, his voice surprisingly even.

Was Claiborne being cooperative, or was he waiting for the chance to help Buttonwood?

The passageway door opened again, and Steve swung around to see Alix appear, her face bone-white.

"Alix, what is it? I told you to stay—"

"I'm sorry, Steve." Her voice shook. "He looked in the bunkroom, made me come up."

"Put that thing down, Gammon," Kolker ordered behind her, "or she gets it right now." He moved his arm, and now Steve saw the muzzle of an ugly military .45 pressed to her neck.

Some choice. Give up Prescott's pistol and gain no more than a few minutes. Or sacrifice Alix and take the chance that he would be faster than Kolker's second shot.

"Gammon, I'm telling you, gun down—on the sofa there, or she goes. Where the hell is Prescott, Mr. Buttonwood?"

"That's what I'd like to know."

Steve backed past Buttonwood and took a two-handed stance. He centered the pistol's blade sight on Kolker's forehead.

Prescott had been overconfident and easily diverted. Kolker was a different story. "You've got to be kidding, Gammon. When was the last time you fired one of those things? Even if you luck out, she'll get it because this trigger is just a hair's width from putting it to her, you understand?"

Kolker was probably correct. Even if Steve nailed him square in the forehead, the reflex jerk would fire his big automatic. Its heavy slugs were capable of stopping a man cold wherever it hit him. The thing would tear Alix's head right off her shoulders.

"Gammon, you dumb bastard, you're turning into more trouble than your brother."

The instant Kolker spat out the words, Steve knew *this* was the man who had killed Jim!

Steve's finger tightened on the S&W's trigger. But he held off. There was no getting around the critical probability of Kolker's reflex reaction to a bullet plowing into his brain.

Kolker jammed the .45's muzzle deeper into Alix's neck and shoved her through the doorway.

What happened then was a heart-stopping blur. Claiborne, hidden from Kolker by the open door, threw himself sideways against it. The door, impacted by the yachtsman's full weight, whipped past Alix's left shoulder and slammed Kolker in the side. The heavyset OmniSecure man was caught totally by surprise. He thudded sideways against the door jamb. The explosion of his .45 deafened Steve. Alix pitched forward and crumpled.

Steve shot a horrified glance downward. No blood. The door's impact had forced Kolker's gun arm up. The .45 had blasted an ugly, powder-specked hole in the white overhead.

Kolker rammed the half-open door aside, jamming Claiborne back into the steering station. The .45 roared again, a panicky shot as Kolker scrambled for balance. The big slug snapped between Steve and Buttonwood, close enough for Steve to feel its flick of heat past his cheek. It exited through the salon's aft window, popping a crystal-edged hole in the heavy glass.

Then Kolker steadied himself and leveled the big .45 straight at Steve's chest, his face as expressionless as that of a robot intent on a programmed assignment to kill.

Without consciously aiming, Steve fired. Jerked the trigger as fast as he could cycle it. Again. And again.

The first 9mm slug caught Kolker in his right shoulder. The .45 blew a long, ragged hole in the salon's carpet, inches from Alix's head. The S&W's second shot hit the door jamb. The third slammed into Kolker's left arm, spun him toward the steering station. The next shot hit him under the right arm, and he went down hard, across Alix's legs. The Colt bounced on the carpet. Steve kicked it away from Kolker's outstretched fingers.

Now the only sounds were the slap of waves against the hull of the broaching boat, the subdued drumming of the engines as Claiborne scrambled to throttle them back, and the whistling shriek a jet of rising wind made through the bullet hole in the salon's aft window.

Steve waved the gun in Buttonwood's direction. "You stay right where you are. Claiborne, there's a man bleeding pretty badly in the bunkroom." He knelt. "Kolker's still breathing, but barely. I'd suggest that you get on the radio in one hell of a hurry."

"Wanted to before, Mifflin, but I realized they'd see the lights go on at the steering station down here. The woman . . . ?"

Steve cupped Alix's shoulder gently. "You all right?"

"Is any of us?" She jerked her legs from under Kolker's inert form and sat up, fingering the red bruise on her neck where he had jammed his gun muzzle.

Then Rustie's tousled head appeared in the stairwell from the master stateroom. "Did I miss anything?" she asked brightly.

Behind him, Steve heard Claiborne's voice, no longer richly baritone, but now high and squeaky, saying over and over, "Mayday . . . Mayday . . . Mayday."

EPILOGUE

The coast guard cutter *Sanibel* reached the *Take Over* at 1214 hours EDT. Horace Buttonwood, Milo Kolker, and George Prescott were taken into custody. Kolker and Prescott recovered from their wounds, though Prescott was badly and permanently scarred about the face. Kolker regained only limited use of his right arm.

All three were extradited to the District of Columbia, where they were indicted, tried, and convicted on counts of kidnapping and assault with intent to murder. Kolker and Prescott were subsequently bound over to authorities in the State of Hawaii, where they were tried, convicted, and are now serving life sentences for the contract murders of James Gammon and Walter Van Hayden.

Throughout the questioning by the FBI, the police in Washington, and the Maui County Police, Milo Kolker insisted that what he had done had been "in the best interests of this nation." He refused to believe that FRETSAW had been no more than an elaborate confidence game, and is currently provided two one-hour psychiatric counseling sessions per week by the State of Hawaii.

Aaron K. Buttler, aka Horace Buttonwood, was also convicted of massive fraud, misappropriation of funds, evasion of income taxes, and conspiracy to commit murder. He is currently serving consecutive sentences in federal prison in Virginia, totaling 174 years.

Burlington Claiborne was found to have been an innocent participant in FRETSAW activities and was not charged. At this writing, he is believed to be cruising off Baja California in the company of Margot "Rustie" Pavlovic, daughter of the late president of Pavlovic Petrochemical International, and owner-of-record of the motor yacht *Take Over*.

Marcie Gammon, widow of James Gammon, was hired by Kinnon Publications as associate editor for *Decor* magazine and moved to New York City.

Andrew Albertson, aka Richardson Pope, reached Miami aboard a Delta Airlines 727 without incident. Because of a tropical depression in the eastern Caribbean, his flight to Grand Cayman was delayed nearly twenty-two hours. When the old Caribbean Airways DC-3 finally took off from Miami International, he found himself breathing a long, shaky sigh of intense relief.

The DC-3 made two intermediate stops before it reached the Caymans. The first was in Nassau, where the tanks were topped off for the much longer haul to Puerto Rico. The Nassau stop was uneventful. Albertson felt comfortable here, out of U.S. territory. The next stop, though, hours later, was back in American jurisdiction, at San Juan's Isla Verde International Airport. Among the people who boarded the plane here and climbed up its sloping aisle were two lean men in business suits. Albertson knew the instant he saw them that they were FBI.

He was extradited to the District of Columbia, tried, convicted and sentenced to fifteen years for fraud, misappropriation of funds, and evasion of income taxes. He was able to convince authorities that he took no part in the planning and implementation of the successful murder plots against James Gammon and Walter Van Hayden, and the attempted murders of Steven Gammon and Alix Cortland. He was not charged in any of those felonies, and he testified as a state's witness at the trial of Horace Buttonwood.

The Internal Revenue Service impounded the assets of FRETSAW, including the two bank accounts in the Bank of the Islands, Grand Cayman. Following the District of Columbia's Federal Court's acceptance of IRS computations, more than half the assets were appropriated by the IRS to settle tax liabilities and levied fines. Nineteen major contributors to FRETSAW filed a class action suit for recovery of the balance for return to donors, but the IRS ruled that the remaining assets were to be distributed per Article 16 of FRETSAW's bylaws, in accordance with the organization's Internal Revenue Code 501 (c) (3) status. The mounting legal expense of contesting that ruling in Federal Court discouraged the FRETSAW litigants, and the suit was ultimately dropped.

Article 16 had been included in FRETSAW's bylaws to meet the IRS requirement that a nonprofit organization name a recipient of remaining assets, should said organization be dissolved. When he and Buttonwood had roughed out the bylaws, Pope had shrugged at Article 16. Buttonwood penciled in a name.

Thus it was that just over a year after FRETSAW collapsed, the incorporated town of Gridley, New York, found itself the stunned recipient of nearly $3.5 million.

Steve Gammon flew to Washington from Fort Myers to testify at the trials of Buttonwood, Kolker, and Prescott. When he returned to Florida, he realized that the last time he was in D.C., he would have sworn that if anyone were to accompany him back to Florida, it would have been Marcie Gammon.

As the DC-9's cabin door closed at Washington National, the woman in the seat beside him asked, "You're sure, Steve? You know what I've been through. What I've . . . been."

The engines rumbled, and the jet began to back clear of the loading dock.

"Alix," he said gently, "I'm sure."